BAD FOR YOUR TEETH

EVAN BAUGHFMAN

D & T
PUBLISHING

DEDICATION

For Mason and Story—
Sweet or sour, you're always my favorites.
(I really hope you choose to read this someday, when you're older!)
Love, Dad

ACKNOWLEDGMENTS

A published full-length novel. Wow! Seriously, this is a childhood dream come true! A lot of hard work went into this book, and I'm grateful for the opportunity to share Jase's story with the world.

First and foremost, thank you to Dawn Shea for being so easy to work with and for giving *Bad for Your Teeth* a home. It's been an honor and a pleasure to contribute to the Little Gremlins line of spooky stories. Young horror fans are lucky to have D&T in their corner!

Thank you, editor James La Chance, for providing your thoughts on this manuscript. Thank you, Ash Ericmore, for designing the book's fantastic cover art.

Pat Dobie read and edited an earlier draft of this novel. Her encouragement and suggestions helped to make this story more vibrant and publishable. Thank you, Pat!

Thanks to Mike Vert, A.E. Santana, Kevin David Anderson, and Mark Tullius for reading this story and for sharing your kind words with me.

Thank you to my parents for supporting my creative writing pursuits. And for paying for my braces. Years and years of braces.

Thank you to my wife, Ashley, for keeping our home and family in order while I'm busy spilling my brains onto the page.

To dentists everywhere: you do important work. Sorry for villainizing your profession, but it was great fun to write. I give you permission to write a story about a nefarious middle school teacher/horror author.

And to You, the Reader: I truly appreciate you. I hope *Bad for Your Teeth* made you smile bright, fangs and all.

IN BLOOD RED LETTERS, the door said, *Dr. Xander Sharp, D.D.S.*

My heart hammered. I knew what those three letters actually stood for.

D.D.S.

Deadly Dr. Sharp.

Out there in the open. So clear. So obvious.

The back of my right hand itched like crazy. It always did when I got nervous. I scratched and scratched.

"Jase, stop that."

I turned to Mom's voice. She and Grandpa stood behind me in the hallway outside the dentist's office. They didn't really expect me to open that door and step inside, did they?

Because I was pretty sure that my first-ever encounter with Dr. Sharp was destined to end in misery. Some tooth on my right side had been nagging me with fire every time I ate. I hadn't told Mom about it yet, but she'd get the bad news soon enough, and a lecture would certainly follow.

We'd recently relocated to West Bay, a town in northern California, and Mom seemed pretty on-edge about the sudden move. So was I, of course. Leaving behind my friends had been awful. I didn't have a personal phone or social media—Mom said I was too young for both. Who knew if I'd ever even hear from my Arizona pals again?

In front of Dr. Sharp's door, Mom said, "It's only a check-up, honey. If you've been brushing and flossing as often as I tell you to, the appointment should be nothing but smiles."

My previous dentist, Dr. Peters, never found a cavity inside my mouth. Regardless, I knew California would continue to produce very little sunshine for me. Dark clouds had been on the horizon since Day One.

"Dana," said Grandpa, "if he brushed and flossed as often as you tell him to, he wouldn't have any time to breathe."

Mom ran fingers through her thick, black hair. "We don't want his teeth to end up like yours."

Grandpa hated going to the dentist more than anyone I knew. He let his real teeth fall out of his head a long time ago, and now he wore fake teeth called dentures all the time. Well, he didn't wear them when he slept, I guess. At night, he kept his slimy smile in a glass of water by his alarm clock.

Grandpa rolled his wise, gray eyes. "Oh, dentures aren't anything to be ashamed of at my age."

Mom argued, "Jase is eleven."

"You have a point." Grandpa stared at me. "Been brushing and flossing as often as your mother tells you to?"

"No. I like to breathe."

Grandpa grinned. "Atta boy."

Mom sighed. "I'm sure you do what's necessary."

I looked away from her and scratched the nervous itch again. I brushed my teeth—*most of the time.* I'd flossed my teeth—*a grand total of three times…I think. Maybe it was four times—no, definitely only three.* Teeth take a lot of work. I'm a naturally lazy kid.

"You've made it this far, honey. Either you open the door, or Grandpa or I will do it."

"Not opening it," Grandpa said. He knew what the letters stood for, too, I bet.

"Fine," said Mom. "I will."

She didn't have to. The door creaked open. A woman about Mom's age stood inside the doorway next to a blonde girl who looked a little bit older than me.

"Excuse us," the woman said to Mom. "Come on, Julie," she said to the girl. "Dr. Sharp suggested we run right out and get you one of those electric toothbrushes, and I need to put the meatloaf in the oven if it's going to be ready for your father when he gets home."

"Meatloaf?" said Julie. *Really?*" She licked her lips and then jumped a little, clapping her hands like a cheerleader. *Really* weird.

"Didn't know you liked meatloaf so much." The woman walked past us, and her daughter followed close behind.

Mom carefully re-shut the door and took a couple of steps toward Julie and her mother as they waited for the elevator. "Hello," said Mom.

The woman turned. "Yes?"

"It's Julie, right?"

The girl nodded. "Hi."

"Julie, this is my son's first day seeing Dr. Sharp. Would you say he's a good dentist? Any reason to be afraid of him?"

My face grew red. I almost hid behind Grandpa.

"Dr. Sharp is *so* cool." Julie grinned at me. "You'll like him."

"Seems to be great with kids," said Julie's mom. "Everyone says nothing but nice things."

Mom said, "Wonderful to hear. Isn't it, Jase?"

I shrugged. "Whatever."

The elevator chimed its arrival. Doors slid open. Julie's mom said to me, "You'll be just fine. Don't worry."

Mother and daughter disappeared inside the elevator. Its doors closed, and the hall was silent once again.

Grandpa told Mom, "Way to embarrass your son there."

"I didn't embarrass…"

"No? Jase turned about as red as Adonis's roses!"

"Adonis…?" I asked.

"In Greek mythology, Adonis was—"

"Dad, please, you know how I feel about that Greek garbage."

Grandpa held his fingers together atop his wrinkled, bald head. "They're interesting stories."

Mom always made the same argument: "They're too violent!"

"This one isn't." Grandpa looked at me. "Adonis was a boy who went hunting one day, and he was gored to death by a wild boar. Skewered by the pig's giant tusks! Anyway, beautiful red roses soon sprouted from pools of Adonis's blood."

"Dad!" Mom hit him playfully on the shoulder. "You said it wasn't violent!"

"Said it wasn't *too* violent. Wasn't *too* violent, was it, Jase?"

I smiled. "Nope."

Mom asked if she embarrassed me. "That girl was pretty, right? You're too young for crushes, though, aren't you?"

I screamed, "There's no crush!" My face felt redder than ever. "Just don't need other people knowing how I feel, is all."

"Really?" said Mom. "Why, then, have I heard so much complaining from you about coming here?"

Grandpa said, "If you can't annoy your family, who can you annoy?"

"Sorry if I embarrassed you," said Mom. "Just wanted to show you there isn't any reason to be afraid."

Grandpa asked, "What if the guy's got a hook?"

"What?" Mom and I replied in unison.

"What if the guy's got a hook for a hand? That would scare me!"

"Dad, why would the dentist have a hook for a hand?"

"His name's 'Sharp,' right? Hooks are sharp."

"Really doubt the man's name has anything to do with his physical appearance. Jase, don't worry, okay? The dentist wouldn't be able to hold any tools if he had a hook for a hand. It's ridiculous. Kind of funny, not scary, if you think about it."

Funny? I didn't laugh one bit.

As Mom went back to the *D.D.S.* door, I imagined a shadowy figure hovering over me in a dark room, the only light around glinting from the tip of a steel hook where a hand should've been.

2

MOM REACHED PAST ME, turned the knob, and the door swung inward. I closed my eyes, one last desperate attempt to escape the inevitable.

Scratch, scratch, scratch.

"Might as well come in," said Grandpa. He patted me on the shoulder as he walked by.

I took a deep breath, wiped sweaty palms against my shorts, and then opened my eyes. I couldn't believe it.

Everything was...normal. The walls were painted white, not black or splattered with blood. The screams of tortured children didn't fill the room. Instead, a movie loudly played on a television mounted high up on the wall.

"My favorite!" Grandpa stood in front of me, beaming. "Nemo!"

He made me watch that stupid fish movie so much, it almost made me sick seeing it up there on the screen. Quickly, I realized much of the movie took place inside a dentist's office. Whoever put the movie on had to have known that. Clever thinking. But, then, why did Grandpa, of all people, like a movie that took part in a dentist's office?

Some mysteries are never meant to be solved.

Ten chairs bordered the waiting room. Seven seats were taken. None of the open seats were beside each other. I'd have to sit next to a stranger. *Just great.*

At the front of the room, Mom leaned over a counter, speaking quietly to the young woman sitting behind it. Grandpa sat beside a man reading a magazine.

I scanned the room for the safest place to sit. Everybody read a magazine of some kind, most likely taken from a small table adjacent to the door. Also on the table were pamphlets that read, *Cavities: Why Eating Sweets Can Be Not So Sweet.* I groaned. Grandpa needed to read one of those.

He wasn't supposed to eat caramel candies, because they're bad for teeth—especially fake teeth—but that never stopped him from eating them whenever Mom was elsewhere. Every time he popped a caramel into his mouth, he smiled and said, "Sweet ambrosia."

Didn't know what he meant by "ambrosia" for a long time, so one day I asked him. "Ambrosia," he said, "is the food of the Greek gods. The most delicious thing one can ever taste. This candy is my ambrosia. Never had anything more delicious, except maybe your grandmother's lips."

I groaned at that. Never met Grandma. She died when Mom was a teenager. Kind of like how my dad died when I was a baby…

"What's your ambrosia?" Grandpa had asked me.

After some thinking, I said, "Mom's chocolate chip cookies."

"My second choice. Unless she burns them, of course."

If Mom was around, Grandpa sometimes paid me a penny to sneak him candy from the bowl in the living room. He hadn't held a job for a while, so he must've been saving those pennies for years. I wasn't the type of person to ask questions when it came to money. As an unemployed kid, every cent counted.

Grandpa once told me, "Even a penny can go a long way."

But no amount of pennies could've helped me at Dr. Sharp's office. Not unless I smashed my penny jar over the dentist's head and made a run for it. Grandpa might've been amused by such a thing, but Mom would've yelled at me until my eardrums burst.

So, there I was in the waiting room, unsure of my next move. Wasn't going to read an anti-cavity pamphlet—that was for sure. The movie couldn't offer anything new to me, although Grandpa's eyes were glued to the screen. I just needed to sit, think happy thoughts, and stop scratching my hand so much.

I sat beside the only other kid in the room. He was short and stout, with brown curly hair and glasses. I was surprised to find him reading the pamphlet from the table.

The boy looked my way. "Wonder if my tooth looks like this," he said. "That would be so *gross*." He pointed to a photograph in the pamphlet. A close-up shot of a yellow—almost brown—tooth with a giant, ugly hole in its middle.

I nodded. "Definitely gross."

"If my tooth looked like that, I'd just ask Dr. Sharp to take it out and give it to me. It'd be awesome for show-and-tell. I can already hear the girls in class screaming!" He giggled. It was summertime, so I didn't know which show-and-tell or class he was talking about.

"Would probably freak them out," I said.

"I know! Wouldn't that be wonderful?"

I inched as far away from him in my seat as I could, but it wasn't nearly far enough.

He leaned over. "The looks on their faces…Priceless! They might even barf!"

I looked to where the other empty seat had been. Maybe I could run over to it and—*too late*. Mom now sat in the chair, writing furiously on a clipboard.

"You don't look so happy to be here," said the boy. An understatement on so many levels.

"Anyone *want* to be at the dentist?" I half-expected him to say that he did, the way he was so excited about possibly having a nasty cavity.

Instead, he nodded. "You'd have to be pretty crazy to want to be here."

Suddenly, Mom said, "Jase, what's your social security number?" She held a pen over the clipboard.

I shook my head. No idea. What the heck was a social security number?

"It's escaping me at the moment…" She smiled. "Never mind. Go back to talking with your friend there." She looked down to what was in front of her and started writing again.

The boy said, "Jase, huh? That short for something?"

"Jason."

"Hi, Jason."

"Jase. Call me Jase."

"I'm Braxton. That's short for Braxton, and you can call me Braxton." He laughed, but I didn't. "So, I've never seen you here before. This your first time?"

"Yes."

"My mom filled out that sheet the first time I came here, too." He paused, thinking. "That was so long ago. Almost three years. The last time either of my parents came here with me."

I thought the woman sitting next to Braxton was his mother, but nope. Her child must've already gone inside to see Dr. Sharp.

"Nervous?" Braxton asked.

I stopped scratching. "A little."

"I remember being nervous the first time I came here, but Dr. Sharp's really nice." He whispered into my ear, "Maybe a little *too* nice."

"What's that mean?"

He leaned back. "No adults are really that nice. At least, my parents aren't."

"Think he's faking it?"

"Maybe. I don't know. Judge for yourself. It's a little fishy sometimes."

"He probably doesn't have a hook for a hand, then?"

Braxton's eyes grew wide. "No way."

Immediately, relief flooded my nervous system. Then, that feeling was drowned out by humiliation. How could I have just let this boy know about my silly, little-kid fear?

Except Braxton added, "Sure wish he had a hook-hand. Totally take *him* in for show-and-tell if he had one." His comment chased away my shame. Braxton didn't seem to care about saying silly things himself.

I didn't think it was possible to take another person in for show-and-tell, but something told me it'd be a pretty normal thing for Braxton to try and do.

"First day's easy," he said. "Just a simple check-up. Dr. Sharp has to see if your teeth are good or bad. Had a perfect check-up my first day. Nowadays, though, my teeth aren't so good." He held up eight fingers. "Here to get my eighth cavity in two years filled."

"Wow!"

"Should be in the record books or something."

"Aren't you scared of the needle and drill?"

"You get used to it after the fourth or fifth time."

"I've never had a cavity before, but today might change that."

Braxton smiled. "Well, if you can go your whole life without ever getting a cavity, then *you* deserve to be in the record books."

I returned the smile, but knew my first day at Dr. Sharp's office would erase all hope of being in the record books for perfect teeth.

3

THE DOOR beside the receptionist's counter opened. Out stepped a woman with long hair like Mom's, but the woman's hair was brown instead of black. She wore a white lab coat over a purple polka dot blouse. A paper facemask hung around her neck. Maybe she should've worn the mask. Would've hidden her scowl.

Braxton said, "That's Dr. Sharp's assistant, Alexis."

"She always look so happy?"

"Usually looks angrier."

Alexis glanced at a clipboard in her hands. Her dark eyes scanned the room. When her gaze fell upon Braxton, she smiled. Kind of. It was like her face muscles weren't used to smiling, so the smile ended up looking more like a cheerful scowl.

"Braxton," she said, "your appointment isn't scheduled for another forty-five minutes. A little early, aren't you?"

Braxton said, "Nowhere I'd rather be." I sensed some truth in that statement.

Alexis then said, "I'm looking for a Jesse Clark."

I stood. "That's me. But I'm Jase, not 'Jesse.'"

Alexis looked back at the clipboard. "Says 'Jesse,' not 'Jase.'"

"I know my own name, lady."

"Jesse! I mean...um...Jase!" yelled Mom. "That's no way to speak to an adult! Apologize right now!"

I looked to Grandpa. He said, "Better do it."

I sighed and turned back to Alexis. "Sorry."

"Indeed. Ready to take you in now, *Jase.*"

But I wasn't ready. Did that count for anything?

Mom said, "I still need to finish this paperwork." She waved the clipboard in her hands.

Alexis pointed to the young woman behind the counter. "Whenever you finish, please hand it to Beth. She'll make sure it gets to the right place."

"What about my son, Andy?" asked the woman beside Braxton. "How much longer will he be?"

"Andy's just about done," said Alexis. She turned to the man sitting beside Grandpa. "Sir, Claire will be out shortly, as well."

"What about me?" Braxton asked. "Can I go in, too, with Jase?"

Alexis thought about it for a moment. "Sure, if he doesn't mind."

All eyes fixated on me. Didn't know if that made me feel bigger or smaller. Just made me feel more uncomfortable, like the walls were closing in around me.

"Yeah," I choked out. "Cool."

"Awesome!" cried Braxton. He practically leaped from his seat.

"Let's go, guys," said Alexis.

Braxton headed straight for the open doorway. Needless to say, I was hesitant to follow. Mom gestured for me to go. Grandpa gave me two thumbs up.

I nodded and somehow forced my legs to move forward. Some eons/seconds later, I was past Alexis, and she closed the door behind me.

Now, I was a few steps closer to my fate. I sweat more, my stomach churned, and my hand continued to itch. But I hadn't come this far only to retreat. Had to get through it somehow...

Alexis stood against the closed door. "Braxton, don't know if we should be happy to have you back with us so soon."

"Believe me," he said, "my parents don't want me here any more than you do."

Alexis asked, "Are they still vegetarians?"

He nodded. "Unfortunately."

"I see. You two, please, have a seat here." She pointed behind us to a small wooden bench resting against a wall.

Braxton and I sat. Wasn't sure why we had been taken from sitting and waiting in one room to sitting and waiting in another room. Sometimes—*a lot* of the time—adults didn't make very much sense.

Alexis said, "I'm going to see if Dr. Sharp is done with his other patients." She leaned over another countertop to speak with Beth. "Get the camera and take a good shot of Jase while I'm gone."

The dental assistant walked by and disappeared down a hallway. Beth glided over to the bench, holding a silver digital camera.

"What's that for?" I asked.

"Like, look behind you," she said.

Posted on the wall were dozens of photographs of smiling kids. Didn't know how I'd missed them before. Each photo had the name of its particular kid written in CAPITAL LETTERS beneath it. In the topmost row was a photo of Braxton, obviously taken a couple of years earlier. Julie, the Girl Too Excited About Meatloaf, smiled somewhere near the middle of the group.

Beth said, "We do this with, like, all the kids on the first day, so we can see how their smiles improve over time."

"Can I take a new one?" asked Braxton.

"Sorry, but, like, no."

"That's what you always say."

Beth raised the camera to her eye. "Okay, wait just, like, a sec for it to, like, focus and stuff."

Braxton wrapped an arm around my neck. I didn't really enjoy it even when Mom hugged me, so I almost pushed him away.

Then he said, "This guy and I are going to be great friends. Please take a picture of us on our first day together so we can look back on it in thirty years?"

Beth brought the camera down from her face. "Not really supposed to do that, but it sounds, like, really sweet. So, um, okay, I guess." She brought the camera back to her eye. "Smile and say, like, cheese or something."

I barely smiled and didn't say anything. Braxton shouted, "Stinky limburger!" and probably had the biggest, goofiest grin on his face. The camera flashed. Spots danced across my sight.

Beth looked at the camera's little screen. "That is, like, so unbelievably precious." She looked at me. "Now, one with just you. Smile as, like, wide as you can."

I smiled, but I probably could've smiled wider if I really wanted to. Just wasn't much to be smiling about. The camera flashed again. More spots.

"Okay, got it." Beth glided back behind the counter.

Braxton said, "Some people think a photograph actually captures a part of your soul. With every photo, another part of it's taken away and trapped forever, frozen in a moment in time."

I said, "You just forced us both to lose another part of our souls?"

"Guess I did."

"Thanks."

He beamed. "You're welcome."

I studied the photographs on the wall. Dozens of souls pinned up in front of me. Soon, mine would join them. I shuddered.

Braxton looked at the wall, too. "Hey, that's strange."

"What?"

He pointed to a blank spot on the wall. "Used to be a photo of a guy named Greg here." He pointed to another blank spot. "Michael's photo was here."

"Maybe their photos were moved?" But we found no Greg or Michael on the wall anywhere.

"Both were on the wall the last time I was here."

"When was that?"

"Friday."

"They could've moved or changed dentists."

"In less than a week?"

I shrugged. "My family moved really quick last month. One day, my mom said we had to go, so we did. Three days later, we were gone." Still didn't quite understand why we had to leave without more warning...

"You're right," said Braxton. "Could be just a coincidence. One problem, though."

"What's that?"

His eyes met mine. "I don't believe in coincidences."

"What is it, then?"

"Don't know. Something else. Something bad."

My heart beat faster. I scratched harder. *What was going on?* Should I believe for even a second what Braxton said? He did appear to be a little, well, *out there.* But the concern on his face looked too genuine to dismiss.

"Shouldn't jump to any conclusions, though," he said.

My heartbeat slowed. If Braxton had doubts something was wrong, there wasn't reason to panic. Yet.

"What we need to do," he said, "is ask questions. See what kinds of answers we get when we ask what happened to Michael and Greg's photos."

I nodded at Beth. "Should we ask her?"

"It's a start." Braxton stood. "Hello? Excuse me?"

Beth looked our way. "Yes?"

Braxton said, "I noticed there aren't photos of Greg or Michael on this wall anymore."

"Yeah, they both, like, left."

"Left how?" I asked.

"All I know is, like, their parents talked to Dr. Sharp, and now they're not patients here."

Braxton said, "*Both* of their sets of parents?"

"They aren't, like, brothers, are they?"

Braxton shook his head. "That's all you know?"

"That's it. Anything else? 'Cause I'm, like, kind of busy over here."

"Go, like, back to it, then." Braxton rolled his eyes at me as Beth turned away.

"She didn't know much," I said.

Braxton peered over at the receptionist. "True. Feeling satisfied?"

"Not really."

"Me neither. Let's see what else we can find out."

4

ALEXIS RETURNED FROM A HALLWAY ENTRANCE, now followed by a boy I assumed to be Andy and a girl I assumed to be Claire. Neither kid looked like they'd just gone through anything too terrible.

Alexis said to the kids, "Wait here." To Braxton and me: "You two, this way."

She led us into a long, narrow corridor. There were six doorways along the length of the hall.

"Jase," she said, "please wait in the room all the way down on the right. Braxton, your room's all the way down on the left."

"Hey," began Braxton, "what happened to the photos—?"

Alexis was gone. She was quick.

We moved down the hall, Braxton in the lead. He stopped at the first door on the right. The sign said:

Dr. Xander Sharp, D.D.S.

D.D.S.

Deadly Dr. Sharp.

The dentist's personal office. The door was slightly ajar. Braxton stood there, as if trying to listen to something inside the room.

"Don't hear anything," I whispered. Sort of a lie. I heard music playing softly somewhere.

Braxton said, "Let's go," and led us down the hall. We passed other rooms with closed doors, and, as we approached the rooms assigned to us, the music grew louder. Braxton turned to me and whispered, "That's no radio, in case you're wondering. Every room has its own personal MyPod set up."

"Cool," I said.

A couple of years ago Mom and Grandpa gifted me a MyPod for Christmas. Couldn't make any phone calls with it, but the device held thousands of songs. Unfortunately, I dropped it one too many times. Thing refused to turn on again after a while. Mom refused to buy me a replacement.

Braxton explained, "A bunch of playlists to choose from on each one. First place I've ever been where the adults let the kids choose the music they listen to."

"That's awesome."

We reached our rooms. The doors were open. Music played.

Scratch, scratch, scratch.

Braxton paused. "Have the chicken pox?"

"What?"

"It's okay if you do. I got them in the first grade. Can't get them again."

"Never had the chicken pox. Think I got a vaccine for that when I was a baby..."

"Oh. Have fleas, then?"

"I'm not a dog!" I did my best to ignore, and not scratch, the itch.

"Werewolf, maybe?"

"What? No!"

"Just checking," said Braxton. "Now, this is where we part. Good luck."

"Think I'll need it."

"Naw, you'll be in the record books, for sure!" He walked into his room.

My feet were cement blocks, my legs forged from the heaviest lead. I stood frozen in the doorway to my room. Not even hearing

Justin Bieber on the MyPod could move me forward to change the song.

A door creaked open somewhere behind me. A large shadow quickly filled the hallway.

I darted into the room and hopped onto the large, plastic-covered patient's chair. Sat there, pulse racing, for quite some time before I realized I was scratching my arm again and that no one was coming for me.

I studied my surroundings. Dental hygiene posters on the walls. Two stools on wheels. A large light hanging above my chair. A tray of—*gulp!*—pointy tools next to me.

Was finally where I'd hoped to never be, and everything looked to be horribly, terribly *as-it-should*.

Only thing out of the ordinary seemed to be the MyPod.

Why would a dentist spend thousands of dollars on MyPods for his patients when a single radio station could work just as well and for a much cheaper price?

Then again, I couldn't think of any way a MyPod could do me harm. Although, the mix playing now was a form of cruel and unusual punishment. What would Apollo think of BTS or Ed Sheeran? According to Grandpa, Apollo was the Greek god of music.

I climbed from the chair and went to the MyPod against the wall. The object was a boring shade of white and plugged into equally boring white speakers.

What I wouldn't give to have another MyPod—even if it were a bland ivory shade. Music made alone time feel less alone. But Mom said any MyPod money needed to come straight from my pocket. Grandpa would have to bribe me for twenty thousand more caramel candies before that happened. Not even his dentures could take that kind of abuse.

I touched my finger to the MyPod. Scrolled the song playlists.

"Changing my mix, are you?" Alexis was in the doorway, looking none too happy.

I lifted my finger. "I could, uh, leave it on this." Even while saying it, I cringed, hoping she wouldn't listen to me.

"Great," she said. "Now, sit down."

Man, I really am an idiot sometimes.

Made my way back into the chair, my ears practically bleeding from the music. Apollo probably had cotton in his earholes.

"Machine's busted, so we won't be taking X-rays of your teeth today." Alexis sat in one of the stools against the wall. She held a clipboard and a pen. "Need to ask you a couple of questions before Dr. Sharp comes in. Answer honestly."

"I've got questions for you, too."

"They'll wait until after mine." She put the pen's tip against the clipboard. "What does your diet consist of?"

"Don't know. Normal stuff."

"Specify, please."

"I eat whatever my mom makes me eat, or whatever she lets me eat."

"Whatever she *lets* you eat? What doesn't she let you eat?"

"She doesn't like it when I eat junk food, I guess, but it's not like I get in trouble if I eat some. Just try not to eat too much around her."

"She ensures you have a well-balanced diet, then?"

"Yes, but I find ways to eat lots of things that might be bad for me, too."

"Figured as much." Her pen scribbled across the clipboard. Then she asked the Weird Question: "Does your family stress vegetarianism?"

I hesitated. She'd asked Braxton almost the same thing earlier. What did the woman have against vegetarians?

"Hmm?" She eyed me suspiciously.

"No," I finally said. "Nobody's vegetarian."

She actually smiled. "Thanks. Should about do it."

I said, "Now you can answer my questions," but that's when Dr. Xander Sharp entered the room.

5

THE DENTIST DIDN'T HAVE a hook for a hand. Not even for a foot or a nose. Did I really think a part of him would be hooked? Okay, so maybe I did, but he was hook-less, and immediately my guard went down.

It almost disappeared completely when Dr. Sharp smiled my way. He didn't have fangs, either. Just normal teeth. Well, maybe not so normal. They were perfect, straight, and white. Like, *white* white. Not light yellow or beige. White. Amazing.

If a dentist had bad teeth, would patients even listen to his advice?

Sharp said, "You must be Jase," as he walked over to me, his hook-less palm extended. I shook his hand.

Alexis said, "Jase and I just went over his diet."

"Oh, yeah?" He pulled over a stool and sat beside me.

He and Alexis looked about the same age. They both had brown hair, and, as I looked closer, green eyes. They wore the same white lab coat, too. Sharp was a bit taller than his assistant, though, and he actually smiled. Alexis only smiled when someone informed her he wasn't vegetarian.

Alexis told her boss, "Vegetarianism isn't a part of his family's lifestyle." She most definitely smiled.

So did the dentist.

"Can I ask a question?"

Sharp said, "Of course, Jase. Ask away."

"Why's it matter if I'm vegetarian or not?"

Both adults looked at each other. Sharp smiled again. Might as well have permanently placed a smile on his face with plastic surgery. Sharp's cheeks probably hurt from all the smiling. Maybe he *liked* the pain.

"Certainly wouldn't judge you if you or any of your family members were vegetarians," he said. "There are many different reasons people are vegetarians, and there's nothing wrong with it."

I didn't know about that. It was kind of weird to eat mostly vegetables. I mean, honestly. *Vegetables*? Gross.

"Then why even ask?" I said.

"Wanted to get the fullest possible assessment of your teeth. A person's diet has a big effect on one's dental health. Not just the amount of sweets someone eats, either. Certain vitamins and proteins are present in meat, for example, that help strengthen teeth. Because of the lack of meat in a vegetarian's diet, sometimes his teeth are a little more sensitive or weak than the teeth of someone more carnivorous."

"Oh, okay." Made sense.

The doctor said, "Not trying to pry into your personal life. Sorry if you felt that way."

"Didn't really bother me. Just thought it was kind of weird."

"Teeth *are* weird." That bright smile again. Tried not to look at it directly, because I didn't want to feel any worse about my dental hygiene than I already did. Also, I didn't want to go blind.

"Any other questions?" asked Alexis. "Sounded like you wanted to ask me something earlier."

"Yeah, Braxton wanted me to ask you something."

Alexis snorted. "He would, wouldn't he?"

"Quite the curious one," said the doctor. "What was it?"

"He said there were photos missing on the wall out there of a couple of kids named—"

"Greg and Michael, yes," the dentist interrupted. "He wonders what happened to their photographs?"

"Yeah, and Beth told us—"

Alexis practically shouted, "*What* did Beth tell you?"

I hesitated. Was Beth not supposed to say anything about Greg or Michael, or was she only allowed to tell a certain story?

"Relax," said Sharp. He was quite calm himself. "Go on, Jase. What did Beth say?"

"She didn't know much, really. Just that they both left for some reason, and that you talked to their parents about it."

He nodded. "I did. I'll have to tell this to Braxton, as well, but the details about Greg and Michael's departure aren't all that mysterious or interesting. Unfortunately, it would be inappropriate for me to share those details with you. Hope you understand."

"It's cool," I said, even though he was clearly holding something back. Maybe Braxton would get more out of him, but I had to stop worrying about a couple of kids I didn't even know and start thinking about myself and which pointy tools were about to be scraping against my teeth and gums.

"Glad it's cool," said the dentist. "Anything else?"

Alexis's eyes burned holes in my face. Sharp's eyes were kinder.

I shook my head. "That's all. I do like the MyPod, though." Talking with the dentist had distracted me from the irritating mix that played, but it suddenly seemed to grow into a deafening roar.

"Glad you like it. It's for you guys." He paused. "Sure this is the music you want to be listening to throughout your appointment today? Or has Alexis somehow persuaded you to listen to this stuff?"

Alexis's eyes said, "Don't you dare."

Mine replied, "Just watch me."

I cleared my throat. "Wouldn't mind if we listened to something else."

The dentist said, "That can be arranged. Alexis, please change the playlist to Jase's liking. Would a mix of, let's say, recent rap music be all right with you? All radio edits, of course."

"Sure," I said.

Sharp smiled. Alexis scowled. I smiled. Alexis scowled more. I smiled even more. Alexis grew scowlier. I almost laughed.

"Keep that smile," said the dentist, "because I want to see more of those teeth. Please, sit back in your seat there, head on that headrest. Let's get started."

He leaned over, and with a push of a button, my chair tilted backward. I started to sweat again. My heart pounded. Guts twisted. Hand itched.

At least the music was a little better now.

6

FOUR MINUTES LATER, I wanted to cry, and I did. Only a little bit. I gripped the sides of the chair so tightly that I thought my knuckles might snap apart.

"Just as I thought," said Sharp, his voice muffled by a paper mask. He pulled his hand from my mouth. In his grasp was a sleek metal tool. On its end was, of all things, *a hook*.

"Cavity?" asked Alexis from somewhere behind me.

"Yep," said the dentist. "Hand me that mirror, will you?"

A moment later, a handheld mirror hovered above my face. Tears collected at the corners of my bloodshot eyes. I drooled some, released my grip on the chair, and scratched.

"In pain, aren't you?" asked the doctor.

I didn't need to answer, but I nodded slowly anyhow.

"The last thing we want. We get no joy from seeing you squirm and tear up in your chair, okay?"

Again, I didn't need to answer, but I nodded once more.

"I have to see what shape your teeth are in, and unfortunately that takes a lot of poking and prodding. Most of your teeth don't mind all that, because they're strong and healthy. But the ones it does bother—well, those teeth aren't so strong and healthy. They're a little more sensitive. Open wide, please."

He spoke to me like I was some little kid, like I'd never been to a dentist before. Like I didn't understand why I was in agony.

I opened my mouth pretty wide. Would've been wider if the right side of my face weren't so sore. The mirror showed something dangling from the back of my throat like a plump little worm.

Sharp's gloved finger touched the mirror. "See where I'm pointing?"

"Yenph." It was difficult to speak with my mouth stuck in the open-wide position.

"Good, good." His finger pressed against the reflection of one of my back right teeth. "That, my friend, is a cavity."

All I could see was a small black dot in the center of the tooth. Teeth shouldn't have small black dots.

And since when was the doctor my *friend*? Didn't really get a chance to even think about that, though, before he pointed to another one of my teeth.

"Another cavity?" asked Alexis. I could almost hear her smiling.

"Yes." He pulled away the mirror, looking down at me, his green eyes behind goggles. "Don't think you've been brushing your teeth as well as you could be."

Scratch, scratch.

So much for the record books.

7

"Jason Kyle Clark, I'm not at all happy with this!"

Knew Mom wouldn't be. Still, I'd hoped she'd understand getting cavities was just part of being a kid. No such luck. When she used my full name, I knew she meant business.

She glared at me as I sat in front of the photograph wall. Sharp stood next to her, as did Grandpa. The appointment was over, but the torture had yet to end.

"Stop scratching," Mom said. I did.

"Mrs. Clark," said the doctor, "I understand your concern, and you should not by any means be happy that Jase has cavities. However, two cavities are hardly the end of the world. I've seen much, much worse, believe me. If anything, you should be pleased with your son for lasting this long without ever getting one."

"Downright admirable," said Grandpa.

The dentist smiled. "Not quite, but nothing to be ashamed of, certainly."

Mom sighed. "I've never had a cavity, and I want Jase to have similar respect for his teeth that I have for mine."

Grandpa snorted. "Come on, as a kid you had about the most uneven set of teeth I've ever seen. Wore braces for six years. Had glasses back then, too, and I remember you coming home crying because kids at school called you a four-eyed railroad track."

Mom definitely didn't look happy now. "Braces for *five* years, thank you very much, and my crooked teeth had nothing to do with my dental hygiene. Just bad genetics." She turned to Dr. Sharp. "Please, continue."

"We'll need to set up another appointment so that we can get the cavities filled. Sooner the better, because we don't want those cavities getting any worse, do we?"

"We certainly do not." Mom turned to me. "From here on out we are going to be eating lots of fruits and veggies, aren't we?"

I half-expected Sharp to say something about vegetarians, but he just smiled. "Sorry to leave you here, but I have another patient waiting for me in the back. A young man whose dental hygiene, I assure you, is far worse than your son's."

Braxton. Eight cavities. Wondered what his mom thought about that.

The dentist gestured toward the counter. "Beth will be more than happy to set another appointment for you. Good day. Nice meeting all of you."

The dentist turned and disappeared down the hallway. Mom stepped up to the counter to speak with Beth, and Grandpa took a seat with me in front of all the photographs.

"Aside from the cavities, how was it? Everything you feared? Kind of get the heebie-jeebies just sitting here with you."

I didn't know how serious Grandpa was about that, but I just shook my head. "It was okay. I survived."

"Survival's important."

"Dr. Sharp seems nice enough."

"That's good, too, I guess."

"It's just…"

"Spill it, boy."

I pointed to the wall behind us. "A couple of kids' photos are missing, and he won't tell me why."

"Why should he?"

"Their disappearance is just…mysterious."

Grandpa narrowed his dark eyes. "Says who?"

"Braxton."

"That kid you came in here with?"

"Yeah."

"Made a crazy friend already?"

"Don't think he's *that* crazy."

"Good quality in a friend. Not being crazy."

Was Braxton really my friend? He was kind of weird, yeah, but I didn't care too much about that. I hadn't really met anyone else since my family moved four weeks ago. Maybe Braxton and I could have fun together. He seemed to like me pretty okay. *More* than okay. I was willing to give him a try.

"Let's go," said Mom. "You're back here on Tuesday." She'd apparently finished with Beth.

Grandpa stood. I stayed in my seat.

"What, now you want to stay here?" said Mom.

"Don't want to go without talking to Braxton."

"Who?"

Grandpa said, "I think he's made a buddy."

Beth was observing. "Isn't it, like, so cute?"

"Very," said Mom. She finally smiled. "Some good has come out of this visit, after all."

I asked, "Can we wait for him?"

Mom looked at her watch. "We're supposed to eat out tonight."

"Can he come with us?"

"Jase, I'm sure his parents are here to—"

"He said they aren't, Mom."

"I don't know…"

"Grandpa?"

He shrugged. "Your mom's the boss, kiddo. I see no harm in it. Boy would be safe with us. Not like we're serial killers."

Mom stared hard at Grandpa. "But the liability. I don't even know the kid's parents."

Beth said, "From what I know, they're, like, totally weird. They don't ever, like, come here with Braxton. I've only ever talked with them on the phone. "

"See, Mom? We could at least give him a ride home. He's getting a cavity filled right now. You can't just let him walk home alone after that!"

Grandpa said, "Your son has a point."

Mom nodded. "Okay, we'll wait for him. Maybe, just *maybe*, he can come with us to get a burger."

My stomach growled. Suddenly felt so empty...

A big, juicy burger?! Sounded fantastic!

Sounded *perfect*.

8

FORTY-FIVE MINUTES LATER, Braxton finally emerged from the dentist's clutches and his drills. Mom, Grandpa, and I were in the waiting room, well, *waiting* for Braxton's arrival. We'd waited so long that the movie ended and started over again. Grandpa was quite pleased.

Braxton waved to me as he stepped through the doorway with Alexis. He smiled without showing teeth. Maybe they hurt too much to display.

Alexis looked down at Braxton and said, "You know what to do. No eating or drinking for at least half an hour."

Braxton didn't even look her way. He just nodded and walked over to me, then winked. Weird.

Alexis said to Mom, "Dr. Sharp thanks you for taking Braxton home. He shouldn't have to walk home alone after a filling."

"It's not that bad," said Braxton. "My face doesn't even feel numb anymore. You really get used to it after about the sixth time."

"In any case," Alexis said to Mom, "Braxton's parents appear to be quite *unconventional* when it comes to how they raise their son, but over the phone they seemed happy that you'd be so kind as to bring him home."

"It's no problem," said Mom.

Braxton beamed. "They even said I could go to dinner with you!"

"Under the condition that Braxton only eat a salad, of course," Alexis said.

"*Salad?*" asked Grandpa. "Do children even like salads?"

"No," Braxton said swiftly.

"Have to obey parents' orders anyway." Mom walked toward the exit. "Come along now."

Alexis locked eyes with me. "See you in a few days, Jase." My spine became an icicle.

I followed Braxton out the door as fast as I could. Freedom. For now. Mom was already at the elevator doors. She must've been just as hungry as I was.

I licked my lips. *Burger. Thick. Cheesy. Yummy. Goodness.*

My stomach not only growled. It bellowed.

"Heard that," Mom commented as we caught up to her.

I shrugged. "Can't help it."

Grandpa said, "Even these old ears heard it. Sounds like you have the Chimera trapped in your belly."

"I know you're not making another Greek mythology reference."

"Dana," Grandpa said, "no reason to be afraid of the lion-goat-snake. It can't get you. It's stuck inside Jase's stomach."

Mom glared. "No. More. Monsters. Got it?"

Grandpa changed the subject. "Good thing I put in extra denture adhesive today. Burgers are tough on the old chompers." He looked down at Braxton. "So, why're your folks making you eat salad? That some kind of goofy remedy for a cavity?"

"If that's the case," said Mom, "you, Jase, are going to have a nice, green, leafy meal."

"No!" No salad. I needed a burger.

"My parents always make me eat salad," Braxton said with a little sigh. "Without dressing, usually."

"Without dressing?" said Grandpa. "Your folks have something against taste?"

Braxton shrugged. "They're vegetarian. My dad wants to go vegan by the end of the year."

Grandpa nodded. "That is indeed a serious problem."

The elevator doors opened. No one was there. The four of us made our way inside. The doors closed, and we descended.

Mom asked, "Your parents have always raised you vegetarian?"

Braxton shook his head. "Only the last couple of years. They saw some show on television about slaughterhouses. It freaked them out."

Grandpa snorted. "I worked in a slaughterhouse from '74 to '81. It was good, honest work."

"We know that, Dad. Don't make Braxton uncomfortable. He's our guest."

"I'm not uncomfortable," said Braxton. "It's cool you worked in a slaughterhouse. Was there a lot of blood?"

"Full of gory livestock limbs, just like a Cyclops's den."

Mom didn't even bother complaining about Greek mythology this time. Instead, she said to Braxton, "I'd like to meet your parents. They sound interesting."

"*Interesting?*" said Braxton. "I think my parents are crazy."

"I think they are, too," said Grandpa.

"Dad! I'm sure they're very nice people!"

Braxton said, "Not really. They call me fat, you know?"

Silence. So much silence.

The elevator dinged. Doors slid apart. We stepped into the building's lobby.

"After they watched the show on slaughterhouses, they watched one on obesity," Braxton added. "Home's been very little fun since that night."

Mom said to Grandpa, "Maybe we should try eating less meat."

"Dana, that's the worst idea you've ever had!"

"I just think our health might benefit from more vegetables, and…"

While Mom and Grandpa argued, Braxton whispered to me, "When we're alone, I have something to show you."

I gave him the what-are-you-talking-about look. He patted his left pants pocket.

Didn't know whether to be curious or kind of scared.

I just settled on both.

9

AT THE RESTAURANT, everyone ordered a burger. Even Braxton. Only his burger was made of tofu or bean sprouts—something strange and disgusting like that. And it came with a huge, vibrant salad.

When the waitress left with our orders, Grandpa said, "A burger that isn't made of meat? Too young to be a hippie."

"Dad, his parents have raised him a certain way."

"Yeah, *they're* hippies. I get it. I mean, I *don't* get it."

"Just because you don't agree with something doesn't make it weird, scary, or wrong."

"Sure about that?"

I laughed, and so did Braxton. Mom looked about as far away from laughing as she could get.

"Wish I could eat a real burger," said Braxton.

Grandpa said, "Who's stopping you?" He pointed to Mom. "Besides her."

"I am. Haven't eaten meat for so long, just the thought of eating it almost makes me want to puke all over the place. Don't want that to happen, do you?"

Grandpa shook his head. "Please, no."

"Last year, my cousin Larry dared me to eat some bacon, and just the smell of it made me throw up all over Aunt Kerry who ralphed into Uncle Gary's—"

"Okay, this isn't very appropriate dinner conversation." Mom put up the roadblock. Just when he was getting to the good part, too...

"That's why I don't eat meat," said Braxton. "My mind and body aren't used to it anymore."

"A tragic tale if I ever heard one," said Grandpa.

Braxton gazed at his hands clasped together on the table. "Guess you can blame all my cavities on it."

"How?" I wondered.

"My parents are so strict when it comes to what I eat. Can't stand it, really. To kind of get back at them, I sneak a lot of junk food into my room. Chips. Candy. Cupcakes. Donuts. Eating all that stuff is my way of being free. I don't care how many cavities I get. I need that freedom."

No one in my family said anything for a few moments. Felt pretty bad for the guy.

Finally, Grandpa slapped him on the shoulder. "A little rebellion never hurt anyone."

Braxton asked, "What about the Shays' Rebellion? That was a brutal part of American history."

Grandpa looked at Mom and me. We shrugged. He said, "I like to say history's history. Better left in the past than brought up again in the present."

Mom snorted. "Except Greek history."

"Greek *mythology*," began Grandpa, "is full of fun stories. Have something against fun?"

Before I could answer "yes" on her behalf, Mom said, "Is History a favorite subject of yours, Braxton?"

"Not really. I like all subjects the same. Expect maybe P.E. I'm a pretty good student, just lousy at sports." Braxton turned to me. "You look like a sports guy."

"Sports are okay," I said, "but I like to read and write."

"Cool! I read a lot, too, but you write? Stories and stuff?"

"It's not epic poetry," said Grandpa. "He's no Homer."

"You'd better be talking about the Simpsons," Mom replied.

"The *who*? Our new neighbors?" Grandpa was only kidding. He watched *The Simpsons* at least once (sometimes twice) every day.

Braxton asked, "Who's Homer Not-Simpson?"

"An ancient Greek writer," Grandpa explained. "He wrote long, beautiful, *epic* poems like *The Odyssey*."

To Braxton, I said, "I've got a journal. Maybe if I have a good story to tell someday, I'll write one."

Braxton's face lit up. "I'd be the first to read it!"

Mom said, "At Jase's old school, he won an essay contest and received a hundred dollars."

"Wow!" Braxton exclaimed so loudly that other patrons paused their meals to glance our way.

I shrugged. "Not a big deal. It was just about recycling."

"Don't be modest," said Grandpa. "Best essay about recycling I ever read!"

"Can I read it sometime?" Braxton's eyes pleaded with mine.

I said, "You really want to read an essay?"

"Not *an* essay. *Your* essay. We're friends now, and I want to get to know you the best I can."

I said, "If you must…"

Braxton nodded. "I want to know everything about you from your stance on recycling to what type of peanut butter you like—I like smooth the best, but chunky's okay—to how you like life here in your new hometown."

I stared at him, wondering if I'd gotten myself attached to an oddball, but Braxton just smiled back at me, his face full of cheer.

I said, "I like it here pretty okay." That was a lie. I wished we'd never moved. Didn't miss Arizona's desert heat, but I sorely missed my pals.

"How's it compare to the old place?" said Braxton. "Where is the old place? Why'd you guys move anyway?"

Before I could say anything, Mom spoke up. "You two, go wash your hands before dinner."

Braxton and I slid out our side of the booth. As we walked away from the table, Braxton said, "Now I can show you what I have."

He didn't say another word until we got into the restroom, where he checked every stall.

What could he possibly have in his possession to make him so paranoid?

He opened the restroom entrance to see if anyone else was coming. Coast cleared.

He pulled folded papers from his pants pocket. What terrible words were written on those pages?

"As you waited alone for Dr. Sharp, I went into his office. He was out front talking to those other kids' parents. Alexis walked in and almost caught me red-handed, but I hid under the desk."

"Why'd you go into his office?"

"To see what I could find about Greg and Michael."

"What did you find?"

Braxton began to unfold the papers. "These were sitting out on top of the desk. Didn't expect it to be that easy."

"What are they?"

"Copies of both guys' files."

"Okay…"

He looked up, his gaze gleaming. "They say a lot, Jase. They say *a lot.*"

10

WE CRAMMED TOGETHER INSIDE A STALL. I pressed in tightly against Braxton, trying to get a good look at what he'd taken. The papers were filled with neatly typewritten information. Which dark secrets would be brought to light?

Braxton pointed to one page. "Here it says Michael's lower jaw is growing much faster than it should. Always thought his face looked too long for a normal person."

"A normal person like you," I said.

He nodded. "That's right."

The itch was back. "I don't care about the guy's weird-looking face. You said these say a lot. What else is there?"

Braxton scanned the page with his finger. "He's only ever had one cavity. The mutant jaw pretty much makes up for that, though."

"Besides the teeth stuff, is there anything?"

"There's a phone number and an address."

"Okay. Is there an address for the other guy?"

"Greg?" Braxton flipped to the other page. "Yes, and a phone number." He looked at my hand. "Are you sure you don't have fleas?"

I kept scratching. "Any reasons for us to use that information?"

"Like I said, man, these say *a lot*."

"Show me, then," I said. "Thought you were going to tell me about Greg's overbite or something."

"How'd you know?"

"You've got to be kidding! If that's all it is, then I don't care." I left the stall, headed for a sink.

"Hey! Wait!" Braxton followed.

"Can't believe you got me thinking something strange is actually going on, when all you've found is a pretty common case of longjaw."

"Technically, I don't think it's called 'longjaw.'" Braxton shoved the papers in my face. "You didn't give me enough time to get to the good parts."

I grabbed the pages, started reading. Just a bunch of big words and numbers I didn't understand.

"Good parts?" I said. "I see lots of confusing parts."

"Near the bottom. The parts that somebody *underlined*."

There they were. Someone found a couple of lines at the bottom of Greg's file to be especially important. They were underlined over and over again. They read:

"*BP PSI consistently increasing at strong rate. Subject near completion of Phase Three treatment. A serious candidate.*"

I scratched my head. "Huh?"

"Exactly," said Braxton.

I flipped over to Michael's file. At the bottom of his page, a single line was underlined:

"*BP PSI highest of all. Definite top of the pool.*"

I read the line twice, then said, "Okay…"

"Weird, right?" Excited, Braxton started bouncing back and forth in his shoes.

"I don't understand it, if that's what you mean."

"Exactly what I mean," he said.

"We're not dentists," I said. "Not supposed to understand what this stuff means."

"Come on! Pieces are falling into place here!"

"What pieces?"

He yanked the papers out of my hands. "These two guys both mysteriously vanish in the same week. Copies of both of their files just so happen to be out in the open on Dr. Sharp's desk, which means he was looking at them for some reason. Both files have the same kind of information underlined. Something about...?"

"BP PSI, whatever that is."

"Exactly!" he shouted. "Whatever that is!"

I stepped up to a sink and turned on the faucet. "You'd better wash your hands, Braxton."

I saw him in the mirror, standing behind me, shocked. "You don't think it's strange?" he said.

"Of course, I do." I squeezed soap into my palms. "It seems strange because we don't understand what it means."

"But both files have the same thing underlined. Nothing else in common except for—"

"It could be a coincidence."

"Already told you, I don't believe in coincidences."

"Maybe you should start believing in them." I put my hands under the warm water. It helped to melt the itch away.

"No. Too easy. Everything happens for a reason." He paused. "Why are you being like this? I thought you felt something fishy is going on, too."

I locked eyes with his reflection. "Something fishy *is* going on. You stole files from a dentist's office."

"Copies of files," he corrected.

"So what? You could still get us both in lots of trouble."

"That's why we play dumb. We don't tell anyone anything unless we have to."

"I don't do this kind of stuff," I said. "I'm a good kid."

"Michael and Greg are good kids, too—probably. I don't know them very well, or maybe even at all, but they're 'top' and 'serious' candidates for something that sounds really, really creepy. Whatever it is, it has phases, Jase. *Phases*. That are near completion! Maybe they've *already been* completed!"

I said, "It could mean nothing."

"But what if it means everything?"

I turned off the water and grabbed a paper towel. All was silent as I slowly dried my hands. Time to get them dirty again?

Yep.

I tossed the paper towel into the trash and said, "All right. Let's try those phone numbers."

11

"BP PSI? Yeah, I've heard of it." Grandpa stood in my bedroom doorway later that night. "A very serious thing."

"It is?" I sat at my desk, the glow of the computer screen staining my skin a light blue. I suddenly felt cold, despite the heat spilling through the vents above my Spider-Man poster.

"Very, very serious."

"What is it?" I scratched and scratched.

He leaned against the doorframe. "Not sure you're old enough to understand."

"Try explaining it!"

Mom poked her head in. "What's going on?"

"Jase is trying to get some information out of me."

Mom stepped into the room, holding a basket full of laundry. "Is he?" She walked across the room to my dirty clothes hamper and opened it. "Jase, you wearing beige? I'm washing beige right now."

"I'm not wearing beige."

"Your boxers?" Mom said. "The ones with the little green polka dots? Don't see them in here." She tossed clothes from my hamper into the basket held beneath her left arm.

I said, "Okay, I'm wearing those."

"Want them washed?"

"Like I said, I'm wearing them."

"So, no, then?"

Grandpa sighed. "The boy's going to keep the underwear he's got on."

"Fine, fine…" Without looking at Grandpa or me—just piling laundry from my hamper into her basket—Mom asked, "What're you guys talking about?"

"Man stuff," said Grandpa.

"Secrets, huh? Keeping Mom out of the loop. I see how it is."

Grandpa looked at me. "Mind bringing your mother into our conversation?"

"Already brought herself into it, didn't she?"

He smiled. "How right you are."

"Well?" Mom stared at me.

"We were talking about BP PSI," said Grandpa.

"BP PSI?" said Mom. "What the heck is that?"

He shrugged. "Was hoping you could tell me so that I could tell him."

"Grandpa, you told me you knew what it was!"

"Jase, you're old enough to know that I like to have a little fun with you now and again."

"*Man.*" I sighed. "You guys don't have any idea what it might mean?"

"Where did you hear about this?" Mom said.

I didn't think it would be a very good idea to pull Michael's file out of my pocket and show her, so I just lied: "In this book I'm reading."

"What's the book about?" she asked.

"Um…A doctor."

"A doctor?"

"Yes."

"Are you sure this doesn't have something to do with Dr. Sharp?"

She is good. So good. *Too* good.

I shook my head. "No, in the story the doctor says something about BP PSI to one of his patients."

"Medical mumbo-jumbo," said Grandpa. "Asclepius would know. He's the god of medicine."

After a few seconds, Mom said, "I guess it could be blood pressure. BP could be an abbreviation for blood pressure."

I nodded, but my mind said, "That's not it." Dentists don't use that pump that squeezes your arm like a python.

Grandpa said, "Blood pressure. It makes sense. PSI...? There's a Greek letter spelled p-s-i. *Psi*." It sounded like "sigh."

"Doesn't make sense in this case, Dad."

"Can't a man think out loud without being criticized? I'm just narrowing down the options!" He fell silent for a little while, and then he muttered, "PSI... That's a TV show, isn't it?"

"Don't think so," said Mom. "Jase, just look it up on the Internet."

Grandpa looked hurt. "I am a one-man Internet," he said. "I am full of information."

"Yeah, you're full of *something*, all right," Mom said as she walked out of the room with the laundry.

"Thanks, Grandpa, but I'll just look it up on the Web, okay?"

He smiled. "Ouch. The ultimate insult." He turned and disappeared into the hallway.

I pulled up Google and typed in "PSI." 444 million results found! Ugh. The most popular options were about random institutes and incorporations. Boring. And wrong.

I had to be more specific. I thought and thought and thought. "Come on, Jase. PSI is an abbreviation for...?"

Desperate, I just typed in, "PSI abbreviation." The search engine searched. My fingertips hovered over the keyboard.

There. At the very top. The first option.

Somehow I just knew it was right. How could it be that easy?

PSI. *Pound-force per square inch.*

"A unit of pressure," it read.

12

BRAXTON HAD GIVEN me his phone number at dinner. It was written on the copy of Michael's file in my pocket. My phone number was written on the copy of Greg's file that Braxton kept.

Our house had three phones. One was Mom's cell, which she rarely let me use. The other two were landlines: one in the kitchen, and one in Mom's bedroom. Grandpa wasn't great with technology, so he only knew how to use phones that plugged into the wall. Mom's easy access to two phones made Grandpa a little jealous, since his room didn't have any phone connection hooked up at all.

I headed for the kitchen, going down the hall, walking through the living room. My housemates watched some local news on the TV. Grandpa sat in his musty recliner, and Mom folded clean laundry near his propped-up feet.

"I'm using the phone," I said as I headed for the kitchen.

"Hold it right there," said Mom.

I stopped next to her. "Yes?"

"Who're you calling?" Mom asked me. Then: "Wait! Let me guess. Braxton."

I nodded. "I have to tell him something."

Mom smiled. "So great that you've made a friend. Haven't been apart for two hours, and you're already running to the phone to talk again. Isn't it great, Dad?"

"Yeah, even if the kid is a little weirdo."

"Dad!"

"What, I can't call the kid a weirdo?" said Grandpa. "He's a little weirdo, plain and simple. Were you listening to him at the dinner table? Would 'freak' be more appropriate? 'Cause I thought that would be too harsh, but if you would prefer it to..."

Grandpa's comments faded as I reached the kitchen. I grabbed the phone, almost pulling out the paper to dial the number right there. But I then decided it was best not to risk a file viewing by Mom. The phone was portable, so I headed back for my room.

"What do you need to talk to him about?" Mom asked when I walked by again.

Grandpa said, "It's the PSI, right? Did you find out what it means?"

"Um...no," I said. "It's about... something else."

"Those are the pauses of a liar," Mom said. She stopped folding, clutching onto one of my shirts. "A very bad liar."

"Taught him everything I know," said Grandpa.

The news anchor on TV was detailing information about a bank robbery. I was a criminal caught in the middle of my own heist, and the file felt heavier every second. The phone almost slipped out of my sweaty, itchy hand.

"What are you trying to hide from us, Jason Kyle Clark?"

"*Mom.*"

"Let him gossip with the weirdo. We can inject him with truth serum later."

Mom's eyes were daggers. I swear, she was a living, breathing lie detector.

"Fine. Go." She turned back to the TV.

I practically ran back to my room and closed the door softly behind me. Didn't need to draw any more attention.

I sat back down at my desk, in front of the computer. I pulled out the file and dialed Braxton's number. He told me he didn't have his own cell phone, either, so I wondered if one of his parents would answer, and if one did, would he or she sound like the strange creature Braxton had described?

I didn't get to find out. Braxton answered after the second ring: "Hello, you have reached the Grunk residence."

"Grunk?" I said.

"Jase! Hi! Grunk's my last name. I don't like it, really. Do you? It sounds like something you scrape off the bottom of your shoe. I wonder if my future bride will take the name as her own?"

I couldn't imagine the type of woman who possibly, on an off-chance, if she had *very* interesting taste, would someday marry Braxton, so I just said, "Can you talk?"

"My tongue hasn't been cut out yet!"

"That's good."

He said, "I'm glad you called, because I was just going to call you!"

"Really?"

"Totally! I found something on the Internet."

"So did I. It's why I called."

He asked, "Did you type 'Dr. Sharp' into Google?"

"No, but I will now."

Google was still on the screen. I erased "PSI abbreviation" and typed in "Dr. Sharp."

860 million options. The extent of Internet information never ceased to amaze me.

Since I didn't want to search through 860 million webpages, I said, "Typed it in. Where do I go from here?"

"Number three on page four."

I found the link and silently read the brief details: "...*doctor faces serious accusations...*"

Braxton interrupted with, "Can you *believe* it?"

"Haven't even clicked on it yet."

"Click it! Click it!"

I clicked. A news article popped up on the screen. Its headline read, *"Portland doctor faces serious accusations about use of controversial methods."*

There was a photograph of the doctor next to all the words. I recognized the article's Dr. Sharp, all right. However, it wasn't my dentist.

It was his assistant.

Dr. *Alexis* Sharp.

13

I DIDN'T BLINK. Just stared at Alexis on the computer screen. Words of wisdom: *Don't stare at a computer screen without blinking.* After twenty seconds, my eyes were on fire.

"Jase?" Braxton said at the pinnacle of my eyeball inferno. "You okay? Doesn't sound like you're breathing."

I blinked and let out a deep breath at the same time. "What is this I'm looking at?" I mumbled.

"Isn't it great?"

Great? I could've thought of a gazillion words that better described my opinion of the current development. Like: shocking, strange, weird, freaky, terrifying, horrifying, confusing, jaw-dropping, insane, crazy, intense, ridiculous, and practically any other word in the English language that didn't mean the same thing as great.

"It's…it's something, that's for sure."

"Great," he repeated.

"No, not great." I scrolled down the page. The article was kind of long. "I haven't read what this is about. Have you?"

"Yes."

Silence.

I said, "Do you want to share what you read?"

"Oh," he said. "Duh."

Silence again.

"Braxton?"

"I'm here."

"So…"

He said, "So, I'm just looking at the picture of Alexis. Now I see…"

"What do you see?"

"How much she looks like the dentist Dr. Sharp."

"Huh?"

"They're brother and sister," he said. "It's why they have the same last name."

"The article says that?"

"One of the last sentences says, 'Until the trial, she plans to stay with her brother, Alexander, in California.' Dr. Sharp's first name is—"

"Xander," I said, "which is short for—"

"Alexander. Don't you love how we finish each other's deductions? Anyway, want to know what she did, or supposedly did?"

"I can read the specifics later, but give me the important details now."

Braxton chuckled. "Oh, man, we are so not supposed to have seen this."

I scratched my hand. "What's it say?"

"Maybe we'll grow up to be detectives, be each other's partners, and stake out the bad guys together!"

"Let's take it one article at a time."

"It says that she is a psychiatrist," he explained. "But this article was written five years ago, so maybe she isn't a psychiatrist anymore? We'll have to look for another article."

"If she was a psychiatrist still, would she be her brother's assistant?"

"Good point!"

Scratch, scratch. I said, "Does the article say which 'controversial methods' she was using?"

"She hypnotized a lady, some patient who didn't want to be hypnotized. The patient told things to Alexis she didn't want to when she was hypnotized, and when she found out that Alexis had hypnotized her without permission... Well, you get it. She complained to somebody. It obviously worked better than when I complain to my parents. They don't do anything about anything!"

"That's it?" I asked.

"A couple of other people complained about the same thing—the hypnotizing." Suddenly: "Doesn't this kind of scare you?"

Um, *yes.* Completely. Utterly.

"I've only been around her once," I said. "Don't think she hypnotized me."

"That's the thing, though! How would you even know if you've been hypnotized? You ever been hypnotized before?"

"Well, no." Braxton wasn't helping me feel any better.

"Exactly! Not to your knowledge! Neither have I! But wait! Maybe Alexis has been secretly hypnotizing me for three years and I don't have any clue! Doesn't it just mess with your mind?"

It really did. My brain hurt. Tons.

He said, "Maybe this has something to do with Greg and Michael! We might have taken the next important step to figuring out what the heck is going on!"

I nodded, and then I stopped nodding, because there was no way he could see that I agreed with him. "Yeah, maybe."

"I hope it's more than a maybe. I hope it's an absolutely-positutely!"

"Anyway, don't you want to know the reason I called?"

"Oh, yeah! Wow! You have something important, too? We're really progressing fast, aren't we?"

"I think I found out that PSI means 'pounds per-square-inch'. It's a way you measure pressure."

"Pressure?" said Braxton.

"Pressure. My mom and Grandpa said—"

"You told *your mom and grandpa?*"

"Don't worry, I didn't tell them anything."

"What didn't you tell us?"

Uh, oh.

It was Mom, listening from the other line in her bedroom.

14

SCRATCH, scratch, SCRATCH.

I couldn't believe it. But, at the same time, I totally could.

How long had she been listening? What had she heard? More importantly, what had she hopefully *not* heard?

"Um...um...I...um...uh..." I stammered. Not exactly smooth, by any means.

"Hi, Mrs. Clark," Braxton said.

"Say goodbye, Braxton."

"Are you sure?"

"Very sure," Mom told him.

"Oh, okay. Talk to you later, Jase."

He hung up, and I was left with my mother's screaming silence on the other line. I wished she would just scold me already. All she said was, "Stay where you are."

Dial tone rang in my ear. I turned the phone off, looked at the computer screen, and yelped. The article about Alexis was right in front of me, and Mom was going to be in my room in less than—

The door opened just as I minimized the window. I turned to the doorway and tried to deflect Mom's glare with a great big smile. The smile bounced off her glare and smacked me in the forehead.

"So?" she said.

"What?"

"Don't you 'what' me, young man."

"Seriously," I said as seriously as I could. "What did you hear? Or what do you *think* you heard?"

"I heard enough to know that you're hiding something."

"Can't believe you were spying on me!"

"I can't believe you're hiding something from your grandpa and me."

"I'm not *hiding* anything!"

"No?" she asked.

"No."

"*No?*"

"No!"

"What's with all the no's?" Grandpa appeared in the hallway behind Mom.

I pointed with not one, but two, fingers. "She was listening in on my phone conversation!"

Grandpa didn't look too shocked. He slowly shook his head. "That's just wrong."

Mom said, "What's so wrong about it? You spied in on *many* of my phone conversations growing up."

"What can I say? Didn't trust those boys you dated."

"What about my dad?" I said, trying to change the subject off me.

"Especially your dad," said Grandpa.

Mom's face was as red as Adonis's roses. "We DO NOT speak about that man in this house, *do you understand me?*"

Grandpa and I both knew better. My dad died when I was a baby in some kind of accident—I think he crashed his car. His death hurt Mom so much that she didn't want to even think about it. We couldn't speak about Dad *ever*.

It kind of bothered me when I was in second and third grades, because I saw all my friends having fun and learning how to play sports with their dads. I really wanted to know more about who Dad was, but Mom only had one really old picture of him in her bedroom, and she refused to say anything more about him. Because of Mom's picture, I at least knew I got my blond hair and blue eyes from my father.

Grandpa told me one day, "Your father was a great man. I know he loved you and your mother very much. What happened to him was a horrible, horrible thing, but it can't be taken back. The more you know about it, the more it will hurt you. There's no use trying to revisit that pain.

"It's a little like the situation with your grandma. She got sick very young, as you know, and I had to take care of your mom alone. I really miss your grandma, but I accepted the fact that she won't ever be able to come back. I was forced to move on, for my sake, and for your mom's sake.

"So, I know you want your dad, but he just can't be here. Your mom and I are here for you, and we do the best we can. Can that be enough for you, Jase?"

It had been enough, but the thought still showed up in my head sometimes: *What about Dad?*

In my bedroom, there was an awkward silence after the Dad comment. Mom said more calmly, "I didn't like the fact that Jase was lying to us. I wanted to know what he was hiding."

Grandpa said, "That's all well and good, but it's hardly the way to build a healthy relationship with your son. Now you're going to have the boy constantly on edge, never sure when his nosy mother might be spying. Going to have some major trust issues with him. Isn't that right, Jase?"

I nodded. "Yes. Very true."

Mom walked into the room, eyeing the computer. I sweated from every pore on my body. I felt so gross, so *itchy*.

"His safety is what I need," she said, "not his undying trust. He can *trust* that I care about his well-being and that I will do everything in my power to make sure he's safe."

Grandpa sighed. "Sorry, Jase, she's a tough cookie to crack. May have done a little too well with her."

She snorted. "I'm more like Mom than I am like you."

He nodded. "Unfortunately so."

Mom walked over to my desk. Her eyes kept going to the computer. *Please don't ask to see what I've been looking at online, please don't ask to see what I've been looking at online...*

She raised an eyebrow. "What's this?"

Oh, no. Even worse. *Incredibly* worse.

She had the copy of Michael's file in her hand. I left it sitting out in the open. For as smart as I am, I can sure be a real idiot sometimes.

I didn't even say anything. Didn't know what to say. If I lied, it would sound like a lie, and if I told the truth, it would sound even more terrible.

Her eyes grew large as she read the file. "Jason Kyle *Clark*," she seethed.

"What's that?" asked Grandpa. He met her beside me.

Even Grandpa looked angry as he read the file. "There's that BP PSI," he muttered.

I knew I was going to get it big time. "It" being something cruel and unusual.

"This is what you heard about on the phone?" Grandpa asked Mom.

"No," she said. "I actually didn't hear much. Picked up near the end of their conversation."

Should've *known* she was bluffing. *Dang it.*

"Well, this right here isn't good," said Grandpa, looking at the file. "No, sir, not good *at all.*"

Mom frowned. "Knew he was hiding something."

"What do you have to say for yourself?" said Grandpa. "After I defend you, it turns out you really are guilty of something. Do you know how much that just curdles my milk?"

That last part was one of those old people sayings that don't mean much to us young people. I didn't know what it meant, but I just figured it meant Grandpa wasn't too happy with me. Grandpa was *always* happy with me.

I felt like garbage. I *was* garbage. Couldn't scratch any of my guilty stink away.

I tried to speak, but it didn't come out too well. "I...uh...um... well...you see...uh...I..."

Grandpa said, "This is serious stuff here. You took this—no, wait —you *stole* this from that dentist's office?"

I couldn't say it was Braxton who stole the file and gave it to me, because I didn't want them to be mad at him. They wouldn't want me to hang out with such a "bad influence."

I sunk in my seat. "Yes, I stole it. I was just bragging to Braxton about it."

"Why would you do such a stupid thing?" asked Mom.

For that, I had no good answer, so I said nothing more. I just stared at my feet. My big, stupid feet.

15

MOM HAD me sit at the kitchen table. In front of me were a piece of paper and a pencil.

"You're writing an apology letter to Dr. Sharp," Mom explained. "You're delivering it in person tomorrow, along with the file."

The phone was back in its cradle five feet from me, but it couldn't have seemed farther away. So much for swapping information with Braxton. So much for calling Michael's phone number.

"Get your eyes away from that phone," Mom scolded. "Words need to start appearing on that page."

I said, "What do you want me to write?"

Mom white-knuckled a steaming mug of tea. She glared at me so hard that, for a moment, I thought she might toss the drink in my face. "How about how incredibly sorry you are for being a thief?"

"I'm not a—" I stopped myself. Almost said that I wasn't a thief, that I was only an accessory to a thief. A minor criminal, only a little bit guilty.

"Don't try to back out of this, Jase. You must take responsibility for your actions. Do you know how hard this is for *me*?"

"Why is it hard for you?" I asked her.

"When you go into that dentist's office tomorrow, people are going to know that you, my son, are a thief. They are going to know that *I* have raised a thief. What will that make me look like?" She sighed. "I'm just so disappointed. So very disappointed."

"Want me to tell you why I did it?"

She said, "Doesn't matter why you did it. No reason you can tell me will be good enough. You weren't raised to be a thief. You know right from wrong."

"Exactly! I do know right from wrong. That means I would only steal something if I had a really, really, *really* good reason for it."

"No. I don't want to hear it."

"I do," Grandpa said as he stepped into the kitchen. "You're right, Jase. You're a good kid. Tell us, what forced you to do something so stupid?"

He leaned against the refrigerator, his arms crossed over his chest. Mom leaned back in her chair, her ears apparently now open to what I had to say. Four eagle eyes locked onto me. There was no escape now.

"I took the file," I said, "because a couple of kids at that office have gone missing."

"*What?*" That was Mom.

Grandpa said, "This is the second time you've mentioned this to me."

I nodded. "One of the kids is named Michael. That file you found—it's his."

Mom said, "You've only had one very short appointment at that office. What would put the idea into your head that somebody has gone missing from there?"

"Braxton," said Grandpa.

"I see." Mom continued to glare. "Should've known this was a joint effort. It's very noble, but very foolish, of you, Jase, to take all the blame."

"But I—"

Mom stood and grabbed the phone. "Perhaps Braxton's parents would like to know about all this, too?"

Before I could protest any further—*really, what good would it have done anyway?*—Mom hit the redial button. She brought the phone up to her ear and waited.

Grandpa said to me, "No reason to take the fall alone. You'd hit the ground twice as hard."

I shrugged, hoping that Braxton's parents wouldn't be too hard on the guy, hoping that he wouldn't think I ratted him out.

After a few seconds, Mom said into the phone, "Hello, may I speak to the parent of Braxton? Oh, hello. This is Dana Clark. Our sons met today at Dr. Sharp's office? I have some information I'd like to share with you..."

Within minutes, Braxton's fate was sealed along with mine. The copy of Greg's file had been found. Braxton would join me for the meeting with Sharp.

I was still doomed, but at least now I would have some decent company.

16

THE DOCTOR AGREED to meet with us at noon the next day. He would take time away from his lunch break for the meeting. Mom tried to make me feel guilty for that, and it kind of worked.

"Lunch is one of the most important meals of the day," she said. "Goodness knows Dr. Sharp probably needs all the strength he can get with all the work he has to do."

Of course, lunch is one of the most important meals of the day, I thought. *There are only three of them!*

I wondered what Dr. Sharp liked to eat. Something with meat in it, no doubt.

A little before noon, Mom and I stepped back into the waiting room. Everything looked pretty much the same as it had the day before, but the air felt much colder. Nemo didn't swim across the television screen, and Braxton was the only other person in the room. Again, he read the anti-cavity pamphlet, and he didn't look upset at all.

"Where are your parents?" said Mom. "I was under the impression that your mother would be joining us, as well."

Braxton put the pamphlet down. "You come to realize that my parents aren't very reliable people."

She said, "They dropped you off, at least."

"I walked."

Mom frowned. "We could've picked you up."

"Exercise is good for me." Braxton looked my way. "Jase, are you nervous? You look nervous."

Did I? What gave it away? The scratching?

But I was less worried about what Sharp would say and more about how much Mom would kill me.

"You should both be nervous," said Mom. "What you've done is unacceptable, and we'll see what happens because of it."

"My parents said I couldn't leave the house for a week, but then they let me walk out of the house an hour ago. Like I said, they aren't very reliable people."

"My computer was taken away," I said. "For two weeks."

"And it will be gone for two weeks," Mom cut in. "You can rely on that."

The door to the back rooms creaked open. Dr. Alexis Sharp stood before us. She was smiling now. She obviously got some kind of pleasure out of our unfortunate situation.

"Hello, Mrs. Clark," she said. "How are you today?"

"Been better," said Mom. "Thank you."

"Will you be the only other adult present for the meeting?"

Mom said, "Looks like Braxton's parents were unable to make it. Jase's grandfather is busy."

Yeah, busy watching TV and eating candy. The last place he wanted to be again was a dentist's office.

"In that case," said Alexis, "if we don't have to wait for anyone else to arrive, please follow me."

She held the door open for us to enter. Braxton led the way. Alexis swept her gaze over Braxton and me as we passed her. Her smile faded. Her normal glare reappeared. She led us down the hallway to see her brother.

The door to his office was open, so we entered. The dentist sat behind a large wooden desk, writing something on a pad of paper. No wonder the files had been easy for Braxton to find. The room was spotless, and even a single piece of paper sitting on a desk would have seemed out of place.

Framed certificates hung on the wall behind the doctor. Thick books lined shelves. Metal file cabinets shined. Sharp's smile glowed.

"Mrs. Clark," he said, "hello." He and Mom shook hands, and then he gestured for all of us to sit in the chairs in front of his desk. We sat, and Alexis moved to stand next to Sharp.

"Hope you don't mind that Alexis will be joining us," said the dentist. "She and I work very closely with one another."

Mom shook her head. "Of course, no problem."

"Fantastic." He leaned forward, looking at me, then Braxton, Braxton, then me. "What exactly has happened here?"

I hesitated, and I looked to Mom for help, but she didn't offer any. She only said, "Go on."

Braxton, for once, didn't seem too eager to speak, either. Maybe he realized how serious the situation was. Maybe he was ready for me to take all the blame. If that was the case, he had another think coming.

I decided that the truth, the whole truth, and nothing but the truth was all I had to say. Lies weren't going to get me anywhere but in a hole I couldn't climb out of.

"Um, well..." I said. Should've been able to scratch a hole in my hand at that point.

"Yes?" said Sharp as he flashed that smile again. I think it was so that I wouldn't feel intimidated. Didn't quite work. Alexis and Mom's stares more than made up for his lack of intimidation.

"You see..." I continued.

He just stared and smiled. Smiled and stared. I was sure he knew —they all knew—why we were there in that office, but he was going to force me to tell him everything anyway.

"Give him the letter and the file," Mom said suddenly.

I had been clutching them in my hands. Mom was trying to make some statement by forcing me to hand them back over to

Sharp myself. Braxton started fishing through the pockets in his jacket.

"Here," I said, breaking eye contact from any adult. I slid Michael's file and my apology letter across the desk.

"Here's mine," Braxton said. He pulled folded paper out of his jacket. "My letter is eight pages single-spaced. Not only do I apologize for stealing, but I also apologize for all the cavities I've ever made you fix."

Sharp accepted the gifts. "Thank you, boys. I will read every word of these letters."

"You're welcome," said Braxton.

"I must say, though, that I was worried about these files."

Alexis nodded. "We were both worried."

The dentist said, "I thought I misplaced them. *Lost* them."

Alexis shook her head. "No, he thought I lost them. I don't lose things."

Sharp looked at his sister. "She doesn't lose things. That's why I thought it was so strange, but I never once suspected that the files had been stolen." He looked at me. "The files are very important to me and for what I do, but why would you want them?"

"Tell him," said Mom.

"Please do," snarled Alexis.

"The thing is—" I began.

"The thing is," Braxton interrupted, "that Jase shouldn't be in trouble. I should be in trouble. I took the files. I showed him the files. All he's guilty of is listening to me."

"That's surprising," said Alexis, even though she was clearly not surprised.

Mom poked me. "Is this true?" I nodded. "Nonetheless," she said, "you have to take some of the blame here."

Like I mentioned earlier, there was no escape for me.

"Braxton," said the dentist, "why did you think it was necessary to take these files?"

I tried to tell Braxton with my eyes that he shouldn't tell the truth, the whole truth, and nothing but the truth. I didn't know how everyone would react to his truth, his whole truth, and his nothing but the truth.

Eyes never speak as well as lips do.

"Michael and Greg are missing," said Braxton. "Why are they missing? Tell us why they're missing!"

The room was silent. Sharp seemed to be saying something to Alexis with his eyes. He was having better success at it than I had. I wasn't very good at listening to eyes, either, though. Didn't know what was being said between the two of them.

Sharp finally spoke. "What makes you think they're missing? Because their pictures aren't on the wall anymore?"

"Yes!" Braxton shouted.

"You should save the detective work for the professionals," said Alexis.

"What're you guys hiding?"

"Braxton," said Mom, "know your place. Demonstrate some respect. You came here to apologize to them, not to accuse them."

"I came here for answers!" said my friend.

The dentist stood. "Thank you, Mrs. Clark, for your concern. However, I think it would be best if we ended this once and for all. If Braxton would like answers, he will get answers."

The dentist pushed the phone on his desk toward Braxton. "I would like for you to call Michael and Greg's parents. They'll tell you exactly why the boys are missing."

17

"*REALLY?*" said Braxton.

He wasn't expecting that offer. Neither was I. Mom looked as if she didn't know what to think. Alexis and Sharp were unfazed.

"Yep," the dentist said to Braxton. He pushed the files back across the table. "The phone numbers are there. Please call."

Braxton looked at me, wide-eyed. "Let's do this!"

"Okay," I said. "You dial."

Sharp said, "I'll put on the speakerphone for you." With the push of a button, he filled the room with dial tone, ready to prove our suspicions wrong. That's what he was doing, wasn't it? Why else would Sharp and Alexis be so willing to let us call Michael and Greg's homes? They knew the answers we received would reveal nothing strange.

Braxton grabbed Michael's file, lifted the phone out of its cradle, and dialed. As the phone rang, he bounced up and down anxiously in his seat.

After three rings, a man's deep voice boomed, "Hello?"

Braxton said, "Hi, is Michael there?"

A brief pause, then: "May I ask who's calling?"

"This is Braxton Grunk."

"Who?"

"Braxton Grunk."

"*Who?*"

"*Braxton Gr—*"

"Mr. Huntley," the dentist interrupted, "this is Dr. Sharp."

"Oh, Dr. Sharp. How are you?" Mr. Huntley wasn't expecting Braxton Grunk to be with Sharp, that was for sure.

Sharp smiled, but not even his smile could be seen over the phone. "I'm doing well, thank you. I know we spoke yesterday to tie up things, but I was wondering if you could do something for me?"

"Yes?"

"With me right now is one of my patients. He introduced himself to you."

"Brandon?"

"*Braxton,*" corrected Braxton.

Sharp continued, "Braxton was a friend of Michael's here at the office. He noticed Michael's photo taken off the wall, and he wanted to know what happened to his friend."

"Okay..." said the man.

"He wanted to hear it straight from you, if that's okay?"

"I guess so..."

Braxton leaned closer to the phone. "This is Braxton Grunk again. You're Michael's father?"

"Yes. Excuse me, Braxton? You and Michael weren't close, were you?"

"Well, no, not really."

"That's good. You'll probably never hear from him again."

"Why's that?" asked Braxton.

"Michael has moved back to Colorado to live with his mother and stepfather."

"Did this happen suddenly?"

"I'm sorry, but anything else really isn't any of your business." Mr. Huntley was not happy.

"Thanks." Braxton leaned back in his seat, and then he nodded to the dentist.

Sharp said, "Thanks for your help, Mr. Huntley. That will be all. Take care."

"Okay, you too."

That was that. Michael was in Colorado. Not missing, but with family. What could have been safer than that?

Over the dial tone, Alexis said, "Would you like to call for Greg now?"

Braxton dialed Greg's number. After two rings, a woman answered. "This is Sharon."

"Mrs. Martinez? Hi, this is Dr. Sharp."

"How *are* you? Is there paperwork I missed?"

"No, nothing like that." He explained the situation to Greg's mom.

"Oh," said Mrs. Martinez. "Is this young man sitting there listening?"

"I'm here," said Braxton.

"Greg had to be sent off unexpectedly to boarding school."

"What did he do?"

"That's really none of your—"

"Did he and Michael do something together?" said Braxton, cutting the woman off. "Is that why they both had to leave?"

"Michael?" said Mrs. Martinez. "Who's Michael?"

Braxton leaned closer into the phone. "Where's the boarding school?"

Greg's mom said, "I don't think that's very impor—"

"I think it is!"

"Braxton!" Mom and Alexis both yelled.

"Who's *that?*" Mrs. Martinez wondered.

"Thank you for your time," said Sharp.

"*Where is the boarding school?*" Braxton repeated.

The dentist reached to hang up the phone, but before he could end the connection with Greg's mom, she said, "Colorado. The school is in Colorado."

18

"What's the name of the school?" Braxton asked the dial tone. Sharp had ended the conversation with the push of a button. With another push of a button, the speakerphone was off.

"So, are we satisfied?" Alexis said as she locked eyes with Braxton and then me.

I looked to Braxton for what to do. My feelings were mixed. What Michael and Greg's parents said seemed to be reasonable, but at the same time it felt kind of *odd*.

Braxton just shrugged. He said, "Guess it'll have to do."

Sharp chuckled. "Were you expecting something more interesting?"

"I thought it was plenty interesting," said Mom. "It was a bit unconventional handling things that way, but perhaps it really did satisfy the curiosity. Has it? Jase?"

I nodded. "I can see it was all just a coincidence."

Did I really see things that way? I didn't think Braxton did. After all, he didn't believe in coincidences. It's what got us into the mess in the first place.

"I...I'm sorry," said Braxton. "What I did was wrong."

"Jase, do you have anything to add?" Mom said.

"Yes, I'm sorry, too. What *we* did was wrong."

"What do you think the consequences should be?" Mom asked Sharp. "There should definitely be consequences. I would completely understand if you decided you couldn't treat Jase any longer as your patient after he displayed such deceptive behavior."

Sharp only smiled more. "No, that won't be necessary. I can understand a child's curiosity. We all at one point in our youth let our curiosity get the best of us. It's not something that should be praised, but in this instance, I think we can tolerate it."

"Very generous of you. Isn't it, Jase?"

I rubbed my side. "Yes, very generous. Thank you, Dr. Sharp. I'm sorry this happened." I knew how to kiss butt just like any other kid.

"What about me?" Braxton wondered. "Do I still get to come here?"

"*Get*" to go there? Did Braxton really see it as a privilege to go to the dentist? Especially to a dentist he didn't seem to entirely trust?

Sharp nodded. "You're in the same boat. Don't mistake what I say, however. What you did was wrong, and if we have problems of this nature with either of you again, then I can't promise such generosity the next time around."

"Sounds fair," said Mom.

I quickly spoke before Mom could glare at me again. "Yes, that's fair," I said. "Very fair. Thanks."

"Thanks," said Braxton.

"Very good." Sharp stood behind his desk and looked at his watch. "Looks like it's about lunchtime."

"We should really be on our way, anyhow," said Mom, standing.

Alexis said, "Wonder if we could have a couple of moments alone with you, Mrs. Clark?"

What did they need to say to her that they couldn't say in front of me? The same thought seemed to run through Mom's head. She agreed to the offer, though.

That Sharp smile again. "Great," the dentist said. "It's just boring paperwork stuff, I'm afraid. Boys, would you mind waiting outside the door? Just stand in the hall for a couple of minutes?"

"Come on, Jase!" Braxton pulled me out of my seat and through the doorway.

Alexis closed the door behind us. "Behave," she said before the door shut tight.

Why were they being so secretive? They couldn't really be talking about paperwork. They were purposefully hiding something from me. There must have been something wrong with my teeth…

I gulped. "Think it's weird they closed the door?"

Braxton snorted. "Very."

"Should we try to listen in on what they're talking about?"

"I don't want to hear about paperwork. You want to get in trouble for eavesdropping on a conversation about paperwork?"

"When you put it that way…"

"Exactly!" He looked down the empty hallway as if to see if we were alone. We were. "Let's move away from the door so *they* can't hear *us*."

He pulled me again, this time down the hall and out in front of the photograph wall. My photo and the one with Braxton and I together were now posted. He pointed to the space where Michael and Greg's pictures used to be.

He said, "They're going to keep that spot empty on the wall, I bet. Just to taunt us."

"What're you talking about?"

"What am I talking about? What am I *talking* about?" Braxton began to pace. "Were you just in that office with me?"

"Yeah. So…?"

"You heard the lies their parents told me?"

"Braxton, it didn't sound like they were lying. Why would they lie to you?"

"*Duh*, Jase. Duh! They didn't know they were lying to me!"

"Huh?" I scratched my head. And then I scratched my hand.

"They *thought* they were telling the truth, or at least what they were told was the truth."

"You've lost me."

He said, "You saw the article about Alexis. She knows how to hypnotize people, right?"

"I guess so."

"I think she hypnotized Greg and Michael's parents. She did something to their brains. They told me what they're supposed to say when someone asks them about their kids. It's not what really happened to Michael and Greg, though."

"Why do you think that?"

"Colorado, Jase. *Colorado.*"

It did seem weird that Michael and Greg both went to Colorado. Out of all the states they could go to, why did they both end up in the same one? It was too much of a—

"Coincidence, Jase. You know I don't believe in it. Alexis gave them different stories to tell: Michael is with his mom, and Greg is at boarding school. But Alexis must've gotten lazy and given them parts of the same story to tell! That's why both Michael's dad and Greg's mom said their sons went to Colorado, and one didn't say Florida, or Tennessee, or Maine. Neither Michael nor Greg is in Colorado. I don't know where they really are, but I don't think it's there."

I wouldn't—*couldn't*—believe it. The itch returned to prove otherwise. "Is it possible that you think too much?" I said. "What if they're both really there?"

"That's why I'm calling Greg's mom back as soon as I can. I wrote the phone number down before I brought the file today. I need to find out what's really going on here."

"Smart," I said.

"I know I am, but what are you?"

"Not convinced. If what you say is true, Braxton, it would be crazy and scary, but what

makes you an expert on hypnosis?"

"The Internet."

"What makes you think Alexis hypnotized Greg and Michael's parents? Isn't that jumping to conclusions? Shouldn't we get more evidence before we start thinking such crazy things are true?"

"Evidence shmevidence." Braxton grinned. "Besides, you already believe me."

He was right. I did pretty much already believe him. Didn't want to, but I couldn't deny that pieces to the puzzle were beginning to fit in the strangest ways.

"What do we know?" I said. "We're only kids!"

"It's what we don't know. It's what the adults won't tell us. It's what we're going to find out." Braxton smiled. "Adults always make this mistake."

"What mistake?"

"They underestimate just how curious a kid can be. Curiosity can't be stopped, Jase. It can only grow and grow. We're going to figure this out. You just have to promise me..."

"What?"

"Don't tell anyone anything. We have to pretend we're done with all this. Pretend we learned our lesson."

"I didn't learn my lesson?" I asked.

"No, but soon enough Alexis and Dr. Sharp will learn *theirs*."

19

BRAXTON WAS CRAZY. Did that make me crazy, too, for believing a lot of what he said? It probably did.

When we got back from the dentist Mom dismantled my computer, unplugging cords and separating the monitor from the hard drive. She then put everything in the garage. I didn't really want to spend time with Grandpa or Mom, so I had nothing to do but write in my journal for a bit and then read books.

Still, all I could think about was whether or not the Drs. Sharp could really be doing something so evil to their patients. The problem was, I couldn't even think what the "evil" thing they might be doing was. Why hypnotize parents in order to kidnap their children?

Were Michael and Greg at some kind of top-secret Bad Dental Hygiene Camp where they learned the hard way how to keep their teeth clean? That theory didn't work exactly, though, considering Michael only ever had one cavity, a near-perfect record. Then, *what?*

At about ten o'clock that night, Mom came into my room to tell me she was going to bed. I was already in bed, staring at the ceiling and thinking about Alexis hypnotizing parents. My mom sat on the edge of my bed.

"I'll be watching you tonight," she said. "Even when I'm sleeping, I have ways of keeping an eye on you."

I blinked up at her, not sure what to say. I didn't think she had a hidden video camera installed in my room, but I couldn't ever be too careful with her. At the very least, she could have bugged the room with some kind of listening device.

"In other words," she added, "don't even *think* about using the phone. The phone bill keeps records of all calls from this house. You do anything suspicious with Braxton again, and that computer's gone until Thanksgiving."

She didn't need to worry. I wasn't going to call Braxton. Although, I couldn't exactly guarantee he wouldn't try to contact me.

"Good night, honey," she said, kissing me on the forehead. "Grandpa is in the living room. Soon enough he'll be sleeping TV."

"Sleeping TV" is what we called Grandpa's habit of falling asleep at night with the television on full-blast. It was usually my duty to turn it off. I sometimes decided to just change the channel and watch cartoons instead.

"Good night," I mumbled.

"Excuse me?"

"Good *night*," I said in a nastier tone.

She looked over to where my computer usually sat. "Don't get all upset with me. You're the one who brought this upon yourself. You're a big boy. You made a wrong decision, you live with it."

"Whatever."

She grew red in the face, and she looked like she was going to say something else, but instead she just walked out of my room and shut the door behind her. *Good riddance.*

"Finally!" I said to no one.

Thump.

What was that?

Thump.

What the *heck*?

I looked at the window. It was closed, but the blinds were open. I couldn't see very far out into the dark night even with the moon hanging so brightly in the sky.

A grinning face suddenly appeared before me.

I scrambled out of bed and landed hard on my tailbone. It felt like I'd fallen onto a beehive, it stung so badly.

Braxton waved at me from outside the window. *Just when the itch had gone away, too!* He held up an open box of Ding Dongs. He wanted to risk sneaking into my house late at night to *eat dessert*?

I tried to wave him away, but he didn't seem to get it. He only waved more.

I walked over to the window. "You have to go home!" I said.

He shook his head. With his other hand he held up a cell phone. Ding Dongs and a cell phone. It looked as if he had wild plans in store for us.

What to do? Take the safe route and send Braxton away, or let him inside to see what kind of trouble he could get us into?

I thought about Alexis Sharp hypnotizing parents, taking their kids, imprisoning them or worse. And for what? Safety wouldn't get the mystery solved.

I tried my best to lift the window open quietly. As I lifted, Braxton pushed up, as well, *slamming* it open. I sat there in silence, just waiting for Mom to rush in. Grandpa's hearing was good for "an older person," but the television was loud.

After a minute's listening, I said, "*What* are you doing here?"

Braxton leaned folded arms on the windowsill. "Did you notice that I threw Ding Dongs, and not rocks, at your window?" His breath was chocolatey.

I only stared at him.

He said, "In movies they always throw rocks, but rocks scratch and could even *break* a window. That's why I threw something softer to get your attention. Ding Dongs."

"I live in a one-story house! There's no reason to throw *anything* at the window! Just knock next time!"

"That could work. That way I wouldn't have to waste any

snacks!" He disappeared from view, then stood up with two dented treats in his hands. "Want one?"

"Not really. I have to go back to see Dr. Sharp on Tuesday. Chocolate and whatever that stuff is in the middle have to be bad for my teeth."

"You already have the cavities, Jase. These can't make them all that much worse."

"Thanks, but no thanks."

"Fine, be like that. More for me." He dropped the Ding Dongs back in the box. The phone, too. "Can I come inside?"

I glanced at the door. Still closed. "I don't know." I didn't want my computer gone 'til November.

"Come on, I walked all this way..." He winced. "My feet hurt."

He did look tired. "How did you even know where I live?"

"I've been walking around for a long time in this neighborhood, looking for the house with your mom's car in the driveway."

I looked at the door again. "My mom's probably not even asleep yet."

"Let me inside and lock the door, then."

"I don't have a lock."

"Get a lock."

"I don't see how saying that will make the door any more locked."

As I said that, Braxton hoisted himself up into the window and practically fell into me, then dropped onto the floor and lay there, panting. Surprisingly, he made it through the window without a sound. It was impressive for someone so graceless. I never tried to stop him. I knew I was going to let him in anyway.

He put the box on the bed and pulled out a Ding Dong and the cell phone. "Let's get to business," he said.

"Business?" I ushered Braxton toward my closet, away from the bedroom door. I asked him to whisper.

He pulled a piece of paper out of his pocket. *Greg's mom's phone number.* "I didn't want to call without you," he explained. "After they talked to your mom, my parents won't let me use the house phone."

"Same with my mom," I said. "You have a cell phone?"

"Of course not. I took my dad's. But he won't even know it's missing. He and my mom have been asleep since eight. Heck, they won't even know that *I* am missing."

"I don't feel too good about this, Braxton."

"Relax. If you think we're going to get caught, then we'll get caught."

I dragged my desk chair over to the door and pushed its back under the doorknob. "Don't know if it's that simple."

Braxton said, "Trust that I'm there for you. You're there for me. We're partners now, Jase. Partners stick together."

Yes, we were partners, all right. Partners *in crime*. From what I knew, criminals usually got their just desserts, and they were never tasty.

Braxton unwrapped the Ding Dong, took a bite, and dialed.

20

WE HUDDLED CLOSE TOGETHER. Braxton held the cell phone between our ears. He had the volume on as high as it could go, which made me increasingly nervous.

Just when I thought no one would answer, the familiar voice of Greg Martinez's mother swam into my ear. "Hello?" said the woman.

"Hi," said Braxton. "You remember me, right?"

"Um...no."

"Are you sure?"

A long pause, then: "Yes."

"Are you really, *really* sure?"

I wanted to strangle him. Instead, I just took the phone away and said into it, "I'm sorry. Mrs. Martinez, we're friends of Greg's, and we would like to know, if you would be so kind to tell us, the name of the boarding school you sent him to."

"Isn't it a little late for you boys to be calling? It's almost—"

"Please, Mrs. Martinez," I said. "We just want to send Greg a letter."

"Well..."

"Which state is the school in?" I asked. "Please?" Adults like it when you say "please."

I knew she would say, "Colorado," again, and she did.

Braxton whispered, "Ask her for the name of the school again."

I asked, "What was the name of the school, ma'am?"

"It's...well, it's..."

I waited for an answer. It didn't come.

I said, "Mrs. Martinez?" Was she still there? I thought I heard her breathing.

Finally, she said, "For the life of me, I *forgot*."

Braxton's eyes grew wide. I'm sure mine did, too.

"You forgot?" I made sure to sound like I didn't believe her. "Did you write it down anywhere? Do you have any information on the place?"

"I...I'm sure I do, but...but I just can't think of where I left it at the moment."

"But it's in Colorado?" I asked.

Braxton said, "Ask her if it's in Fruita. My cousin lives in Fruita, Colorado."

I didn't want to ask her that. Colorado's a big state. I'm sure the-school-that-maybe-wasn't-a-school wasn't located in some random town out of hundreds that Braxton just happened to know about.

I asked her anyway, because Braxton wouldn't stop poking me. I didn't like being poked. "Is the school in Fruita?" I asked.

"Fruita?" she said. "No. That's a real place?"

"Denver, then?" Denver was the only city I could think of that was in Colorado. Home of the Broncos, Nuggets, and Rockies. The Mile-High City. It was a pretty big place, so maybe the school was there...

"Denver?" she said. "I thought that was in Idaho?"

We were getting nowhere fast. Heck, I think we were already there. *Nowhere. Population: Us.*

Braxton pulled the phone out of my hand and said into it, "You're really, really, really, super duper *duper* sure you can't remember the name of the school?"

"I would like to say it sounds like…" She never finished what she was going to say. "Oh, never mind. Isn't it terrible that I can't think of it?"

"Well, it's mysterious," said Braxton. He looked at me. *"Very, very mysterious."*

"I'm just tired," she said. "I've been so busy. I'm sure I'll be able to think of it later. Could you call back at a different time? Tomorrow maybe?"

"Maybe," said Braxton, and he hung up.

We just stared at each other. Well, Braxton also took bites out of a Ding Dong and I scratched my hand.

"That was weird," I said to break the silence.

He replied, "You're surprised? I'm not."

"I don't know what it means," I said.

"Don't say it's a coincidence, Jase!"

"I won't, because I'm starting to think it isn't." I stood. "But how are we going to know for sure? We have to call back again tomorrow."

He nodded. "Of course, but we also have to do something else. Something to help us get a better idea of what we're dealing with here."

"Like what?"

"We need an expert's opinion. We're going to find a hypnotist."

21

USING Google on his dad's phone, Braxton found a guy who called himself "Chip the *Hip*notist." His advertisement claimed that he "put the *hip* back in hypnosis." First of all, no one had used the word "hip" to describe anything that was "cool" or "awesome" for as long as I'd been alive, so I didn't have any idea how "hip" the "*Hip*notist" could actually be. Secondly, "hip" wasn't technically a part of the word "hypnosis."

We still decided to see him above anyone else. Mostly because the ad promised his services would be "oh so cheap, yet oh so valuable." Also, Braxton knew the way to Chip's office by bus.

The next morning, Braxton called the house and asked politely if I could come over to his place. His unreliable parents must have already decided to let him use the house phone. Mom and Grandpa had no idea that he had been at our home the night before, so it looked like we hadn't planned out his invitation beforehand. It worked out perfectly. Mom allowed me to hang out at Braxton's house for the day even though she was disappointed with what we had done. She must've been excited for me to have a friend of some kind, even if he was sort of a troublemaker. Plus, taking the computer away was brutal enough.

Mom drove me to Braxton's house early in the afternoon. He stood at the curb waiting for our arrival.

Mom said she'd pick me up at six o'clock for dinner.

As she drove away, Braxton said, "Come on, it's time for a bus adventure!"

I was less excited to ride a bus, but how else would we get to the hypnotist? Mom wouldn't drive us. Braxton's parents were almost nonexistent.

Braxton agreed to pay the bus fare if I promised to pay Chip. I knew it wasn't a very fair deal, but I was the one with the jar full of Grandpa's pennies. Finally, an opportunity had come to spend them.

While Braxton ran down the sidewalk, I tried my best to follow close behind. Even though the penny jar made my backpack heavier than usual, Braxton didn't go very fast. Pennies jingled with our every step.

I don't know why we ran to catch the bus. It showed up seventeen minutes after we got to the bus stop. And it smelled like sweaty cheese.

Fifteen minutes later, we got off the bus in front of a shop that served donuts, hamburgers, and ice cream. I could survive okay in a place like that. A couple of blocks down from Super Donut Burgerland was a small building with "Chip the *Hip*notist" painted on a bright yellow sign.

"Here is where we get answers," Braxton said proudly.

He walked through the door without hesitation. A bell rattled as we entered, but it wasn't needed. The hypnotist stood right there before us, like he was waiting for someone to come in.

The room was empty of other people, but not of stuff. Besides a desk and some chairs, there seemed to be lots of posters on the walls, and books and T-shirts on countless shelves.

"Hello, guys," Chip said. "How may I help you?"

He was younger than I thought he would be. He was in his twenties, wore glasses, and had a goatee. A large gold chain hung around his neck. It made his ugly, shiny blue shirt even uglier and shinier. Not very "hip."

"You know how to hypnotize people?" asked Braxton.

Chip smiled. "It's what the sign says."

"Very good," said my friend. "We need information on hypnosis from an expert."

Chip's smile faded. "I'm an expert," he said, "but that's all you want? Information? You're not here to book me for your birthday party?"

Braxton shook his head. "We just want cold, hard facts. Or opinions. Probably both."

"What about?" Chip looked at a gold watch that I was sure wasn't made of real gold. "I'm busy."

I said, "Sure looks like it." I took off my backpack and unzipped it. "We can pay you if that's what you want."

"Yes, that's what I want." He grinned. "Very much."

I lifted the jar out of the backpack. Held it out to him. "Here you go."

The hypnotist didn't reach out for the pennies. Just stared at them. "Guys, you're serious?"

Braxton nodded. "We will seriously give you *all* these pennies, Dorito."

He backed away from us. "I don't know…"

"But we need your help!" I said.

"How can I help you?" said the man. "What could you possibly want with what I have to say?"

I decided to just get it all out in the open. "Our dentist is hypnotizing people, and we don't know why or how!"

Chip stopped and looked at me. "Whoa. What?" He began to chuckle. "Explain." He gestured to some chairs against the wall. "Let's sit and chat for a bit. How much money did you say was in that jar, anyway?"

22

"WHOA," the hypnotist said after we filled him in on our situation. "That's a gnarly story, guys. I mean, *crazy* gnarly."

"Can you help us?" I asked.

He leaned forward in his seat across from us. "I don't know what you think I can do for you. I hypnotize people for parties and corporate events. What you've described to me is something out of my league. It's something you should go to a professional hypno*therapist* about."

"We don't know what a hypnotherapist is!" said Braxton.

Chip snorted. "That would explain why you came to me..."

I said, "Do you at least believe us?"

"Something seems to be going on, all right. It's a little more sinister than plain old hypnosis, though." The man stood from his seat. "It's hypnosis taken to an extremely unnecessary level."

An icy spider crawled down my spine. "What does that mean?" I asked.

Chip began to pace. "Hypnosis is primarily used for two purposes: entertainment and health. I do the *fun* hypnosis. I can make people think they're dogs or have them dance like a TikTokker."

"Awesome!" cried Braxton. "What kind of dog do you think I would be, Cheeto? I'd say a bulldog. What do you think?"

Chip did his best to ignore the outburst. "Hypnosis can also be used for medical practices. Someone can be hypnotized to quit smoking, for example. It can also be used to eliminate intense fears of certain things like—"

"Sharks!" Braxton interrupted again. "I'm so scared of sharks, I can't even take a bath without looking for one!"

I could see Chip was getting annoyed, but he continued. "Then there are those people who can use hypnosis *for evil*. When people are hypnotized, their defenses are stripped away. They say or do things they wouldn't normally say or do. Some people abuse that privilege by getting private information from those they hypnotize. That sounds like what this Alice did in Portland years ago."

I was so wrapped up in what he was saying that I didn't bother to tell him that Alice wasn't Alice, but was Alexis. Braxton, on the other hand, corrected him.

"It's what *Alexis* did in Portland years ago," said Chip, nodding. "What she's doing now, if indeed she is toying with people's minds, sounds like advanced hypnosis. Something more in the area of *brainwashing*."

My body froze as the itching increased. Never thought I would hear that word in real life. That was something that only happened in books and movies!

"I don't know too much about brainwashing, to be honest," said Chip. "Quite frankly, it's a little too freaky, a little too gnarly for my tastes. But I do know some things."

"I think we're getting our pennies' worth," said Braxton. Didn't he mean *my* pennies' worth?

"In order to brainwash someone," said Chip, "you need lots—*lots* —of time and preparation. It's not a simple hypnosis that can take over a mind in a matter of minutes. No, brainwashing, complete *mind control*, takes days, weeks, or maybe even months of work.

"People wouldn't usually let themselves get brainwashed, either. They won't sit there for days and days while their memories, behaviors, and beliefs are changed. Unfortunately, people can sometimes be brainwashed without knowing they're being brainwashed."

"How?" I asked.

"Subliminal messages," said Chip.

"What're those?" Braxton and I wondered aloud at the same time.

"They're messages that your brain can pick up without you knowing they're being picked up. Like, during a movie, an image of popcorn and soda could flash on the screen. It would flash so fast that your eyes wouldn't see it. Your brain, though, can see more than your eyes can, and your brain would see and receive the message. Then you would maybe get hungry for popcorn and thirsty for soda, and you would buy some from the snack bar. You wouldn't know it was because you were just told to buy popcorn and soda. You'd think it was just because you got a sudden craving for that kind of snack."

"That's kind of scary, Frito," said Braxton. "I thought I just ate popcorn and drank soda because I liked to."

"Maybe you do, or maybe you don't," said Chip. "And, please, the name is Chip, not any type of greasy fried snack."

"What could Sharp and Alexis be showing people to brainwash them?" I asked.

"I don't know," said Chip, "but there's another way to send subliminal messages. Through *sound*."

"Sound?" I said.

Chip nodded. "Like music. Messages can be hidden in songs."

Braxton got it before I did. "The MyPods," he said.

I almost fell out of my chair. *Of course.* The MyPods in each room could be brainwashing patients without them even knowing it! I shivered. What messages were they sending out, though?

"I don't get it," said Chip. "What are MyPods?"

We told him, and he said, "This seems more like something that's really happening every second."

"Great! Someone believes us!" shouted Braxton.

"Not completely," Chip said. "Need more proof. What you have is a lot of maybes. I think I believe you as much as I do because I want to believe you. Other people, like the police, would laugh at you without proof."

"Where's your phone?" asked Braxton.

"Why?"

Braxton pulled out a familiar piece of paper. "Could you call this number and see if you can find out where in Colorado Greg goes to school?"

"I guess so..."

We listened as Chip talked to Mrs. Martinez. Their conversation was almost *word-for-word* like the one we had with her the night before. She couldn't "find" the information again. She asked Chip to call her back the next day.

When he hung up, Chip turned to us. He said, "It doesn't sound like she's hiding anything. She just... doesn't know anything more."

"You really think she doesn't know where her son is?" I said.

The hypnotist shrugged. "She *thinks* she knows, at least. But I agree. How could a mother not know the name of the place she sent her son? That doesn't seem right. It's pretty gnarly."

I said, "It's freaky." *Scratch, scratch.*

Chip nodded. "It could be the freakiest part about this whole thing. Where are these kids if not where their parents think they are?"

23

CHIP SENT us out to get more evidence. He said that any time we wanted to see him or talk to him, we were welcome to drop by or call. He said he would help us any way that he could, but he couldn't really go to the police for us because of "things he did back in college."

He also gave the pennies back to me, saying it would be unnecessary to charge friends for his services. If we were his friends, he was even less "hip" than I thought. However, it did feel good to know that there was somebody out there who might believe what was happening.

As we waited at the bus stop for our ride back to Braxton's house, I said, "I have to get one of those MyPods."

"Steal one, you mean?"

"Yes, Braxton, steal one."

He munched on a bear claw he bought from Super Donut Burgerland. "When you go in to get your cavities filled on Tuesday?"

I nodded. "That's the next time either of us will be there. It's only three days from now."

"Sounds like a good plan, but it's also very risky."

"Completely risky," I agreed. "They'll notice as soon as I leave that one of the MyPods is missing. No way they won't catch me."

"Switch their MyPod with mine."

I said, "You have a MyPod?"

Braxton smiled. "I have a MyPod, you don't have a MyPod. You eat meat, I don't eat meat."

"Yours looks enough like the ones Sharp uses?"

"He didn't bring in the MyPods until last year," said Braxton. "When I saw how cool they were, I asked him all about them, and I got the *same exact kind* he did."

"That works out, then," I said. "I'll just switch yours for his."

"Yep, a classic switcheroo!"

The bus arrived and took us back across town. We were the only passengers. The air inside was warm. Stifling.

Braxton asked, "Where did you used to live?"

I hesitated a couple of seconds and then said, "In Arizona. A city called Mesa."

"Arizona's hot. Hotter than this bus!"

"Yeah, but I liked it there. I had some good friends."

"Still talk to them?"

I shrugged. "Not really. Hard to keep in contact with people when you don't know if you'll ever see them again."

"Why did you move here?"

I looked out the window at all the California license plates. "Because my mom got a better job."

"What does she do? She's smart, so I guess…A lawyer!"

I snorted. "No, she works at a preschool."

"Couldn't she have worked at a preschool in Arizona?"

"I would think so. It's just…"

"What, Jase?"

"There has to be some other reason we left. You don't move to a different state to become a preschool teacher. You especially don't pack up and leave everything behind in three days for that."

Braxton scratched his head. "That is strange. What do you think the real reason is?"

"I don't know. All Grandpa and Mom tell me is that we were 'in need of a change.'" An Arizona license plate flashed by, and I had to turn away from the window after seeing it. "I didn't see any need for changes. I was fine. But it's not the first time it's happened."

"What do you mean?"

I explained, "Before we lived in Mesa, we lived in Las Vegas. Halfway through first grade, we suddenly had to move, and we ended up in Arizona. For all I know, in a couple of years, we might have to suddenly move to Antarctica."

"I hear it's beautiful there." Braxton looked serious. "But I wish you stay here for a long time. For your sake." I'm sure he counted his own sake in there, as well.

As we walked to his house from the bus stop, Braxton said, "Don't think any less of me when you meet my parents, okay? They work from home."

"Yeah, no problem," I said.

I wanted to tell him he shouldn't worry. He was strange at times, yeah, but he was smart and nice, too, and he wanted to be my friend. I didn't have a closer ally, and I appreciated his friendship. Nothing and nobody could take that away.

Of course, it's hard to tell most people what your true feelings of them are, because you're usually too worried about how weird and cheesy it'll make you look.

"My parents aren't funny like your grandpa or even as nice as your mom," he said.

He thought Mom was *nice*?

"Mostly, they'll ignore us, and it's probably better that way."

I asked, "They're that bad?"

"Just don't make any eye contact with them."

Don't make eye contact? Were they his parents or rabid wolverines?

When we reached his driveway, he said, "My mom will offer snacks. It's okay to ignore her and go with me to my room. I have some Ding Dongs, Twinkies, Ruffles, Pringles, and pumpkin pie under my bed."

"Okay," I said.

On the porch outside the front door, he said, "My parents don't believe in locks. Someday a psycho is going to figure that out and go on a rampage here."

He turned the knob without inserting a key, and the front door opened. Standing right there before us, waiting and watching, was Mrs. Grunk. So much for ignoring us...

I made the mistake of looking into her horrible, horrible eyes.

24

Did I say "horrible"? I meant "amazing." Braxton's mom was—dare I say it?—the most beautiful woman I'd ever seen. She made my hand itchier and my heart beat faster than any uncovered secret could.

I had never met Mrs. Grunk before. I had stayed in the car while Mom talked to her the couple of times we dropped Braxton off at home. From the way Braxton talked about his parents, I imagined his mother as some terrifying beast, like a harpy, which is some super-hideous, flying monster from Greek mythology. *I did not expect her to be an angel.*

Her hair was the color of fire, her eyes emeralds. Her skin was vanilla ice cream. Her smile shone with little stars.

"Hi, you must be Jase," she said.

"Um... yeah... That would be...uh... me." So *smooth.*

She shook my hand. I forgot I had hands until she took one of mine in a feathery grasp. "I am so grateful that Braxton has met you," she said. "It's so hard for him to make friends."

Braxton closed the door behind us. He didn't say anything, but he looked annoyed. I got the hint that I really shouldn't take too long speaking to his mom. *Say hi and move on...*

But those eyes. And that smile. Mrs. Grunk asked, "Would you like a snack?"

I didn't need to look at Braxton to know what he was thinking. *No snacks! Flee! Run for your life!*

But those eyes. And that smile. What harm could there be in taking snacks from those eyes and that smile? No harm at all...

"What would you like?" she said. "I have organic celery and soy peanut spread."

Never mind! *No snacks!*

"Mung bean dip and organic potato slices?"

The word "organic" scared me. Did it mean "good for my organs"? *Flee!*

"How about slices of vegetable loaf on organic wheat bread? I have hummus. If you don't like hummus," said Mrs. Grunk, "I have soy peanut spread like I said before."

Run for my life!

I turned to Braxton for help. He smiled and said, "Mom, he's not hungry. We just came from a donut shop."

Even though I didn't eat any donuts, I nodded. Mrs. Grunk's smile vanished, and she no longer looked happy to see me. She frowned, putting ugly wrinkles in her once-perfect face. *There was the harpy.*

"Donuts?" she shrieked. "The ultimate insult!"

Her scream wasn't aimed at just Braxton, either. I felt her harsh, citrusy breath on my cheek. I took a step back, right into the closed front door.

Forget the harpy. She was a Siren, beautiful and hypnotizing until you got too close to her true colors. Then she would decapitate you in one bite.

"Chad!" she yelled. "Braxton ate a *donut!*" Mrs. Grunk's eyes bulged out of her head. I could have still gotten lost in those eyes, but now if I got lost in them, I would probably never find my way out again. It was surprisingly easy to look away.

Mr. Grunk appeared from a doorway behind his wife. He was

tall, muscular, and blond. He had a scary mustache. His eyes were small and dark.

"A *donut*? You've got to be kidding me!" he cried. "What have we told you, Braxton? What have we *told you*?"

Did Braxton eat a donut or kill someone?

"Your teeth!" screamed Mrs. Grunk.

"Your weight!" boomed Mr. Grunk.

If I was Braxton, I would've cried. Or yelled back. Cried and then yelled back. But I wasn't Braxton. He just stood there, staring.

Mr. Grunk slapped the wall with his palm. A framed portrait of the family fell to the floor. Glass cracked. "This makes me so *sick*!" he bellowed.

"Don't you ever *learn*?" spat Mrs. Grunk. "You are not a healthy boy! All we want is for you to be healthy!"

"Who's *this*?" Braxton's father said as he pointed a long finger at me. I furiously scratched at my hand.

"That's Jase!" yelled Braxton. "He's my friend, and he likes me for who I am! He doesn't try to change me!"

"Jase? The co-conspirator? Did I say he was allowed in my home?" Mr. Grunk looked to his wife. "Well, *did* I? Olga?"

Olga Grunk nodded. "Unfortunately, you did."

"This was before he took our son to eat a donut!"

Braxton grabbed my arm. He pulled me past his parents. I didn't think they would let us by. I expected Mr. Grunk to grab me by my hair and throw me *through* the front door.

"We're going to my room," Braxton said calmly.

"Oh, are you? *Are you*?" The veins in Mr. Grunk's neck looked like snakes about to squeeze the breath out of him.

Mrs. Grunk yelled, "Don't think we don't know about what you hide under your bed!"

Braxton said over his shoulder, "Are you talking about the chips, candy bars, cupcakes, or pie?"

"Pie? Chad, did he just say *pie*?"

"Stay in your room!" Mr. Grunk thundered. "Don't you dare come out of there!"

Braxton turned me down a hallway, toward a door covered in yellow caution tape. The caution tape should have been on the front door. *Caution: Stay Out—Nasty People Inside.*

I liked Braxton at that moment more than I ever had before. I didn't know how he kept his spirits so high with parents like his. It said a lot about him. I *was* glad he was my friend. He didn't have to change at all for me.

No wonder he thought my mom was so nice. She was a million times better than Chad and Olga Grunk. At least she loved me.

25

"THEY MIGHT NOT BELIEVE in locks, but I do," said Braxton as he closed his bedroom door behind me. He secured a fat padlock to the door to keep it locked from the inside.

I asked, "They let you put a lock on your door like that?"

"No. This is my ninth lock. I'll buy a trillion if I have to."

"They try to get in when you have the door locked?"

He shrugged. "Sometimes. Not so much anymore. They like to keep their distance from me. This one time my dad climbed through my window to get in here. It was kind of funny. He tripped on my bookshelf."

Sure enough, under the window was a small bookshelf crammed with comics, novels, and other reading materials. The room itself was crammed with stuff. There were too many science fiction and horror movie posters on the walls. Too many blankets on the bed. Too many action figures in the toy box. Too many spaceship models hanging from the ceiling. Too many clothes on the floor.

It was every child's dream and every parent's nightmare.

"Cool room," I said.

"I don't leave this place much, so I try to make it as awesome as possible."

Braxton walked over to the bed, kneeled next to it, and pulled out a trunk. He had painted on the side of the trunk in big white letters "STAY OUT OR STAY OUT."

"What's in there?" I asked.

He turned the dial on a combination lock that kept the trunk shut. Without looking up, he said, "My stash."

"All that food you were talking about?"

"Yes, my treasure."

He popped the lock open and lifted the lid. The trunk contained stacks and stacks of junk food. And half a pumpkin pie.

"Want a slice?" Braxton asked as he pulled out the pie.

"No, thanks. Pumpkins are only good for carving."

"That's fine. More for me!" He dug his hand into the pie and pulled out a big, gooey chunk. He shoved it into his face.

I said, "Shouldn't that pie be in a refrigerator?"

"Probably. Doesn't taste any worse, though." He shoveled another handful into his mouth. "This one time, back when I had my first trunk, I kept deviled eggs in there for a week. Man, were they gross! They smelled so weird! And eggs aren't supposed to get crunchy, right?"

I was going to ask him for a Twinkie, but the thought of a desperately hungry Braxton scarfing down rotten eggs took away any appetite I might have had. So I just looked around for some place to sit that wasn't covered in socks or underwear.

"Want to sit?" he said. "Yeah, that's cool. Let's see if anything interesting's online."

Braxton pulled something else out from under his bed. He brushed a pair of pants off a laptop, and then he wiped the pumpkin pie off his fingers and onto the pants. He sat on the bed and patted the space next to him. At least the bed was covered in blankets and not tightie-whities.

I sat next to him as the laptop warmed up. "Have to find more information on Alexis," he said.

I nodded. "See if there are any boarding schools in Colorado."

"Oh, and more about subliminal messages and brainwashing!"

Once the laptop was done loading, we Googled "Dr. Alexis Sharp." The screen froze while in mid-search for information.

Braxton clicked on the mouse, pressed keys on the keyboard. Nothing worked. Just a frozen screen.

"Restart the computer," I offered.

"Okay, good idea."

As he reached for the laptop's restart button, the screen suddenly went completely black. Three blood red heads popped up in the middle of the darkness. The snarling pit bull heads were all attached to the same red, muscular body.

"What the *heck*?" said Braxton.

"Cerberus?" I guessed.

"What-er-what?"

"My grandpa tells me all this stuff about Greek mythology. Cerberus is a three-headed dog that guards the Underworld."

"Underworld?"

"The place you never want to go if you don't have to."

Braxton scratched his head. "Aunt Mary and Uncle Terry's house?"

I almost laughed. "No! It's where people go when they die. It's a creepy place full of tortured souls."

Braxton clicked his mouse again and again. He pushed more keys on the keyboard and said, "Why is this ugly dog staring at us on my computer?"

"I don't know. Maybe you accidentally clicked on a weird link. Just turn off the laptop."

Braxton pushed the power button. The screen still had Cerberus's drooling faces glaring at us. He pushed the power button again and again.

Nothing. Still more ugly guard dog faces than I could stomach.

"What's *wrong* with this thing?" Braxton shrieked. He hit the laptop with the palm of his hand.

I pulled his hand away. "Don't do that. *Look*."

Words began to form below Cerberus on the screen. Very bad words with very bad news.

"*You've been infected by Serverus,*" I read aloud.

"Oh, no!" cried Braxton. "A computer virus!"

More words formed: *"You've been warned."*

Then the screen went completely blank. We didn't get the laptop to turn back on again.

26

BRAXTON MANAGED to sneak away the house phone without his parents yelling at him. We called the "hip" hypnotist. Braxton had memorized Chip's number, because he knew we'd need it again.

The phone was set on speakerphone. I heard Chip pick up after the first ring. It was like he waited by the phone for somebody to call. "This is Chip. I put the 'hip' back in 'hypnosis'. How can I hypnotize you today?"

I said, "This is Braxton and Jase, the kids from earlier."

"Of course, it is." He sounded more than a little disappointed. "More questions already?"

"Something else has happened," I said.

"Of course, it has." Chip sighed. "How pathetic am I when eleven-year-olds have more exciting lives than I do?"

Braxton offered, "I don't know, Tostito… Pretty pathetic?"

Chip said, "Well, fill me in. I want nothing more than to live through your adventures."

We described how Serverus had attacked the computer. Chip agreed the laptop now had a virus on it.

"What do we do?" I asked.

"To be honest, guys, I don't know very much about computers. I know a lot about hypnosis and how to ride a unicycle blindfolded, but only the basics about everything else."

Braxton said, "Can we use your computer?"

"So you can get a virus on it, too? I don't think so. I need my computer for business."

"You have a lot of business?" Braxton wondered.

"I have enough. I put the 'hip' back in 'hypnosis,' after all."

I said, "I didn't know someone could put a virus on an Internet search."

"Yeah, it sounds kind of impressive," said Chip. "Someone has some very big, very bad computer skills."

I asked, "Why would Alexis and Sharp go to all that trouble?"

Braxton said, "They knew we suspected something, and they wanted to cover their tracks."

"Exactly," said Chip. "There might be other ways to find out the information—like other words you can use to search—but it sounds risky. You might crash and burn another computer."

I would've offered my computer as a possible guinea pig, but it was in pieces in the garage. I quickly realized how angry Mom would be if I got a virus on the computer. I could only imagine how angry the Grunks would be when they found out what happened to their son's laptop. If eating a donut was an insult, wrecking a thousand-dollar computer certainly equaled death.

"Why use Cerberus?" Chip pointed out. "That's saying something in itself. Cerberus is literally a guardian, right? That means the virus is guarding something. Something that's obviously valuable to these people. Something *big*."

"Brainwashed people," I said.

"No, it's *got* to be bigger than that," Braxton insisted.

"I agree," said Chip. "Things are getting seriously serious. The mystery grows bigger every second. You guys have a plan?"

"Yes!" Braxton was excited to share. "We're going to take a MyPod and—"

"Whoa, hold on there," said Chip. "Not so fast. I don't want to know your plan."

"Why not?" I asked.

"Whatever your plan is, I hope you succeed with it, if for nothing else than you finally getting answers. But if I know what you plan to do, I might have to report it. If things get all gnarly and the cops come around looking for me later on, I don't want to be held even partly responsible for anything you guys do. The cops don't like me. Got it?"

"Not really," said Braxton, "but okay. We won't tell you that we're—"

"Whoa," said Chip. "Whoa! That's enough. Let's not say anything else. If you need an adult to believe anything in the future, contact me again. Until then, though, go ahead with your plans." Chip seemed ready to hang up, but he added, "I can only tell you what I would do in your situation. If I was still a fairly innocent kid, of course."

I asked, "What's that?"

"Whatever it takes. Be as safe as possible, but do *whatever it takes.*"

27

BRAXTON and I didn't do whatever it took. We kind of chickened out. The Serverus virus stole some of our courage. We didn't dare Google more information. Well, Braxton dared. He suggested using the computers at the public library, until I convinced him of the risks involved. It seemed irresponsible to put the well-being of innocent computers in jeopardy. Especially ones that people in the community relied on to make their lives easier.

The Plan, however, stayed the same. Go in for filled cavities and switch the MyPods. It would be so easy... *to mess up*. My appointment with Sharp was either going to be painful or extremely painful, depending on how well things went.

The day before I was to be tortured by the dentist, I sat in the living room with Grandpa, eating caramels and watching Nickelodeon. Mom had taken the bowl of candy away once my cavities were found, but I knew where she hid bags of the stuff. She loved the candy herself, so she could never completely part with it. Whenever she was gone, it was up for grabs, and Grandpa gave me a dozen pennies to sneak the caramels to him.

"Good thing your mother's at work," he said during a commercial break. "This is the life." He began to chew on a caramel. He closed his eyes and smiled. "Ah, sweet ambrosia."

Then his smile went away. He opened his mouth, and I could see the chewy candy had yanked the dentures right off his gums. "*Jrmph*," he muttered as he looked at me.

I knew what he needed. It was not the first, or even seventeenth, time this had happened. I walked down the hall to his bedroom, went over to his nightstand, and grabbed the tube of denture adhesive he kept by the alarm clock. Denture adhesive's literally a type of glue Grandpa put on his fake teeth to hold them in place.

My hand knocked over the glass of water that was also on the nightstand. The glass spilled and rolled onto the floor, under the bed. "*Dangit*," I said between clenched teeth as I began to scratch my hand.

I got down onto my stomach and reached under the bed. The glass hadn't broken in its fall, but it had rolled behind a couple of boxes. I pulled the boxes out and grabbed the glass. In order to get the glass, I had to soak my left arm in a spreading puddle of water. "*Dangit*."

I sat up on the floor and put the glass back on the nightstand. I pushed a shoebox under the bed, careful to keep it away from the puddle of water. The other box I'd pulled out had no top to it, so I was able to see what it held inside.

A pile of yellowed newspaper articles. The top article read, "*Bank robbers to rehabilitate in mental health institute*," and the one beneath that said, "*Another body added to Phoenix murder toll*."

There were a couple of dozen articles in the box. They were mostly from Arizona or Las Vegas newspapers. There were some California articles that were fifteen years old. The newest article was only five months old and was from the paper we used to get in Mesa. There seemed to be a link between all the articles. Each one dealt with crime or, to be more specific, *criminals*.

Why would Grandpa want to keep these articles?

"Jrmph."

Grandpa stood in the doorway. He must've gotten tired of

waiting for his denture adhesive. He walked over to me and held out his hand. I put the adhesive in his grasp.

"Spilled your water," I said as I pointed to the empty glass by the alarm clock. "There's a puddle under the bed. I should get a towel."

I began to stand, but he gestured for me to stay put. He put a hand to his chest as if to say that he would handle it. He then walked out of the room, and I heard him moving around in the bathroom next door.

That was another difference between Grandpa and Mom. If I spilled something in Grandpa's room, it didn't faze him. If I spilled something in Mom's room—which I had never done and hoped to never do—Mom would've probably scolded me for a half-hour and then made me lick it up.

Okay, so she never really made me lick anything off the ground, but once at our house in Mesa, I dropped a burrito on the rug under the dining table. Beans, salsa, cheese, beef, and sour cream splattered in a nasty pattern. Mom scolded me very loudly.

My thing was, why have a beloved rug under the place we ate anyway? Wasn't it in danger of getting stained every time we sat down for a meal? Not very good decorating sense Mom used there, but at least there was no rug under the dining table now. She'd learned her lesson.

I started to read the article from five months ago about the bank robbers in Tempe, Arizona who had to be placed in a mental hospital because of something "traumatic" that happened to them at their apartment. The article did not say what that traumatic something was.

It was an interesting article, but I didn't understand why Grandpa thought it was important to keep forever.

"What're you looking at there?" Grandpa was in the doorway, holding a towel. His dentures were back in place. "Some old junk?"

"Old newspaper articles," I said. "Why'd you keep them?"

He came over, looking down at what was inside the box. "Oh, it's kind of foolish reasoning, really. Thought I'd keep a collection of articles that showed why where we used to live wasn't such a good place to be. So that in the future I'd be able to show your mom why we shouldn't return to those places, just in case she ever thought of going back."

I nodded. "Guess there were a lot of bad things happening back in Arizona. I never noticed."

"You're a kid. What would you have to notice that stuff for?"

"All this time, I've been kind of angry we moved. I thought it was stupid. Didn't know why we needed to 'change' anything. Now I guess I see why."

"You don't have to worry about all that now. We're in beautiful California." He bent over to push the box back under his bed.

"I've got it, Grandpa." I placed the box back under the bed, again doing my best to avoid the puddle of water. "Hand me the towel."

"What a guy," he said as he handed me the blue cloth. "We'll keep this our little secret. We all remember how your mom acted during the IBD."

As I soaked up water under the bed, I said, "IBD?"

"Infamous Burrito Drop. If we call it 'the IBD,' we can talk about it whenever we want around your mom and she'll never know what we're even talking about. She won't have an opportunity to get upset about it."

I smiled. "Good idea." I wiped up the rest of the water and climbed out from under the bed. Felt good not to have to inhale any more dust or dead spiders.

Grandpa smiled at me. He said, "That's the way to live up to your namesake."

"What?"

"Don't tell me you forgot who you're named after."

I said, "Mom's friend, Jason, from college?"

"Well, there's *him*." Grandpa put a hand on my shoulder. "I like to think you were named for the Greek hero, Jason. You know that."

"Yeah, but Mom thinks Greek mythology is a waste of time."

"And she's the one who reads all those romance novels, too." He shook his head. "I know your parents named you after your mom's friend, but I look at it my own way. You're named after a hero. He wasn't a great hero by any means, but he was good enough." Grandpa paused. "It's the little things that help make someone a hero, Jase. You saved me from breaking my back under that bed. That's heroic."

I rolled my eyes. "But I spilled the glass."

"No one said heroes are perfect. But when a hero makes a mistake, he'll do his best to fix it, right?"

"Grandpa, all I did was clean up water."

"It certainly wasn't getting the Golden Fleece, but it was something."

The Greek hero, Jason, went on a quest to retrieve a golden ram's wool so that he could become the ruler of some kingdom. The wool was referred to as the Golden Fleece. I liked the story, not because it had some guy named Jason in it, but because the ram whose fleece was fought for could fly.

Grandpa smiled very wide. "You know what I just thought of? Jason had his Argonauts, and you have your own Argo*not*. Or Argo*nut*. Get it?"

The ship Jason sailed on to get the Golden Fleece was called the *Argo*. The men who helped Jason on his quest were called the Argonauts. Grandpa seemed to be twisting the word around to make fun of Braxton. I didn't like it very much.

I said, "Please, don't tease Braxton anymore." After meeting Braxton's parents, I didn't want any other adult to put him down.

Grandpa put his hands up. "Okay, I'm sorry," he said. "That was a bad joke. Didn't even really mean it."

"No?"

He shook his head. "Every hero needs a companion, a sidekick. If the hero can't help himself, he's going to need his friends to get him out of trouble."

"That's right."

"Tomorrow, however, you will have to help yourself in that dentist's office."

I scratched my hand. "Yeah…"

"You're a hero, kiddo. You have to be strong. Don't surrender to the fear like I would. A hero never surrenders."

"Okay, Grandpa."

"Because tomorrow will be legendary. Jason and his quest for the Golden *Floss*."

I groaned. "No way. Flossing makes my gums bleed. I'll never floss again, even if it is made of gold."

"That," said Grandpa, "is just another reason I am proud to be your grandfather."

28

THE NEXT DAY at Dr. Sharp's office, I sat by the photograph wall as I waited for Alexis to take me back to almost certain doom. Surprisingly, the spot where Michael and Greg's pictures had once been was now filled up with new smiling photos of a young girl and some boy with braces.

It was like Michael and Greg were never there. That's what the Sharps wanted us to believe, wasn't it? The boys were gone, nothing more than former patients who had simply moved on "to Colorado."

I didn't buy it.

It was then that I wondered what had happened to the missing photos themselves. Where did they go once they were off the wall? Into the trash? Or were they kept somewhere else?

Beth the receptionist typed on the nearby computer. I stood up and walked over to the counter she sat behind. She didn't look up at me. She just typed more.

"Excuse me?" I said.

"Well, if it isn't, like, the bad kid," she said without a glance in my direction. "What kind of trouble are you, like, trying to get into today?"

Braxton's MyPod was becoming a heavy stone in my jacket

pocket. She couldn't see what I was hiding, could she? I figured that, no, she couldn't, because she wasn't even looking my way.

Apparently, the Sharps had made Beth aware of what Braxton and I had done. Had they given her instructions not to give me any information, or would she still be willing to answer the questions I had for her?

"I'm not a bad kid," I said.

"That's what bad kids say. They, like, deny everything. I should know. I have, like, three bratty little brothers and sisters. They got me in trouble, like, all the time when I was growing up."

"Braxton and I didn't get you in trouble with Alexis and Dr. Sharp, did we?"

Her fingers stopped typing. She brought her eyes to mine. "All they, like, told me was that I shouldn't talk about patients with other patients. My parents have lectured me, like, way worse. Don't worry."

"That's good. I don't want you to get in trouble."

"But what *do* you want?" She leaned back in her chair and crossed her arms over her chest.

I said, "I do have one question. Can I ask it?"

"Sure, but I probably won't, like, answer it."

"What do you do with the photos once they are taken off the wall? Where do they go?"

Beth hesitated for a brief moment, and then she said, "I guess it's okay to tell you... Dr. Sharp, like, keeps them for his records or something."

So Sharp still had Michael and Greg's pictures in his office somewhere. I wanted very badly to see those photographs, if for no other reason than to figure out what the missing guys looked like. I didn't want to walk by them on the street and not even know I had.

How could I get those photos in my hands?

Behind me, Alexis's voice suddenly said, "Beth, may I steal Jase away from you?"

I turned to find Sharp's sister staring at us. My jaw dropped. Even though Alexis's appearance came at a somewhat unexpected moment, it was not she who made my eyes almost pop out of my head.

Standing next to her, dressed in gold chains and a pink collared shirt, was Chip the Hipnotist. *What the heck was he doing there?* I decided to ask him just that.

I looked right at him and said, "What are you doing here?"

He looked at me strangely, as if he didn't recognize me. "What do people do at the dentist's office, man?" he said. "Have fun? I don't think so."

Beth said, "Do you two, like, know each other?"

Before I could say anything, Chip said, "No."

My hand itched. Why was Chip lying? Did he want me to play along for some reason? He gave me a slight nod with his head that I interpreted as meaning, *You had better be quiet.*

I said, "I thought only kids went here?"

"For the most part, you'd be right," said Alexis. "But we do treat some adults."

I went over to the photograph wall. Sure enough, it displayed about ten pictures of adult men and women. I had never really looked at the wall too closely, except to focus on the empty spots that had once been there.

"Let's go, Jase," said Alexis. To Beth, she added, "Please help Mr. Quinn here schedule a full cleaning for later on in the week. Take a picture of him for the wall."

It seemed to be Chip's first time at the office. Was he there to spy on Dr. Sharp? Or did he really just need to go to a dentist, and the story Braxton and I told him about Sharp reminded him of that fact? I really hoped it was the first choice.

"Make sure you get me at a good angle," Chip said to Beth. "I mean, I look great from all angles, but some work better than others."

Beth giggled. "Is that right?"

Chip walked over to her at the counter. "Should I take the chains off for the shot?" he asked. "They could reflect some gnarly light."

"Are they, like, made of real gold?"

"Don't know. Got them from some machine in Taco Bell."

Beth smiled. "Wow, they are, like, super shiny. I like shiny."

"Hey, so do I!" said Chip.

Looked like they were flirting, but since I had so little experience in that area I wasn't quite sure what I was witnessing at that moment. I didn't get why Chip was ignoring me and talking to the dumb receptionist so much.

"Jase, come on," Alexis said again. "The sooner we get this done, the better."

I turned to follow her down the hall, but I looked back at Chip one last time. He definitely was not looking in my direction at all. He laughed with Beth. It was as if they were in their own creepy, confusing, little world.

I didn't know what to do or think. I decided to just push it all to the back of my mind until later. Braxton would have some ideas about what had just gone on.

At any rate, the last thing I needed was some major distraction, because, as I walked behind Alexis toward my room of torture, the music grew louder and louder. The Plan was officially about to go into effect.

29

THINGS STARTED off as smooth as creamy peanut butter. *Too* smooth. I suspected something was up. Alexis acted perfectly toward me when we got to the room. Again, suspicious perfection had always been the dentist's problem from the start, but now it was, oddly, Alexis's problem, also.

As we sat in the room waiting for Sharp to appear, Alexis smiled at me. She made lame jokes and comments about the weather. Something was *definitely* up.

I found myself missing her scowl. The new and "improved" Alexis freaked me out. She was trying her best to be nice to me, and I knew it was all an act to steer my suspicions away from her. What Braxton and I did with the files must've put the Sharps on edge. It made them destroy Braxton's computer, and it forced kindness out of Alexis.

What had Braxton and I really found? What was Alexis trying to hide behind that smile?

She even said, "You can change the music. I know we don't share similar taste."

I looked at the MyPod. I wanted to erase One Direction from the room, but couldn't. Luckily—and unsurprisingly—Braxton listened to the same stuff Alexis liked. It was necessary to switch the MyPod with another that had at least some of the same playlists. It was the only way the switch could happen without Sharp and Alexis finding out about it... *right away.*

Oh, well. Even if we did get caught, we would have whatever information the MyPods held. The subliminal messages would be ours. And then the police's. Hopefully. *If there were subliminal messages even on there...*

"Jase?" said Alexis. "Are you okay?"

I snapped out of my thoughts. "Oh, um, yeah, I'm fine. You can... leave it on this." It was so very hard to get that out.

"I can?" she said. "It doesn't bother you?"

I said, "I'm getting used to it." What a lie. "I like the... harmonies." An even bigger lie.

"Harmony" was the way the voices sounded all together. I only knew what it meant because Mom told me years ago that if I was born a girl she would've named me "Harmony Ruth" after her grandma. *Harmony Ruth Clark.* Could you imagine?

Alexis nodded. "Yes, the harmonies are very nice. Especially on 'Story of My Life.'"

I nodded even though I didn't know what she was talking about. That worked a lot with adults. Nod your head when you don't know what else to say.

"Are you nervous?" she asked, looking at my scratching fingers.

Braxton's MyPod felt heavier in my pocket every second. It was a lead weight holding me in the seat. Not getting the switch done in time made me nervous. Alexis hadn't left my side since I left the waiting room. She didn't want me to steal another file, I guessed.

I knew there was something else I should have been a little nervous about, though. Something else I was there for...

"These are your first cavities," said Alexis.

Bingo. The cavities. I hadn't given much thought to them even though they were the reason I was at the dentist's office in the first place. I was too focused on my mission.

Alexis tried to assure me everything would be okay: "The filling procedure is far less terrible than people make it out to be."

I said, "My grandpa says it's pretty terrible."

"Does he?"

"But he has over twenty cavities."

"Let's hope that doesn't run in the family."

"It won't."

A chill ran up and down my back. I was suddenly hit with the realization that I was going to get *holes* drilled into my *teeth*. A needle was going to *pierce my gums*. Pain was coming my way, and *fast*.

The itch was intense. *I wanted my mommy*. She was in the waiting room, ignoring Nemo, reading a book. She could save me. She could get me out of that chair and back home to safety.

But she would also take me away from the MyPod, away from The Plan. *Unless there was some way I could get away with both things...*

"I want my mom," I said.

"Your mom?"

"Yes! My mom!"

Alexis frowned. "Why?"

"I can't go through with this!"

"You want to leave?"

"Yes! I can't be here!"

"Um... *okay*. This kind of thing happens. Maybe it would be better if she sat in here with us during the procedure?"

"Yes! No! Maybe! Just get her! I won't do this without talking to her!"

"Fine. No problem. Stay put."

Within seconds, I was alone in the room, listening to One Direction begin to harmonize. I'd just given myself the perfect opportunity for an old-fashioned MyPod switcheroo.

I jumped out of the chair, slid across the tiled floor, and bumped into the table holding the MyPod. Its speakers almost toppled off the table, but I held them steady. I fished Braxton's MyPod out of my pocket. The devices really were identical.

Even with sweaty palms and one itchy hand I managed to work quickly. I turned the power off Sharp's MyPod and pulled it out of its stand. The room was eerily silent. I placed Braxton's MyPod into the stand, and—

"Jason Kyle Clark."

Mom had arrived.

30

How long had she been standing there? What had she seen?

I turned to her and tried not to look incredibly guilty. But, like I said before, she was a

living, breathing lie detector. She did nothing but glare at me from the doorway.

"What're you doing with that thing?" she asked.

I almost fell to my knees and begged for forgiveness. That was until I realized her glare was aimed at the MyPod—*Braxton's* MyPod —on the table. She didn't even see the other one I hid behind my back.

Before I could even lie, Alexis and Sharp entered the room. Sharp, of course, smiled. He said to Mom, "Jase didn't mention our MyPods to you?"

Mom shook her head. "What should he have told me about them?"

"Nothing much," said the doctor. "We let our patients choose the songs they want to listen to during their appointments."

"Yeah," I said. "I was just searching for a new song."

Mom looked at the dentist. "Didn't think he was supposed to be touching something that wasn't his, seeing how he, you know, has had a problem with that in the past."

"Really," Sharp said, "it's no problem whatsoever. If he wants to change a song, that's fine with us."

As the adults made eye contact with each other, I tried my best to quickly slip the switched MyPod into my right pants pocket. I padded it beneath a wad of tissues. Mom must've seen me move out of the corner of her eye—she was like a freaky *hawk*—because she immediately turned her attention back my way.

"Can I choose the song now?" I asked.

The adults all stared at me. Mom said, "Sure."

I turned on the MyPod's power. Braxton had a playlist called "*So What If Girls Like Them? So Do I!*" He claimed the mix of songs included "every hit of every boy band legend."

I went with a safe bet and selected the song Alexis had mentioned earlier. "Story of My Life" crawled out of the speakers. The silence we'd just experienced had been so much better.

Wait. That gave me an idea. Didn't know why I hadn't thought of it before. It was so *simple*.

"I adore this song," said Alexis.

"Actually," I said, turning off the MyPod, "I think I would like it better if there wasn't any music on at all."

There was that scowl again. Was it because Alexis wouldn't be able to listen to her precious One Direction or because my mind wouldn't be receiving any subliminal messages? Probably both.

Why hadn't I thought of it before? Make the switch and don't play any music at all off Braxton's MyPod. That way things looked the same *and* there would be no chance of the MyPod accidentally playing a song that wasn't part of the Sharps' playlists.

I officially amazed myself.

Alexis burst my bubble with, "We can't have that. There has to be music."

What? The hairs on the back of my neck stood tall. The itch was back.

Mom asked, "Why does there *have* to be music?"

Go, Mom! Fight for my right to silence!

Alexis frowned. "It helps us with what we do."

"How so?" Mom inquired.

The two women looked about ready to go for each other's throats. Mom would win that fight hands-down. I'd bet a jar full of pennies on her any day.

"Mrs. Clark." The doctor deflected Mom's glare with another smile. "What Alexis means to say is that the music serves a certain purpose in what we do. It helps to take our patients' focus away from what they are here for and refocuses it onto something more positive. An upbeat or familiar song can help relieve even the worst discomfort, right?"

I almost believed that Sharp almost believed what he said. He was obviously far more experienced at thinking of things off the top of his head than I was. But I knew his real reason for wanting the music on. It was the same reason Alexis had. It had nothing to do with patients' focus.

"No, the music isn't going to help me," I said. They wanted to control my brain without me knowing it. Too bad for them I knew all about it.

"Jase," said the dentist, "I understand you're uneasy about this whole thing. We brought your mom back here to help you out. We want this to go as well for you as possible. From my experience, the music really does help to calm patients down. Perhaps your mom would agree with that?"

I immediately realized he'd been able to accomplish what Alexis failed. He brought Mom over to his side, the *Very* Dark Side.

Mom nodded. "I don't really pay attention to what the dentist is doing so much. I try to sing along in my head with the radio instead."

"But it's not what I want to do," I whined.

Alexis said, "You'll probably change your mind."

"No, I won't! No. I. *Won't!*" I tried my best to be as annoying as possible. Most adults would do almost anything to get a kid to stop annoying behavior.

I forgot that Mom wasn't like most adults.

"Jase, you stop that right now," she said. "You do not talk back to an adult that way, do you understand me?"

"Yes, I understand, but—"

"*Butts* are made to be in seats, and that one right there"—she pointed to the plastic-covered chair—"has your name written all over it."

"Where? I don't see it."

Bad move. Dumb move. *The worst move possible.* Mom walked up to me and grabbed my itchy wrist tightly. I thought my bone was going to snap in two. She got right in my face.

She fumed, "It's bad enough they made me come back here because you wouldn't cooperate. It's even worse now that, with me here, you still won't cooperate. How do you think that makes me feel?"

"Angry?" I said.

"You're right about that. So pick some music you want to listen to, because—"

"Mrs. Clark," interrupted the dentist.

She turned to him. "Yes?"

"The music isn't necessary. If he really doesn't want to listen to any music he doesn't have to listen to any music. Remember, his comfort is what is most important here."

Alexis didn't look happy with what her brother decided without her permission. Was that how it usually worked? Sharp said how things went and Alexis did whatever he decided? She didn't seem like the kind of person who'd like that very much.

"Okay, then, Jase," said Mom. "You're sure you don't want any music on? I think it'll help."

I shook my head. "The music would just hurt my brain."

Mom seemed confused with what I said, but the other two just stared at me as if they hadn't heard me or cared. I'd picked my words so carefully, too.

"We'll honor your request," said Sharp. "Now, if you would get into your seat, that would be great. We're already behind schedule."

31

I SAT BACK in the plastic-covered chair. Alexis walked over and clipped a blue paper bib around my neck. What was I, a *big baby*?

From the look Mom gave me, I could tell her answer would have been, "Yes, a very big baby." She stood against the wall with her arms crossed, watching my every move.

"Try to relax now." The dentist's voice floated from somewhere close behind me.

Relax? A needle was about to be plunged into my gums! A drill was about to dig into my teeth! I was about to scratch a hole straight through my hand!

My throat closed up. Only tiny bits of air would come in or out. *Breathe through your nose, Jase, breathe through your nose!* Oh, no! Why was I a mouth-breather? *Why?*

A strong hand gripped my right shoulder. The dentist smiled down at me. "Ready to begin?" He held a metal tray with his other hand. On it were pointy tools that included a pointy needle.

I shook my head and said, "I can't do this." Now I wasn't saying it to get Alexis out of the room. Now I was serious.

"I blame his grandfather," said Mom. "He's put ridiculous thoughts in Jase's head about dentists."

Sharp nodded. "I understand. Jase, would it be okay if your Mom stood beside you and held your hand?"

First, a bib. Now, Mommy holding my hand. Yep, a big baby, for sure. Maybe the bib would soak up my tears, too.

Mom now looked sorry for me. "It's okay, baby"—*Did she have to say* baby?—"I'll hold your hand if it'll make you feel better."

It seemed like a good option at the time. I nodded.

Mom walked over to where I sat. Sharp asked her to stand on the left side of the chair so that he could work from the right side. When she grabbed my left hand, I barely felt any better. Plus, I couldn't even scratch.

"Jase, honey, your hand is so cold," Mom said. "You're sweaty, too." She ran her other hand through my hair. "It's going to be okay."

"It's going to be a breeze," said Sharp. "I've filled hundreds—*thousands*—of cavities. I've never had a problem. Not even once."

I sensed that was a lie. A perfect record? Yeah, right! He never once accidentally drilled an extra hole in some kid's face?

"He knows what he's doing," added Alexis. "He's a very good dentist. One of the best."

Like I was going to believe her!

"How about this?" said the doctor. "Let's work our way up to the cavities. We'll start off slow."

He rolled a stool over from against the wall. He sat next to me, placing the tray on a table by my knees. Alexis handed him a pair of latex gloves he slid over his hands. At least they were hands, not hooks. He strapped a paper mask and goggles to his face.

He said, "The wax, Alexis." He held a hand out to the assistant. "Thank you."

The only wax I knew about came from candles. He was going to pour candle wax in my mouth? What kind of dentist was this guy?

He held what looked like a sports mouthguard in his gloved hand. "This," he said, "is a special kind of wax. What you need to do is bite down on it as hard as you can when I tell you to."

"Why?" I asked.

"Since our X-ray machine's broken, we need another way to see what your teeth look like. When you bite down on the wax, we'll have a clearer picture of how your bite looks. We want to see if you have an overbite or if your teeth are growing in funny. Stuff like that."

"Okay," I said.

"That's cool with you?" the dentist said. I nodded. "Good. Open wide."

He gently placed the "mouthguard" over and between my teeth. It was so light that I hardly felt it resting there. He moved the wax around with his gloved fingers, which poked the inside of my cheeks.

I flinched and moved in the seat. Mom grabbed my hand tightly. "It's okay, it's okay," she repeated over and over.

Sharp said, "All right, bite down as hard as you can for thirty seconds."

I bit down on the wax so hard that my jaw muscles hurt. My eyes became watery. The wax had no taste. They should have at least given it some flavor, like chocolate or sour apple.

Tasteless wax. Aching jaw muscles. Breathing through my nose. Thirty seconds felt like thirty minutes. Thirty *centuries*.

Finally, Sharp said I could open wide again. He pulled the wax out, some drool following it out of my mouth. It oozed down my chin, really nasty and warm. Alexis leaned over and wiped the drool off with the bib.

"Isn't that cool?" asked the dentist.

He held the wax in front of him like he was showing me a piece of priceless artwork. All I saw was a semicircle of holes in a mouthguard.

"I can tell you have a very strong bite." The dentist looked to Mom and added, "Must be hard to tear food away from him."

Mom said, "Sometimes it is." She squeezed my hand.

"Alexis, please take this." Sharp handed his sister my bite, and then he pushed a button on the side of the chair.

The chair tilted back. *Uh, oh. Here we go.* Time to look at the ceiling. There were lots of holes on the ceiling tiles. Maybe I could try to count all of them.

"Squeeze as hard as you want," said Mom.

I tried not to squeeze her hand too hard just yet. As soon as I saw that needle, I was going to probably break her fingers.

"Let there be light," said the doctor as he pulled down what looked like a submarine periscope high above my face. With the flip of a switch, the periscope shot light down onto me. Now all I could see was that thing staring at me. It never blinked.

"I don't want to surprise you," said Sharp. "Here comes the needle."

My entire body trembled. The unattended itch burned. I began to break Mom's fingers in my grasp, but she didn't scream, so I probably wasn't actually breaking her fingers. Not that I wanted to, anyway.

What had Grandpa said? *A hero never surrenders.*

I wasn't getting poked with a needle without a fight. Well, *another* fight. I closed my mouth shut as tight as I could.

"You have to open your mouth," said Alexis.

I shut my eyes. If I didn't see the needle, it couldn't exist. If I kept my mouth shut, no needle would come my way.

I envisioned the wax in my mouth. I bit down as hard as I could. They would have to pry my lips apart... or wait until I had to breathe again.

Darn mouth-breather. *Mouth-breather!*

"Jase," said Mom, "your face is getting red. Calm down."

Keep biting, keep biting... I bit so hard I thought my teeth were going to explode from the force. The pressure I put on each tooth from another was almost painful. The pressure was almost not worth the—

Wait a second. *Pressure.*

The "BP PSI" from Michael and Greg's files. I couldn't ever figure out why "blood pressure pounds per-square-inch" was so important to a dentist. But what if it didn't mean *blood* pressure? What if, instead, it meant—

"Bite pressure!" I screamed.

32

I JUMPED UP SUDDENLY in the seat without first opening my eyes. I didn't know that Sharp had been leaning over me. My eyes shot open when I felt the dentist's chin crack against the top of my head.

When our skulls collided, the doctor jumped up, as well... *into the periscope shining light down on us.* The top of his head connected with the lamp, and he fell forward... *onto the tray of pointy tools.* The dentist and the tray both crashed to the floor beside my seat.

All was silent for a second or two. And then Mom and Alexis started yelling.

"*Xander!*" Alexis shouted as she raced to the side of her fallen brother.

"*Jason Kyle Clark!*" Mom shouted as she yanked me out of the seat and over to her, clutching my shoulder.

I pretty much ignored the rest of what Mom shouted in my ear, because I could do nothing else but stare at Sharp crumpled face-down on the floor. He didn't move.

Scratch, scratch, SCRATCH.

I killed him.

Then he moved. Slowly, but he still moved. He also groaned.

Alexis kneeled on the floor beside him, helping turn him over. He gave a quick shriek of pain.

I wondered if he fell on any of the pointy tools themselves, or if he just knocked all of them to the floor around him. Pokers, scrapers, and thingamabobbers were scattered like wounded soldiers on the battlefield.

I couldn't see some of the doctor because the chair was between us, so I struggled against Mom's grip to get a better look. Even though I didn't really trust the guy, or even like what he did for a living, I honestly hoped I hadn't hurt him.

Alexis pulled the paper mask and goggles down, away from the dentist's face. Amazingly, he still smiled. However, his smile was less amazing than usual. It was a sleepy grin. I couldn't see any of his blinding teeth.

"Try to ignore it, Xander," said Alexis. "Breathe. *Breathe.*"

Ignore *what*? I looked up at Mom, and she released one of her hands from my shoulder to cover her mouth. Her eyes grew wide.

"What is it?" I stood on my tippy-toes to get a better look over the chair.

"I'm okay," said the dentist. "For the most part."

Alexis helped him stagger to his feet, and then I saw the needle sticking out of his right elbow. His arm was limp against his side, as if it were made of rubber.

"Do you want me to pull it out?" asked Alexis.

"No." He said as he waved her away with his left hand. He fell into the chair I'd just been sitting in.

"I'm sorry!" I said, because I was. Why did his arm hang like that? Had he broken it in the fall?

The dentist said to me, "Don't think this has ever happened before." He chuckled.

"Is your arm okay?" asked Mom.

He looked down at the right arm that lay in his lap like a dead snake. With his left hand, he grabbed the needle, grunted, and pulled it out slowly. He bit his lip as he pulled it out.

"Oh, *Xander.*" Alexis looked genuinely concerned for her brother. The look on her face made me feel a lot worse.

"Think I'll live," Sharp said once the needle was out. "Everything from the elbow down is just numb. The anesthetic should wear off in a while."

Anesthetic. The stuff injected into his arm from the needle was the stuff that was supposed to be injected into my gums.

"Right now, though," said the doctor, "I'm not going to be able to do any kind of dental work with my arm like this." He turned to Alexis. "Tell Beth to reschedule all of today's appointments."

"*All* of them?" said Alexis.

"I want to make sure my arm's one-hundred percent. It's not worth the risk."

"What about what's happened here?" asked Mom. "Is there any way we can reschedule?"

"It was an accident," said the doctor. "I don't hold grudges. Talk to Beth out front about rescheduling."

Mom said, "How could we help with all this?"

"Mrs. Clark," said Alexis, "thank you, but the most help you could give us would be to go home and enjoy the rest of your day."

"Oh, okay." Mom grabbed my wrist and pulled me towards the door. "Come on, Jase."

I put my hand in my pocket to make sure the MyPod was still there. It was. The Plan hadn't gone without a hitch, but at least I'd been able to make the switch.

33

LATER, in our living room, Grandpa high-fived me. With his other hand, he popped another caramel candy into his mouth. "That," he said, balancing the candy on his tongue, "is something I have always wanted to do to a dentist." He began to chew. "Ah, sweet ambrosia."

I'd just finished telling him what happened at Sharp's office. Mom wasn't home. In fact, she never technically made it inside the house before leaving again. My accident at the office must've really made her angry, because she didn't say a thing the entire way back. When we got there, she dropped me off at the curb and sped away. She went somewhere to "cool down." She probably wouldn't be back for hours.

"I don't know, Grandpa." I looked down at the floor. "I feel kind of bad about it."

Grandpa leaned back in his recliner. He chewed loudly. I didn't want his teeth to fall out again. Between chews, he said, "You've got a good heart. It's not black or made of coal like mine."

I smiled. "Thought you told me you have a baboon heart!"

"Oh. I'm old. I get things mixed up sometimes."

I pulled one of Mom's numerous decorative couch pillows over to me. I hugged it tightly. "You're really not mad?" I said.

"Please, this is Grandpa you're talking about here. Dentists and I are mortal enemies. Imagine me as Theseus and a dentist as the Minotaur. We're always going for the other's throat."

The Minotaur was a half-man, half-bull beast that killed all its victims in a giant underground maze. It did this until the Greek hero Theseus came along and disposed of the monster...

"You and Mom both got mad at me, though, the last time that—"

"What you did with that file angered me because it was a dishonest and stupid thing to do," Grandpa said. "Stealing is not okay, even if what's stolen is something valuable to a dentist."

The MyPod began to feel heavy in my pocket again. I couldn't imagine how angry Grandpa would be if he found out I stole something else. And Mom would—*I didn't want to* think *about what Mom would do to me.*

Grandpa said, "Don't look so sad. Raise your head up. Have candy." He paused. "And

stop scratching your darn hand for once, will you? You've been doing it for months, and it can't be good for your skin."

I did my best to stop, but it didn't last long. I was scratching again within seconds.

Grandpa took another caramel out of the bag in his lap and tossed it to me on the couch. "Your mother may be angry with you," said Grandpa, "but I bet she's almost as angry with me. She didn't come in the house for a reason. She didn't want to be around you *or* me. This is far worse than the IBD."

I smiled and nodded as I popped the candy into my mouth. "She thinks you've put bad ideas about dentists in my head."

He said, "Have I?"

"Yes."

"Then I've done my job."

I wanted to tell him right then about everything I'd found out about Sharp and Alexis. But, even as much as Grandpa hated dentists, he probably wouldn't believe most of what I told him. It was a crazy story, and Grandpa was an adult. He would want "more proof."

I knew the proof was in my pocket. But if I showed him the MyPod without knowing for sure what it said on it, I was doomed. He'd ask where I got it from, and I'd have to tell him the truth, because when he found out the lie I told him was a lie, I'd be in deep dung.

There was little time to waste before Sharp and Alexis found Braxton's MyPod instead of theirs. I got off the couch.

"Where are you going?" Grandpa asked.

"My room." I turned to leave, but stopped when I remembered Mom wasn't there. Grandpa was easier—or more willing—to crack.

"Yes?" he said. Adults can tell when a kid has something more to say.

I said, "I know we've gotten in some trouble, but I was wondering if Braxton could come over?" He deserved to be solving the mystery right next to me.

"Okay…"

"Grandpa, *please.*"

He stared at me. "What would your mother say? She isn't happy, as is."

I groaned. "Forget it." I began to walk away.

"Hold on. I wasn't finished speaking. I wanted to know what your mother would say, because you know me. She and I agree less than Theseus and the Minotaur do."

I could begin to see why the Greek references annoyed Mom so much. "What's the answer?" I said.

Grandpa chewed loudly. "Of course, your friend can come over if he can find his own way. If your mother doesn't like it, she can talk it over with me."

"Thanks!"

I raced to the phone in the kitchen. As soon as Braxton walked over, we'd listen to what terrible words the MyPod was *really* singing to us.

34

I SPENT TOO many minutes on the phone with Braxton, filling him in on all that took place at the dentist's office. I was paranoid that his crazy mom or dad would eavesdrop on our conversation (as my crazy mom liked to do), but he assured me they were gone for the day at some health spa. Still, I didn't quite understand why we couldn't just discuss everything in person when he got to my house. Finally, Braxton said he'd heard enough and that he was leaving to meet me.

He arrived at the house within an hour. Grandpa was in his bedroom with the door shut, so I greeted my friend. It was probably for the best, considering that Grandpa might have called Braxton "Argonot" or "Argonut" to his face.

"Braxton's here," I yelled at Grandpa's room as we walked by it.

There was no reply from the other side of the door. Grandpa must have fallen asleep. Old people liked to nap.

Once we were in my bedroom, I closed the door. "No lock?" said Braxton.

I said, "Sometimes I wish I could lock my mom out of here. If I tried to, she'd probably cut down the door with a chainsaw."

Braxton giggled. "Yeah, that would be so awesome."

I didn't see how Mom screaming at me and slicing through my bedroom door with a deadly weapon could be awesome, but I still said, "For sure."

"Should we get to it, then?"

"Totally. Take a seat."

He sat down in the chair in front of my desk. I didn't have much of anything out of order in my room—Mom made me clean it often —so Braxton was in little danger of sitting on any underwear or socks. I wondered if being out of his element made him uncomfortable, but then realized that only in the presence of his parents had I seen my friend anywhere near uncomfortable.

"Are you hungry?" I asked.

"Do you have any pumpkin pie?"

I shook my head. "Not in my junk food trunk."

"You have a trunk, too?"

"What I mean to say is, I don't have a trunk. I have a kitchen with a pantry and a refrigerator."

"Asking me if I'm hungry is like asking Bigfoot if his shoes are too small. The answer is always yes."

I began to pull the MyPod out of my pocket, but stopped. "I can go get you something."

"You're such a good host. The pumpkin pie can wait. I came here because of the MyPod, right?"

I didn't have the heart to tell him we didn't have any pumpkin pie. It was the summer, so pumpkin pie was out of season anyway. Just how old *was* that pie in his trunk?

I didn't want to think about it, so I said, "You brought the speakers and the stand?"

He'd brought a red and green plaid backpack. Kind of hurt my eyes to look directly at it. My backpack was just a boring shade of blue. Braxton seemed to deliberately try to be different from everyone else. But, really, what was so wrong about that?

He pulled the speakers and stand from within the plaid monstrosity. I told him to put the stuff on my desk and to plug it all into the nearest outlet. Now that my computer was dismantled and collecting dust in the garage, the empty outlets peered up at me like grinning skulls.

Once the equipment was set up, I placed the MyPod into the stand. I turned the power on, and a number of playlists popped up on the screen. Did it matter which one I chose?

Braxton said, "The message would be on anything, right? They don't play the same songs for everyone."

I picked something called *"Easy Listening."* A guy named Seal started singing. I immediately wondered what the name of Seal's brother was. *Walrus?*

Braxton and I sat there for a couple of minutes, not saying anything to each other, only listening to Seal sing a love song. I was pretty sick of love songs, but then remembered something I read on the Internet a long time ago: seventy-five percent of all songs are love songs. The odds that the next song I chose wouldn't be a love song weren't very good.

So we listened to more scratchy Seal until I finally said, "Other than the song itself, nothing is wrong."

"Let's listen to another one," Braxton said.

The next song was a love song by the Cranberries. It left a bad taste in my mouth and ringing in my ears.

The song after that was a love song by Mariah Carey. *Ouch.*

"The only message I'm getting," I said, "is that I don't want to listen to any of these songs ever again."

"What if," offered Braxton, "we turned on the volume full-blast?"

"To make our ears bleed even more?"

"If there are messages, we wouldn't be able to hear them easily. That's what Chip said. On low volume, we really won't be able to hear them if they're there."

I shrugged. "Okay."

"Your grandpa won't be angry?"

"He has old ears. Plus, he's a deep sleeper. He can't hear us in here."

"Let's do it!" said my friend.

I cranked the volume up as loud as I could. Those little speakers packed a mighty punch. I had to back away from them, because I thought my eardrums were going to explode. Every high note was a knife to my head.

Braxton and I shared disappointed looks after about thirty seconds of Mariah Carey at high volume. Everything I heard was pretty terrible, but not in the way we hoped it would be.

"What are we going to do now?" I screamed.

"What?" said Braxton.

"What are we going to do now?"

"What?"

I had to scream: "WHAT ARE WE GOING TO DO NOW?"

"WHAT?"

I walked back over to the MyPod, about to turn it off, when a voice suddenly said a couple of words over Mariah Carey's shrieks. It was so quick that I didn't catch what was said, but not quick enough for me not to hear it at all.

My head snapped over to look at Braxton. He'd heard it, too.

I rewound the song back a few seconds, waited for the words again. There they were. There they went. It was literally that fast.

I paused the song. "Do you know what it's saying?" I asked.

"Something about 'east,' I think."

East? What the heck could that mean?

I rewound the song again. Again. Again. Again.

"Eat," I said once I paused the song the fourth time. "I know it says 'eat.'"

"That's it!" cried Braxton. "What's the other word?"

Within a couple of more tries, we had it figured out, and it made little to no sense at all.

35

"Eat meat," I said.

Braxton nodded and repeated what we had heard: "Eat meat."

The hidden, subliminal message was confusing, but that didn't make it any less frightening. It made it *even more* frightening. Always scarier to not know something than to know it.

I scratched my hand and said, "Why do they care so much about us eating meat? I mean, all those questions about being a vegetarian, and—"

"We need to tell someone *now*." Braxton definitely looked more scared than I was. "Can I call Cheeto from your phone? He wants proof, and now we have proof!"

I said, "Yeah, I guess we should call him."

"But, first, let's show your grandpa!"

"He's sleeping."

"So, wake him up! This is too important! He won't get angry, will he?"

I shook my head. "He's the one who usually wakes *me* up."

But, would Grandpa believe everything we had to say even with the new evidence? Would his old ears even hear the message when our young ears had trouble picking it up?

I shrugged. "It's worth a shot."

Braxton jumped out of his seat. I was close behind him. We slammed open my bedroom door and practically ran down the hall to Grandpa's room.

I knocked on the door, but there was no answer. Like I said, he was a deep sleeper. I knocked again, but louder this time. "Grandpa!" I shouted.

When there still was no answer, I looked over at Braxton and said, "Maybe we should just wait."

Braxton shook his head. "No way. This is too important." He grabbed the knob, twisted it in his hand, and the door slowly creaked open. He said, "Yeah, this family definitely needs to invest in some locks."

The window blinds were cracked open, and sunlight spilled into the room. From the doorway, we could see Grandpa on the bed, unconscious.

I think most old people snore, but Grandpa had always been silent in his slumber. His chest and belly lifted and fell peacefully beneath a blanket. His closed eyes faced the ceiling. Dentures rested in the glass on his nightstand.

Braxton pointed. "Are those his teeth?"

"Yes."

"Cool. Would he let me try them on?"

I just stared at my friend for a few seconds before saying, "No, Braxton, he wouldn't." I paused. "Now, just wait here. I'll wake him."

I left Braxton at the door. I walked over to the bed, reached out a hand to shake Grandpa awake, and then I stopped when I noticed papers spread out on the bed beside him.

"What is it?" said Braxton.

I didn't immediately answer. I recognized the papers as some of the newspaper articles I had found stored under Grandpa's bed the day before. Why had Grandpa taken them out of the box? He'd obviously been looking at them before he fell asleep. I thought he'd said they were no big deal...?

There were only three articles next to him. What was so special about them? I had to find out, so I reached over Grandpa's heaving stomach, snatched the papers off the bed, and walked back to the door.

Braxton looked confused as I approached him. "What are those?"

"Old articles."

"Why didn't you wake him up?"

I said, "Just wait. I want to look at these before he puts them away again." I slowly pulled the door shut. "Back to my room. Quick."

"This is kind of like when I took those papers off Dr. Sharp's desk," said Braxton.

I didn't want to compare what I was doing to his earlier stealing, so I said nothing.

"Let me see one," he said.

I handed him a piece of yellowed paper and turned down the hall. Braxton didn't follow me. He stood outside Grandpa's door, beginning to read.

"Come on, let's go," I urged.

Braxton's jaw dropped a little. "Oh, wow... Jase..."

"What?" I was getting irritated.

He looked up at me slowly. "Why does your Grandpa have an old article about Dr. Sharp?"

36

THE ITCH WAS AFLAME. "What're you talking about?" I said. "Let me see that."

I ran up to Braxton and snatched the article out of his hand. It was dated fifteen years earlier. The headline read, "*College student caught trespassing, killed.*" Below the headline was a faded photograph of a large, yellow house surrounded by tall, spiked iron fence posts.

I asked Braxton, "Where does it talk about Dr. Sharp?"

He pointed below the photograph and read the caption aloud: "'*Early Wednesday morning, Jason Root, 21, accidentally impaled himself on the fence enclosing the property of plastic surgeon and local celebrity, Dr. Alexander Sharp.*'" Braxton paused. "Impaled? That means he shiskabobbed himself on one of those spikes. Gross."

I shook my head. "This can't be right. Dr. Sharp is a dentist, not a plastic surgeon."

"Maybe he used to be one."

"No," I said. "He's too young."

Braxton nodded. "You're right." He looked at the top of the page. "This is from our paper, *The Daily Gust*, but it's from before we were even born."

I looked back through Grandpa's open door. He was still asleep.

What was he *hiding*? Why would he have a newspaper article dated so long ago from the town we just moved to?

I closed the door softly and said, "My room. Now."

As Braxton followed me down the hall, he said, "What do you think is going on?"

I scratched my hand. "I don't know. We have to read this whole thing."

"This can't be a coincidence, Jase."

"I know. I *know*."

Back in my room, with the door closed, we stood near my desk. I had a bad feeling about what I held. I was too itchy. I couldn't sit. I felt like I had to run away.

But from *what*?

"I'll read it out loud," said Braxton.

"Okay." I handed the article over to him with a trembling hand.

He read: "'*Dr. Alexander Sharp earned fame for donating his free time toward the reconstruction of pets disfigured by Kirk Mason and Eric Christopher, local teens who terrorized the West Bay with vicious attacks against animals in the summer of 1997.*'" Braxton looked at me. "Why would they hurt pets? Pets are nice. My parents won't let me have any, but I once played with a turtle at a pond. I pretended he was mine. His name was Shelly."

"Keep reading," I said.

He continued: "'*Because of his dedication to assisting man's best friends, Sharp quickly grew to be one of the most successful and respected figures in the community. The doctor also made local headlines in 1971 when he returned home to the West Bay as a wounded Vietnam War veteran and recipient of the Purple Heart.*

"'*In a surprising turn of events, the surgeon became the mentor of both Mason and Christopher after the boys inexplicably turned themselves in for their horrific crimes during the winter of 1997. They had both come from broken homes, and Sharp, a devoted father, took on the task of helping turn around the misguided youths as they spent time behind bars.*'"

"It's not the Dr. Sharp we know," I interrupted. "It has to be

Xander and Alexis Sharp's *dad*. That's why it says he is a 'devoted father.'"

"Yeah, very smart," said Braxton. "Okay, so why does your grandpa have an article about their dad, then?"

I scratched harder. "I don't know. Continue."

Braxton started up once more: "*After years out of the spotlight, Sharp is once again in the news—not for something he has done, but instead for something done to him. At the time of this article, Sharp could not be reached for comment about the events that took place at his home early Wednesday morning.*

"*At approximately 2 a.m., authorities were called to Sharp's estate in North Hills. A statement released by police confirmed that Jason Root, a recent graduate of Los Caminos Community College, had been caught trespassing on the doctor's property, but, when he attempted to flee the scene by scaling a twelve-foot fence, the man fell onto one of the enclosure's spikes. Little is known about Root's motive for breaking into the estate, but a backpack full of spray paint was found on the premises.*

"*Root earned an associate's degree in Psychology in June, and he has been described by professor Valerie Nunez as 'good-natured and timid.' Nunez is 'surprised and saddened by the news.'*

"*No family has come forward to speak for the young man, but his roommate, Kyle Clark, who shared a Florence apartment with Root, stated, 'Jason [was] a great guy. Really great. I don't know what he was doing [at that house], but he had to have had a good reason to be there.'*

"*'Clark's girlfriend and Root's other roommate, Dana Goodman, added, 'We'll figure out why this stupid, stupid thing happened. We have to know what Jason was thinking. He didn't deserve this.'*

"*At this time, the police are working diligently to figure out why 'this stupid, stupid thing happened,' as well.*"

I don't think I took a single breath as Braxton read the last three paragraphs of the article. They had revealed too much, and, also, too little.

When his eyes lifted from the paper to look at me, Braxton said, "You're going to scratch yourself to death, Jase."

I shook my head slowly. "No, I'm not."

"You okay? You look sick. Think you should sit?"

"No," I said. "If I sit, I might never get back up again."

"Did the article say something…?"

"Yes!" I screamed. I had my breath back. "It said the guy I'm named after died on the fence of the Sharps' dad's house!"

"Huh?"

"I'm named after my parents' college friend, Jason," I explained. "I didn't know until now that his name was Jason Root."

"Why do you think you were named after *him*?"

"His roommates—the ones quoted in the article—they were *my parents*!"

As Braxton stared at me, I felt like I was going to cry. I blinked back tears. So *stupid*. Why was I even upset?

"My dad," I said, nearly choking on the words, "is Kyle Clark. Clark's my last name."

"I know it is," said Braxton.

"My mom's name before she got married was Goodman. My grandpa is named Zane Goodman, Braxton."

"So…" said my friend. "This really isn't a coincidence."

37

"I SAW this article yesterday in Grandpa's box," I said. "Should've looked at it more closely. I barely even read the headline."

Braxton said, "Does this mean your family knows Dr. Sharp, Jr. and Alexis?"

"I don't know what it means." I sighed. "Why would my mom and grandpa hide this from me? Why didn't they tell me they lived here in this town before?"

"Maybe those other two articles can explain something?"

"What other two articles?"

Braxton said, "The two you're still holding."

I looked down and saw two other pieces of paper bunched up in my clenched fist. I had been so focused on what Braxton read that I'd forgotten about the other articles I held.

I spread the articles across my desk, smoothing out the creases I had put in them. They were only a couple of paragraphs each and were dated shortly after the first article. Neither had photographs to accompany them.

One article was titled, *"Trespasser forgiven by doctor."*

The other read, *"Restraining order put against friends of deceased criminal."*

Braxton and I exchanged glances. He said, "These are related."

"Read them to me," I said. "The one about the forgiving doctor first."

Braxton replaced the first article with the next and read: "*A trespasser accidentally killed during an escape attempt earlier this week has been pardoned for his crime by the owner of the trespassed property. Dr. Alexander Sharp publicly forgave Jason Root, 21, of Florence, for breaking into his North Hills estate.*

"*In a brief statement given to local press, Sharp said, 'I do not know the young man who entered my property Wednesday morning. I wish to forgive Mr. Root for what he did. He seemed to be confused, not threatening, when I confronted him. What happened to him was tragic for his friends and family. I hope they know I am sincere when I say I am truly sorry for what happened to Jason.'*

"*Police located spray paint at the scene of the crime. Authorities believe Root was there to vandalize the home.*"

"Why would he try to spray paint the house?" I asked.

Braxton picked up the third, remaining article, began to silently read it to himself, and said, "Maybe you should ask your mom about that."

"Is that article about her?"

He nodded. "And your dad." Braxton paused. "Hey, how come you don't talk about your dad?"

"He... died when I was a baby." I gestured to the article in my friend's hand. "Now, what does it say?"

Braxton read: "*Friends and roommates of the deceased trespasser of a North Hills home have been issued restraining orders by the owner of the estate. Kyle Clark, 22, and Dana Goodman, 20, of Florence have been told by police they are not allowed within five hundred feet of, or allowed any type of contact with, Dr. Alexander Sharp.*"

I said, "A restraining order means that if they got too close to the Sharps' dad they would've gone to jail, right?"

"Yeah," said Braxton. "What'd they do to him to get punished like that?"

I furiously scratched my hand. "Just read the rest."

Braxton continued: *"Last week, Sharp released a statement of forgiveness to Jason Root, 21, for coming onto his property uninvited. Root was killed while attempting to run from police.*

"In the days that followed Sharp's statement, Clark and Goodman began to harass the doctor with phone calls. The nature of the calls is unknown, but a source close to the North Hills Police Department reports that the calls were not ruled out as threats against the doctor. The restraining order was put into effect after the two Los Caminos Community College students were found loitering outside the Sharp home late at night."'

I said, "When you 'loiter,' that means…?"

"You're hanging out, looking suspicious, I think," said Braxton. He put the article on the desk. "That's it. That's what your grandpa was reading before he went to sleep."

"My parents threatened this old Dr. Sharp? Why would they do that?"

Braxton offered, "My guess is that they thought he could tell them more about what happened to their buddy."

"It does all seem very fishy."

"Hate to say it, Jase, but it also seems like your *family* is a little fishy. Fishier than you could have ever imagined." He paused. "Not as fishy as mine, though."

"Don't know about that," I said as I attempted to eliminate my nervous itch.

"I mean, you were connected to the Sharps all along! Your mom didn't just pick the dentist's name at random."

My head felt like it was going to burst. I was so confused, angry, and even a little bit scared. I had just stumbled across a huge family secret, and I didn't want it to remain a secret any longer.

I said, "I need to get this cleared up. I really need to wake up my grandpa, and—"

The door slammed open. Grandpa stood before us, his hair rumpled and his dentures in. He was also red in the face. He was redder than Adonis's roses. He was red with *anger*. I didn't know what to think. I had never seen my grandfather like that before.

"You really need a lock on your door," said Braxton.

"Jase, you took the articles?" said Grandpa in a deadly serious tone. "You came into my room and took them? Don't you lie to me. Don't you *dare* lie to me!"

"I did. I won't lie." Didn't want him to be any angrier than he already seemed to be.

"You read them?" He didn't wait for me to answer. "What am I saying? *Of course*, you read them."

"We did," said Braxton.

"*Leave*," Grandpa said to my friend. "Do not speak another word, young man. I shouldn't have allowed you to come over. Get out of this house *right now*."

Braxton said, "Oh... okay... Let me get my MyPod and stuff. Please?"

"Better make it quick."

"No problem." Braxton began to collect his speakers and Sharp's MyPod into his backpack. Good thinking. Mom and Grandpa would notice the MyPod didn't belong to me, and I didn't want to try to explain to them about the device. Not after what we'd found in the articles...

"Sorry, Grandpa," I said. "I thought the articles weren't that important."

He shook his head. "Your mom is going to throw a *fit*."

"I've got it all," said Braxton. He said to me, "Think we should tell him about what we heard on the MyPod?"

"Now is not a good time," said Grandpa.

"But you really should listen to it."

"Braxton," said my grandfather, "I don't care about that right now. Something very bad has just happened here. You need to go."

Braxton looked at me. "Jase? What do you think? Should it wait?"

I nodded. "Think it has to. We'll do it later."

Grandpa said, "You'll be lucky if there even is a later."

"What do you mean?" said my friend.

"I thought I told you not to say another word?" Grandpa said. "Go home. *Now*."

Braxton briefly hesitated, but then he just waved good-bye to me, walked past Grandpa, and disappeared down the hall. I heard the front door open and close a few seconds later.

"I'm so disappointed," said my grandfather.

I didn't know what to do other than to get angry back. "*You* are disappointed?" I said. "I just found out you've been hiding some really important things from me!"

"Don't you take that tone with me," he said. "You know better."

I picked up the articles from the desk. "What does all this stuff *mean?*" I said.

He walked over and took the papers out of my hands. "Guess we'll have to explain

some things when your mom gets home. Until then, stay here, door closed. Unfortunately, I'm going to have to hide all these articles somewhere else now."

"I just didn't know they were so secret. You didn't tell me they were!"

He stared at me. "Thought I wouldn't have to tell you to stay out of my stuff, Jase. But now I guess you're such a snoop... Like Pandora!"

Pandora was a woman in Greek mythology given a sealed jar by Zeus, the king of the gods. Zeus told Pandora to never ever open the jar, but he didn't tell her what was inside of it. (I'd always imagined the jar in the story to be like the one I kept my pennies in.) Pandora was a very curious person, and she couldn't resist opening what was in her possession. A bunch of horrible things—disease, famine, evil creatures, et cetera—flew out of the jar, where they had been trapped for years and years. They created chaos on Earth.

In other words, the world had been a pretty peaceful place until a curious human accidentally brought bad things into it. Perhaps Grandpa's comparison of Pandora and me wasn't so wrong, after all.

Grandpa stepped out of the room and shut the door hard behind him, leaving me more confused, angry, and scared than I had been before.

38

WHEN GRANDPA LEFT, I collapsed onto my bed. I didn't care if I ever got back up again. I closed my eyes, trying to sleep, but I had too many questions going through my head:

Why did we move back to the place where Jason Root died so many years ago? Why hadn't I ever known that the guy I was named after even passed away?

Why didn't Mom tell me she knew Xander and Alexis Sharp's father? Especially the little fact that he had a restraining order put against her and my dad?

Why was Grandpa reading those articles now all these years later? What was that box of articles *really* about anyhow?

Of course, I knew I didn't have the answers to any of those questions for one specific reason: Mom and Grandpa didn't trust me with the information.

Or, maybe, they didn't want me to lose my trust in *them*...

Oh, well, too late for that.

Mom arrived home about ten minutes after I first lay down. I heard her and Grandpa's voices out in the living room. Mom's voice was the first one to get loud. Grandpa eventually met her in volume. I couldn't make out their words, just the anger and frustration.

I dug my face into a pillow. I attempted to muffle the screaming even more by folding the pillow over my ears. Didn't work as well as I'd thought it would.

They never argued like that. Their arguments had always seemed playful before. Now their harsh voices were somehow more real.

I have to admit some tears slipped out of my ducts and were absorbed by the pillow. Couldn't help but to think Mom and Grandpa were only fighting because of what I had done.

Eventually, the arguing stopped. A couple of minutes later, the talking started again, but this time it had a more calm, peaceful ring to it. It was at this point that I pulled my head out of the pillow.

There was a knock at the door. I sat up and said, "Yeah? Come in."

The door opened, revealing Grandpa with a sad smile on his face. "Hey, pal," he said. "I come begging forgiveness."

I said, "I'm not some plastic surgeon named Dr. Sharp. I might not forgive so easily."

Grandpa winced. "Glad to see some of the sarcasm has worn off on you." He stepped into the room. "Well, I've brought gifts to help you forgive me."

"Bribes, you mean?"

He smiled wider. "Yes, bribes." He closed the door behind him. He opened a fist, revealing caramel candies he'd apparently saved up and a few pennies. "You accept my bribery, Jase, in exchange for your forgiveness?"

"Well, I guess the bribery's a start... But you'd better explain some stuff, too."

"That's what I'm here for." He gestured to the foot of the bed. "May I sit?"

I nodded, and he took a seat by my feet. He handed over the pennies and a couple of caramels. He took one of the remaining candies, unwrapped it, and placed it on his tongue.

"Why'd you guys lie to me?" I asked.

"That's the tough part to explain. We didn't ever really lie to you, Jase. We just didn't tell you everything."

I didn't think there was that much of a difference between the two. I knew because I followed the don't-tell-everything strategy often.

"Okay," I said, "why didn't you tell me everything?"

He hesitated. "I'm not going to tell you everything. Not right now. You're not ready. Believe me, the time has not come yet."

"Is it really that bad?" The itch was back. Had it ever left?

"Let's just take it from the top, okay? I want to first say I'm sorry for yelling at you and Braxton. It wasn't your guys' fault. I was just angry with myself for being so careless. I shouldn't have left those articles on the bed like that for you to see. I let my frustration come out against you, and that was wrong.

"But, Jase, if my door is closed, you can't just come into my room. That's not polite."

"I know. We tried to knock first and wake you, but you were asleep. And we had something really important to tell you."

"What was it?"

I didn't want to switch subjects just yet, so I said, "Doesn't matter right now."

"Fine." He chewed on the caramel for a few seconds. "Ah, sweet ambrosia."

"Going to tell me about the articles?"

"I'll try to." He closed his eyes, as if trying to think of where to begin. "You were never meant to see them. The articles. Yesterday, when you stumbled across them, I thought the worst, but you didn't seem to recognize them for what they were. That's why I tried to steer you away from them, make you think they were nothing of importance. I can't blame you for reading them if you thought it wouldn't be a big problem."

"You said they only 'showed why where we used to live wasn't such a good place to be.' So that Mom wouldn't want to 'return to those places.'"

"That's all true, Jase. What happened here in this town long ago was a bad, bad thing. I convinced your mom and dad to leave. That I'd move with them wherever they went. They had to get away so they wouldn't be tempted to break the restraining order put against them. So, we did. We left. I kept those articles as a reminder to never return."

"But we returned all these years later," I said. "Why?"

He nodded. "That's part of what I can't tell you today. Sorry."

"Then, why did Mom and Dad keep bothering the doctor? Did they think he knew something about what happened to their friend?"

"I guess they did."

"Like what?"

"If your mother wants to tell you that, she can."

"Where is she? Why isn't she in here right now?"

Grandpa shrugged. "She just needed some more time alone to think. Been a rough day for her."

"For me, too."

"For all of us, Jase." He swallowed his candy. "You know, it's not the same guy in the article who does your teeth. It's not the same Dr. Sharp."

"I know. The dentist's dad, right?"

"To be honest, I don't know. They might be related somehow."

"It's not a coincidence I ended up in that dentist's office, Grandpa. You guys knew going in that—"

He raised his hand to stop me. "We found his name online. That's all I'll say about that."

I gave a nervous grin. "You do realize you're not telling me anything I want to know."

He chewed on another caramel. "Okay. Ask me questions, then. No guarantees on answers, however. I'll leave a lot of that for your mother. Don't want her left out on this."

"The three articles I read involve our family." I gulped. "Are all those articles in that box about us? Mom and Dad got a restraining order against them when they were in college. Was that just the beginning of the family crime spree? I saw stuff about bank robbers and mental hospitals *and murder* in other articles in the box. We're not a family of fugitives, are we? Is that why we keep moving from one place to the next?"

My hand itched as Grandpa took a while to reply. Finally, he said, "We're not criminals. We leave places where crimes occur. We try to get away from all that kind of garbage."

He'd taken too long to answer. Once again, he wasn't telling me everything, and this time it really started to scare me.

"Grandpa," I said, "*please* tell me! Mom and Dad got in trouble with the law before. Was that the only time?" I hesitated, holding back a sob after a crazy thought popped into my head. "Did Dad die doing something illegal?"

He grabbed me firmly by the shoulder. "Your father died in an accident."

"An accident like Jason Root's?"

"No," he said as firmly as his hold on me. "It wasn't like that."

"*Tell* me!"

He released me. "I'm sorry. I can't do this. You can't know everything yet."

"Why not?"

Grandpa stood. "You just... can't." He walked over to the door. "Your mother might come in later. I don't know. Just stay here."

I was crying now, more confused than ever. "Grandpa!"

"Jase," he said, looking down at the floor. "Not now, okay? We love you, but not now."

He left me alone again. Alone with my questions and his non-answers.

If Mom and Grandpa really loved me, they'd tell me everything, no matter what.

Right?

39

I WAITED FOREVER for Mom or Grandpa to re-enter and explain something. *Anything!*

No one came, and I eventually fell asleep. You would think that with all the questions swimming through my brain I would dream something crazy. I didn't. There were no dreams.

Only darkness.

When my eyes opened again, the darkness had left my head and enveloped the day and my room. A sliver of the moon winked at me from the night sky outside my window. I sat up on the bed and, after my eyes adjusted to the dark, noticed that someone had moved the chair from under my desk to in front of the door. I carefully walked over to the shadowy seat and flipped the light switch on the wall.

Sitting atop the chair was a plate with a peanut-butter-and-grape-jelly sandwich in its center. Even though I enjoy PB and J as much as the next kid, I found myself wishing I had a ham or turkey sandwich in front of me instead.

Next to the PB and J was a small bag of chips and a can of soda. The chips reminded me that I needed to talk with the Hipnotist, and the soda proved that Grandpa had made me this special dinner.

After getting cavities, soda was not on Mom's list of beverages-for-Jase-to-enjoy.

However, Mom had contributed to the meal. Next to the food was a note written in her neat, flawless handwriting. It read:

"Jase, sorry that we can't talk. It's my fault. What's happened is harder for me than you can imagine. We will clear things up for you very soon. I had to go out and do something important. I won't be around for a while. Please forgive your grandfather for whatever he's served you for dinner. Love, Mom."

I was really worried now, scratching all throughout the note. This wasn't typical Mom behavior. Wasn't like her to run away from problems. Problems ran away from her.

I picked up the sandwich, almost took a bite, and then realized that my stomach felt full. It contained too many butterflies. Grandpa's efforts would go to waste. I put the sandwich back down.

Then I remembered the pennies and candy he had given me hours earlier. I walked back over to the bed. Miraculously, I had not rolled over and squished the caramels into my blanket. They lay untouched next to the pennies.

I scooped up the bribes and went over to the desk, where I placed the caramels. I unscrewed the lid on my penny jar. I loudly dropped each cent in with its brothers. Every penny was another question about my family I did not have answered.

Knock, knock, knock.

I turned first to the door, thinking for a second it might be Mom or Grandpa, but I quickly realized the sound came from the other direction. Once again, Braxton stood outside my bedroom window.

The guy just never gave up, did he? I suppose it was a blessing and a curse. A blessing because it meant he got things done, and a curse because it meant he constantly got me in trouble.

I went over to the window and slid it open. "Hey," I said.

"Your mom's still gone?" he said. "Don't see her car out front."

"Well, she came back, but she left again. I never got to see her."

"Is your grandpa asleep?"

"Don't know. Maybe. But he did nap earlier."

He said, "Want to come with me?"

I pressed against the windowsill. "Why aren't you home?"

"I went back, and then my parents called and told me they were spending the night at the health spa. I decided it was the perfect opportunity."

I sighed. "What are you planning to do tonight?"

"You mean, what are *we* planning to do tonight?"

"Braxton, haven't we done enough damage already?"

"Jase, haven't your mom and grandpa already damaged *you* enough with their secrets?" He leaned closer. "Did they explain anything to you yet?"

I looked down to my feet. "Not really."

"Then blame what you're about to do on that."

"Huh?"

"You're confused and angry, right?"

"Pretty much."

"They can't blame you for rebelling after what you've just learned. Or *not* learned."

"You mean they'll understand I left the house without their permission because I was mad at them?"

"Exactly."

"You obviously don't understand my family."

He locked eyes with me. "Hate to tell you this, buddy, but neither do you."

After a few seconds, I said, "Fine. Tell me about this plan."

He smiled. "I called Pringle when I got back home. Told him about what the MyPod said. He told me he wanted to hear it for himself."

"Go on…"

"So, fifteen minutes ago he picked me up, and—"

"Picked you up?"

"Yeah, he has Sharp's MyPod in his car as we speak. We listened to it at full blast. Man, the speakers in his car are awesome! You can hear 'eat meat' so clearly!"

I stuck my head out the window and tried to look toward the front of the house. "Chip brought you here?"

"Yep. We came to get you."

"Why, exactly?"

"We're going to the yellow house. The one where Sharp's dad lived. The one where Jason Root died. The one where your mom and dad—"

"Okay, I get it."

"Well, I told him about the articles. Apparently, he knows where the house is. I guess it's kind of well-known."

"Why are we going there?"

"Maybe Dr. Sharp, Sr. still lives there. He could tell us something."

The itch burned. "That definitely doesn't sound like a good idea."

"Cheeto's an adult. He could help us out if things get crazy."

"I don't want things to get crazy."

He backed away from the window. "Well, I'm going. If you want me to be alone on this after all we've done together, I guess I'll have to respect that."

I growled in frustration. "Fine, Braxton, but I'm going to leave a note for my mom and grandpa just in case. I don't want them to worry too much."

I turned from the window, went over to the chair by the door, and lifted Mom's note from the plate. At the desk, I turned the piece of paper over and wrote my note. Figured I could use a little of what Mom used and some of what Braxton suggested:

"I left for a little bit. Don't be too mad. I'll be back soon. We can talk then. This is hard for me, also. I need to get away and think. You should understand. Thanks for the dinner, Grandpa. Love, Jase."

I placed my note face-up on the plate, and Braxton said, "Is that food?"

"Yeah, my grandpa made me a PB and J sandwich. I'm not hungry, though."

"Can I have it?"

"Sure," I said. "There are chips, too. Want those, right?"

"Bring them here, and let's go. Dorito's waiting."

I placed the soda can into my pants pocket and put on socks and shoes. Leaving the light on so my family thought I was still in my room, I went over to the window and passed the food over to my friend. His eyes lit up at the sight of an unhealthy meal.

I pushed the window open as far as it could go. I swung my legs over the windowsill and dropped down to the ground next to Braxton. I had never sneaked out of my house before. My itchy hand told me I was more nervous about it than I thought I would be.

Braxton said, "Leave the window open just enough for your fingers to slip back under it. That way a raccoon or mountain lion can't get in. At worst, you'll just get a hive of wasps flying in there."

He wasn't so skilled at making me feel any less nervous, but I followed his advice. I left the window ajar only a couple of inches. Just enough for me to push back open when I returned.

"Okay, cool," said Braxton after taking a bite of my sandwich. "Come on, they're waiting. I'm surprised they haven't honked at us."

"*They* are waiting for us?" I thought he said *Chip* picked him up…?

"Oh, yeah. I forgot for a second. When Frito got me he was in the middle of a date."

I followed Braxton toward the front of the house. "He brought his date along for this?"

"Well, she's curious," said my friend. "You know her. It's Beth, from Dr. Sharp's office."

I rolled my eyes. This was going to be, like, interesting for, like, all the wrong reasons.

40

We entered the lawn from the side of the house. Sitting alongside the curb, engine on, was a white car with a smashed left front end. Its headlights glared, but the left light seemed to shine a little weaker, and hang a little lower, than the right light did. Needless to say, it didn't seem so hip. I could make out two people waiting in the vehicle for us.

"Hurry!" said Braxton, sandwich already half-eaten.

He told me to hurry like I wasn't right beside him, step for step. I wanted to get out of there just as much as he did. Last thing I wanted was for Mom to show up and foil the escape plan.

We reached the car. It only had two doors. Beth looked up at us from the passenger's seat, her window rolled down.

I anxiously looked up and down the street and said, "Please, let us in."

Beth smiled. "So, the bad kids take, like, forever, yet they still want to, like, hurry to go do some bad things."

"*Please,*" I said through gritted teeth. At the far end of the block, a car's headlights lit up the dark street in our direction.

"You are, like, so less innocent than you pretend to be, Jase."

"Yep, that's him," said Braxton.

Beth opened her door and stood on the sidewalk. She was in a flowery dress and a tiny jacket. Braxton leaned forward to get into the car, but he didn't get in right away.

The approaching headlights grew larger and brighter with each passing second. I nudged my friend a little from the back. "What's taking so long?" I said.

"How do I get this stupid seat to move forward?" was Braxton's reply.

As he struggled with the seat, the headlights got closer. Closer.

"Let me do it," I said, trying to push Braxton aside.

He said, "No, I think I almost have it."

The car was eight houses away. Seven. *Six…*

I groaned. *"Braxton."*

Five houses. Four. *Three.*

The passenger's seat slid forward. "Got it!" said Braxton as if he had never been prouder of himself.

I brushed past him and dived into the backseat. Headlights washed over the interior of the vehicle as the car outside drove by, not stopping at my house or even at the next. *So much for the close call…*

Chip, smiling, looked at me over the back of the driver's seat. He wore the same outfit from earlier in the day. Good to know he dressed to impress. "You okay?" he said. "That was a gnarly dive. I give it an eight-point-seven. Work on your form just a little bit."

I quickly straightened myself in the seat as Braxton climbed in next to me. Chip turned to Beth as she pushed her chair back about as far as it would go. Braxton's legs almost became accordions, but he didn't seem to mind.

Once Beth was back in the car, and her door was shut, Chip said, "Are we ready? Everyone's buckled up? Safety first, people."

The seatbelt across my chest confirmed I was locked in and ready for the journey ahead. However, I wished the belt would do a better job of smothering my belly butterflies.

"Let's go be, like, accessories to these kid criminals," said Beth.

"You won't get in trouble for helping us," said Braxton. "We won't ever tell anyone you helped us spy. Right, Jase?"

I nodded. "Right." Although, *ever* is not really the same as *never*.

Chip looked over at his date. He said to her, "Baby, if you don't want to want to be involved with this, you don't have to be."

Beth stared at him for a few seconds. "First of all, *Chip*, I am not, like, your baby. It's going to take, like, a lot more than bowling for me to ever, like, be your baby. Especially since you can't even, like, beat a girl at rolling a ball at, like, some pins."

"I let you win," said the Hipnotist.

"I, like, doubled your score, like, three times in a row." Beth looked at us in the backseat. "Second, this is not, like, good first date etiquette. Have you ever even, like, been on a date before? It's supposed to be, like, all about me. You need to, like, do your best to impress me, and you are, like, so failing. You can't, like, accept phone calls from random children and, like, invite them on some stakeout when I'm, like, sitting next to you, telling you, like, with my eyes that I'm not, like, okay with it. You are, like, so clueless."

Chip was silent through the entire speech. I bet he had to concentrate as much as he could to figure out what she was, like, saying to him.

Braxton said, "Should we go?"

Instead of driving, Chip said to Beth, "So you're not cool with it? Why didn't you tell me any of this while we sat here waiting for these guys? Now I'm embarrassed."

Beth crossed her arms over her chest and stared at her date. "I thought you would, like, get the hint or something if I didn't, like, talk to you very much. But, no, you were, like, too busy talking about you making people think they were, like, poodles or Chihuahuas."

Braxton said, "How far away is the big yellow house again?"

"Yeah," I said. "If it's far, we should leave."

"It's not that far," said Chip. To Beth, he said, "So, I'm taking you home?"

She looked back at us again. "No, we can, like, go, I guess. What

Braxton said on the ride over was, like, kind of interesting. And what we, like, heard on the MyPod is, like, really freaking me out a little. I knew Dr. Sharp and Alexis were, like, strange, and I guess I could, like, find out some more things about them. I just don't want to, like, know too much. I don't want to get, like, fired or anything."

"Cool," said Chip. "Our second date won't be as gnarly as this one. I promise." He finally began to drive.

"Better be, like, really glamorous."

The Hipnotist said, "Do you enjoy miniature golf? I go all the time and even have my own personal clubs I take with me."

"I bet I could, like, kick your butt at miniature golf."

Chip laughed. "Oooh, I might like that."

Braxton and I looked at each other. Maybe this wasn't such a good idea, after all. Someone needed to stop the awkwardness, and I guess it was going to have to be me.

"How do you know where this house is?" I said.

"Everyone, like, knows it," said the receptionist. "It's supposed to be, like, haunted. There are, like, all these weird stories I've heard about it. If you grew up here, you, like, heard about that yellow house in North Hills."

"I never heard anything about it," said Braxton.

"You're an exception to the rule," said Chip. "The exception to *many* rules."

"What kind of stories did you hear?" I said, scratching. "Anything about Jason Root?"

"Who?" said Beth.

"I've never heard anything too specific about the place," said Chip. "I've lived here almost half of my life, and the house has always looked pretty gnarly, pretty abandoned. The stories I've heard are about a mad scientist who did bloody experiments in the basement."

Beth added, "I've heard stuff about, like, vampires and ghosts in the attic, I think. It's, like, all ridiculous."

Mad scientists, vampires, and ghosts *are* ridiculous, but hearing about them didn't make me any less itchy. And could the old Dr.

Sharp be considered a "mad scientist"? The thought made me even itchier.

"It's just, like, some old building. You guys think, like, Dr. Sharp and Alexis's dad is there? Like, maybe it's where Dr. Sharp and Alexis grew up? I never, like, thought anyone lived there. And I, like, didn't even know Dr. Sharp and Alexis were related. I've only been at the office, like, seven months, but still..."

Chip said, "You didn't know I was a hypnotist or that I knew these two, either."

"Well, I did just, like, meet you a few hours ago."

"Your lucky day," he said.

"Why were you at the office?" I asked the Hipnotist. "Are you working undercover or something? Is that why you pretended you didn't know me?"

Chip looked at me through the rearview mirror. "Well, yeah. *Duh*. But I also had this gnarly toothache I needed checked out."

I said, "Did you find out anything while you were there?"

"Not really," said Chip. "I wasn't there for very long."

Beth said, "Please, like, stop talking about this in front of me. I can't, like, know about all this stuff if I'm going to, like, keep my job. Thank you."

I could tell Chip about trying to retrieve Michael and Greg's photographs later. There was a *crunch* next to me. Braxton had opened the bag of chips.

He said, "Frito, if you eat chips, does that make you a cannibal?"

"If I eat human flesh, that makes me a cannibal." He paused. "And, please, the name is Chip."

"Oh, I think the nicknames are, like, kind of cute."

Chip looked at Beth. "Well, if *you* like them..."

Beth turned to Braxton. She pointed to the bag he held. "Can I, like, have a couple? Bowling alley hot dogs are, like, not so great. I need to eat something that has, like, some actual non-barfy taste."

Braxton allowed her to snatch a couple of chips. After he ate a couple of his own, he said, "What do you guys think the MyPod's message means?"

The device sat between Chip and Beth. It was plugged into the dashboard. I didn't wish to hear it again.

"Personally," said Beth, "I don't, like, get it. 'Eat meat'? Like, why? Meat makes you, like, fatter." A chip snapped apart between her teeth.

"Alexis did ask me if I was a vegetarian today," said Chip.

"Isn't that weird?" I said.

"I guess," he said, "but maybe they think chewing meat makes your teeth stronger or something?"

"That's what they told me!" I said. "Does that sound believable to you?"

"I think it does," said Beth. "Maybe they just, like, want everyone to have, like, really strong, healthy teeth. Is that, like, so bad?"

I continued: "On those reports we stole, they really seemed too interested in 'bite pressure.'"

"You guys are, like, so paranoid. Dr. Sharp and Alexis are, like, sort of weird, but they're not, like, evil. They let me sometimes have, like, really long lunch breaks."

"But," I said, "bite pressure doesn't seem strange? Chip?"

"Might not seem like it, but this is a date," he said. "You guys are here, I know, but let's not talk about this stuff until the lovely lady is dropped off, okay? She's requested we switch subjects. That's the least we could do. Cool?"

Braxton rolled his eyes my way. We both said, "Cool," at the same moment.

Beth said to Chip, "You think I am, like, how lovely? On, like, the lovely scale?"

Chip didn't hesitate. "You are the loveliest."

It was official: visiting the yellow house was not worth this torture.

41

To ignore Chip and Beth, I stared out the window, pondering a theory about my family's current connection to the Sharps. But it just didn't make any real sense to me:

Mom was some kind of criminal. It was why we kept moving —*escaping*—and now we had returned to the town where her friend died so many years ago. Why did we move back? Possibly for some kind of revenge against the Sharps' father?

Grandpa's articles supported the theory that something seriously shady might be going on—or at least had gone on in the past —but Mom was about the exact opposite of a criminal. She may have done something illegal back in college, but nowadays she lived a boring life. Heck, earlier in the week, she punished me for kind of stealing a piece of paper from the dentist's office! She was not a supporter of crime. No way.

But why were she and Grandpa acting so weird?

"There it is," said Chip as the car climbed a hill. "The gnarly yellow house."

I snapped out of my thoughts. Braxton and I leaned forward to look out through the windshield. Up ahead, at the top of the hill, was a lone building. It appeared to grow taller the closer we drove toward it.

"That's not just a house," said Braxton. "It's a mansion."

The homes leading up to the yellow house were nice, and some were even pretty large, but they didn't appear to be as vast as the building at the top of the hill. It sat alone, the nearest home about one hundred yards away from it. It seemed very important, all by itself there at the top.

Chip passed the last neighboring house and continued toward the mansion, finally parking on cracked asphalt outside a monstrous gate that blocked entry to a long, twisted driveway. A chain and padlock held the gate shut.

"Very gnarly," the Hipnotist said as he turned off the engine and headlights.

"It's, like, kind of spooky," said Beth.

The building was three stories high, but it also had an attic with a dark rectangular window just below an inclined roof. There were many other, larger windows on each floor, but every one of them was boarded up. The attic window was the only one left uncovered. No vampires or ghosts watched us from behind the dirty glass.

In the moonlight, peeling yellow paint looked like decaying bone. Overgrown weeds and dead grass littered the large front lawn. A massive, leafless tree towered behind a tall brick wall on the left side of the house, branches creeping over to the front lawn.

"What's on the other side of that wall?" I said.

"Probably an empty pool," said Chip.

Beneath a crumbling front porch, two large, shadowy doors sat atop the crooked tongue of a staircase. If the attic window (eye) and front doors (gaping mouth) were taken into account, the house looked like the fat head of a sick, demented Cyclops.

Beth said, "Are you going to go, like, knock and see if anyone's home?"

"That seems to be a little impossible to do," said Chip.

It was impossible to do, because giant spears of iron fence surrounded the property. I imagined—and then quickly tried to wipe from my mind—Jason Root stuck on the fence, bloody, screaming, life leaving his body.

Then I saw Mom and Dad standing in front of the gate, yelling at the house. Police lights approached them from behind. That image faded when Chip said:

"I don't think anyone is here, dudes. I have to admit, I was intrigued after what Braxton told me about the old newspaper article, but this place is as abandoned as it's ever been."

I looked over at Braxton. His eyes still studied the house. Was he looking for someone? Obviously, no one was there. Plastic surgeon, Dr. Alexander Sharp, had been there fifteen years ago, but at some point since then he left. (His children left the house, too—but they at least stayed local.)

Our trip had been for nothing.

"There!" Braxton cried, jumping forward, almost into Chip's lap. He jabbed a finger toward the house. "There! Did you see him?"

"Who?" said Chip. He and Beth looked where Braxton pointed.

"Dr. Sharp! He's there, in the tree!"

I practically stood in the backseat, leaning forward, pulling on Chip's seat with my itchy hand. Thought it would give me a better angle, but all it did was provide me with another view of a bare, skeletal tree.

"He *was* there!" Braxton said.

"The dentist?" said Chip.

"No, his dad!"

"Wouldn't his dad be, like, an old man?" said Beth. "How could he, like, climb up and down that tree so quickly?"

"Maybe he's really strong," said Braxton, calming down.

"Where'd he go?" I said.

Braxton said, "I think on the other side of that wall."

"Yeah, he, like, went for a dip in the pool," said Beth, laughing.

"What'd he look like?" I said.

"I don't know. He was all covered in shadows." Braxton slumped back down in his seat. "I saw a dark figure."

"A dark figure could be, like, a stray cat."

"Beth," said Braxton, "it was too big for a cat, okay?" He paused, thinking. "But I guess it maybe could have been a tiger…"

I sat back down. Sounded like he saw something, all right. Something that had never been there.

"Jase, you believe me, right?"

Braxton stared at me, his eyes pleading. Chip and Beth looked back at me, as well.

I said, "If he was there, he's not anymore."

"We could go after him," my friend suggested.

"Doesn't look like anyone is here."

"But, Jase, you have to believe me. I saw—"

"Excuse me, but can we, like, go now?" said Beth. "My parents want me home, like,

really soon."

"Place is abandoned," said Chip. He said to Braxton and me, "Sorry. Was kind of fun, though."

The car's engine rumbled back to life. Headlights bounced off dying bushes. We began our descent back down the hill. Defeated, Braxton had fallen silent.

I looked out the back window, trying my hardest to see what he had seen, but I didn't see anything new. No doctors named Sharp. Not even a tiger.

42

BETH LIVED ONLY a few blocks away from me. She could have had Chip drop her off before we made the trip over to the yellow house, but I suppose curiosity got the best of her.

Outside her plain-looking home, she said to Braxton and me, "This was, like, kind of fun. My lips are, like, totally sealed." Still, I wondered if she would mention anything to Sharp or Alexis.

"Let me walk you to the door," Chip said.

"Like, what a gentleman." Beth giggled and got out of the car. Chip followed her toward the front door.

Braxton had been quiet ever since we left the yellow house. I was startled when he said in his best Beth impersonation, "She is, like, so annoying."

I played along. "Yeah, and she was, like, trying to make fun of us, like, the whole time."

Braxton smiled. He said, "Like, what does Chip *like* about her?"

I smiled back. "Like, she is so totally *like* a goddess. She is, like, as beautiful as Aphrodite." Aphrodite was the Greek goddess of love and beauty.

"Don't know what that means," said Braxton, "but I know you're making a joke, and I couldn't agree with you more."

Through the passenger side window, I saw Chip head back toward the car. Beth shut the front door behind her. The Hipnotist did a little skip across the lawn. He whistled some tune.

"Think they kissed good night?" Braxton said.

I said, "Don't know, and don't care."

Chip opened the driver side door and slid into his seat. He turned to us in the backseat, smiling wide. "We kissed good night," he said.

"Wow," said Braxton. "How was it?"

I gave him the why-don't-you-shut-up look. Why would he want to know the gory details?

"It was delicious," said the Hipnotist. "No tongue this time. But next time there will definitely be some tongue!"

"Be careful," said Braxton. "Don't bite her. Really hurts when I bite my tongue."

"Yeah, I'll try not to," said Chip.

He turned back around in his seat, re-started the car's engine, and we were off. Now that we were alone with him, Braxton and I could speak freely.

"Speaking of biting," I said, "do you have any idea why Dr. Sharp would care about Michael and Greg's bite pressure? It was mentioned on their reports."

"Maybe the stronger the bite, the healthier the teeth?"

"That's all you have?" said Braxton. "I kind of thought Dr. Sharp wanted their bite pressure to be high so that they could... bite things really hard."

Chip snorted. "Bite what things?"

"I don't know? Metal? Rocks?"

"That doesn't make sense," said the Hipnotist. "Think you have to look elsewhere for evidence of bad stuff going on."

"So, is the message on the MyPod good evidence?" I asked. "You said we needed to get more evidence so you could help us out more. Think it's enough?"

"The message is definitely supposed to be hidden," said Chip.

"It's subliminal. They really want people to eat meat." He paused. "But maybe it's like Beth said: meat builds stronger teeth."

"Come on, that's exactly what they want us to think!" I said. "There has to be more to it."

"I go back to the office in a couple of days," said Chip, looking at us in the rearview mirror. "Should I bring up what we heard? Would they give me a straight answer?"

"You have to ask!" said Braxton. "You aren't going to chicken out, are you? You're an adult. You're our best hope."

"Man, don't call me a chicken. I did infiltrate the office with the purpose of helping you guys out. Don't accuse me of wimping out."

"Then don't wimp out," I said.

"Look, I'm all for getting this solved," said Chip, "but it has to be done right. It takes time. If we rush through this, it will backfire."

I said, "If we don't rush through this, Michael and Greg will never be found."

Chip pulled up to a stop sign. "Or maybe they're just in Colorado like their parents said."

Braxton said, "Dorito, why are you being like this? Thought you were a team player! Is this because of Beth?"

"Beth is a special girl. I like her a lot. If I screw things up at the office, it could be her job on the line. She already knows more than she should. That's my fault. Probably should have taken her home from the bowling alley, but I didn't. I want to continue seeing her, and I can't risk that by asking stupid questions."

"Are *you* brainwashed?" said Braxton. "You're acting all weird now!"

"I'm in love."

"Really?" I said. "With *her*? You only met her today!"

We were on my street now. "You guys need to know: love at first sight exists."

Braxton rolled his eyes. "You must have *seen* her before you *heard* her."

I said, "So, you probably won't go into Dr. Sharp's private office and see if you can find photos of Michael and Greg?"

"What?" said Chip. "No, now is not the time."

"When *will* it be the time?" said Braxton.

"Need more intel. Just let me work at my own pace."

I said, "Chip, I need to know what Michael and Greg look like! Have Beth get the pictures, then, if you don't want to do it. She likes you, I think. She'd help you out."

"No way," said Chip. "She already said she doesn't want to be any more involved in this."

"You put the 'hip' in 'hypocrite,' you wimpy liar!" said Braxton. "You aren't helping us!"

"That's offensive," said the hypnotist. "I just drove you to that house even though I knew no one would be there."

"But someone was!"

"Braxton," said Chip, "that's enough. Get out. I don't need this."

He stopped the car in the middle of the street. We were only a half-block from my house now. Braxton and I shared confused looks.

"Both of you," said Chip. "Let's go. I'm sick of being your chauffeur. Don't accuse me of this garbage. That's gnarly, dudes. So gnarly. Get out."

I didn't understand. Did "gnarly" mean "cool," or did it mean "bad"? Chip switched the use of the word around so often, it was difficult to know sometimes.

"Fine," said Braxton. He unplugged the MyPod from the dashboard. "You're a jerk, Pringle."

"If you call me another chip name, I will—"

"Frito."

"I swear, if you don't shut—"

"Cheeto."

"Braxton," I said, "be quiet. Let's get out of here already."

"Yeah, please do exit the vehicle." Chip reached across the passenger seat and flipped the side lever, sliding the seat forward.

Braxton squeezed into the front, opened the passenger side door, and climbed out. I began to follow him out, when Chip grabbed my itchy hand. The hypnotist's eyes bulged.

"Let me do things my way for a little while," he said.

I shook free of his grasp. I scratched my hand and said to him, "Don't think we need your help anymore."

I scrambled out of the backseat. Once in the street, I slammed the door shut. The car just sat there for a few seconds, and then Chip drove off, leaving a smoggy cloud behind.

Braxton shook his head. "He's gone crazy, Jase. Completely insane!"

"I've heard love can do that to a person."

"I don't get it. I just don't get it."

We walked over to the sidewalk. I said, "You going home now?"

"I guess. But, first, I'll make sure you get back okay. If you get in trouble, I want to help explain things."

I said, "Don't know if that will help any," but Braxton was already walking back toward my house. I jogged to catch up to him.

He looked down at the MyPod in his hand. "Maybe I should just smash this," he said.

"Why would you do that?"

"Dorito doesn't think the message means anything. Maybe it doesn't."

"Don't smash it," I said. "Not a good idea. Chip's acting all different now. Just hold on to it. We can still have my grandpa listen. We'll see what he says."

"Yeah... Okay..." He pointed ahead. "Hey, your mom's still gone."

We were only a few houses away from mine. Mom's car was not in the driveway. It meant one of two things: she was still out "thinking" or she had left looking for me.

I scratched my hand. "Let's hurry. Maybe nobody noticed I was gone."

I ran home. Braxton's footsteps clapped against the ground behind me. I hit the lawn, dodged a flower bush, and sprinted to the side of the house. Light still shone through the glass of my bedroom window.

Maybe I had gotten away with it, after all...

Braxton caught up to me and said, "You're fast! Like a camel!"

I ignored him and just stood silent and frozen in front of the window. It was wide open.

43

"I LEFT it open only an inch or two," I said. "Why is it open all the way?"

"Maybe wasps got in," he said.

"No," I said. "But someone did."

"Your mom?"

"That's dumb, Braxton."

"Your grandpa opened it to get some fresh air inside? I have to admit, it smells kind of funky in there."

"*My* room smells funky?"

"Hey, I didn't say mine smelled any better than a skunk's behind."

"If my grandpa opened the window, that means he knows I left. Let's see what's going on."

Putting the itch in the back of my mind, I climbed through the window, trying to be as quiet as possible. My feet barely made a sound as they hit the floor. Braxton entered, an unlikely, silent ninja. The MyPod poked out of his pants pocket.

My chair had been pushed aside from the door. The note I left behind was no longer on the plate. Grandpa must have come in and read it. But why did he open the window? Did he want to make it easier for me to get in? Was it evidence that he was okay with my leaving?

"Come on," I said to Braxton. I went over to the door and opened it.

The lights were on in the living room. Television played loudly. We walked down the dark hall. In my mind, I began to prepare an explanation.

We entered the living room. There was Grandpa. On the floor. *Unconscious.*

My dentist stood over him, holding some kind of white rag in his *right* hand. The anesthetic in Sharp's arm must've worn off.

But, *wait a second.* Dr. Sharp was in *my house. What was going on?*

Suddenly, the open window made horrifying sense.

"There you are," the doctor said when he saw Braxton and me. He wasn't smiling anymore.

"Why are you here?" screamed Braxton.

At least he was able to say something. My body was stiff. Words wouldn't form in my
throat. Couldn't even find the strength to ease the itch.

Braxton cried, "You hurt his grandpa!"

"He'll live," said the doctor in a tone that suggested he didn't care if Grandpa lived or died.

"Get out of here! We're calling the cops!"

Sharp smiled now, but it looked much different from any other smile he'd ever made in my presence. His smile was not a happy smile anymore. *It was an evil one.*

"Braxton, shut up," he said. "For once in your life, just *shut up.*"

The harsh words worked. Braxton did shut up. But only for a second. When Sharp stepped over Grandpa and toward us, Braxton screamed as loud as he could, "HELP US!"

We turned to go back down the hall, but there was Alexis. She'd sneaked up silently behind us. She, too, held a white rag.

"Going somewhere?" she cackled. She must've been in Mom or Grandpa's room.

She grabbed Braxton by the shoulders and pressed the rag

tightly against his face, over his nose and mouth. I realized then just how tall and strong she was. Braxton was no match for her. He struggled for only a couple of seconds, and then he collapsed to the floor in front of me.

I wanted to scream. SCREAM! Braxton and Grandpa were dead! MURDERED! But my body wouldn't work, it just wouldn't!

I was so focused on Alexis that I almost forgot about her brother. When I remembered he was behind me, it was too late. One muscular arm wrapped around my waist, pulling me close to the dentist. The rag pressed firmly over my face.

My body decided to work then. Better late than never, right?

Wrong.

Despite my efforts, the man was just too strong for me. Might as well have stayed still. I tried to scream, but no sound was going to get through. As a matter of fact, something wet was on the rag. Something that smelled and tasted like fire.

I was choking on fire, *choking on it*!

I sank to the floor, my legs no longer working like they should.

Everything went black.

44

WHEN I OPENED MY EYES, everything was still black. Thought for a second I was blind, but quickly realized I was just someplace very dark.

The image of Grandpa lying on the living room floor popped into my brain, and a bolt of lightning struck the middle of my forehead.

I tried to raise a hand up to massage the headache, but both of my wrists were strapped tightly to the arms of a chair. *The itch was going to have keep on itching.* As it turned out, my shins were strapped to the chair's legs, too. At least the seat was cushioned and wasn't covered in plastic like the chair at the dentist's office.

But that wasn't enough to make me feel even the slightest bit comfortable. Again, I found it hard to breathe. I shivered from the sweat oozing out of my pores.

Things were majorly bad.

My eyes started to adjust to the darkness but not quickly enough. All I could make out were blurry shapes. Didn't know if Braxton was anywhere near me, if he was even in the same room. I tried to listen for his breathing, but all I could hear were my own wheezes.

I took a deep breath. Knew I had to stay calm. If I stayed as calm as possible, I would be able to think more clearly. Would be able to figure a way out of the situation, although I'd never been kidnapped by a dentist and strapped to a chair in a dark room before.

As I began to control my breathing, the wheezing continued. *Someone else was in the room with me.*

"Braxton?" It came out too softly, so I called his name again.

There was no answer, only wheezes. Braxton was there with me. He had to be. Just wasn't conscious yet. At least he was breathing. Breathing was good. Breathing meant that he was still alive.

Then he called out my name. But it was soft. Too soft, like it wasn't even coming from the room I was in.

It wasn't. His voice was coming through the walls around me. If Braxton wasn't in the room with me, who was wheezing only a few feet away?

"Braxton!" I screamed back. "Can you hear me?"

"Jase! I can hear—"

A door slammed shut, cutting his voice short. Now there was silence. Well, except for my roommate's wheezing. It now sounded louder and deeper, more like an animal's growl than anything else.

"Hello?"

The only answer I received was the sound of a door creaking open behind me. I tried to turn my head to see the door, but the chair faced away from it. The opening doorway, however, spilled a rectangle of light on what was ahead of me.

A big-screen TV.

A shadow crept across the light. Heavy footsteps thundered on the floor behind me. It was either Sharp or Alexis. I made a guess.

"Alexis," I said, "please let us go." She always made an appearance before her brother did.

"Don't think so," replied the dentist, not showing himself. "It's not even my sister's decision to make."

"Please, Dr. Sharp, *please*." I hoped he would hear the tears in my voice. "If this is about knocking you into the needle, I'm sorry!"

"Just watch," he said coldly. *So much for not holding a grudge against me.* The television zapped on.

Pale blue light filled the room. There were no windows I could see. I was definitely not home. Something played on the TV screen, but my attention was first drawn to the other chair only six feet to my right.

A boy was strapped to it. He was about my size, maybe a little shorter. His longish hair was messed up, as if it hadn't been combed for days. His T-shirt and shorts were torn in some spots. He stared at the TV, never blinking, never turning his head to look my way. He wheezed/growled as he watched.

I said, "Who's he?"

"Shouldn't you know?" said the doctor. "You've tried so hard to find him."

It was Michael or Greg. I'd never seen photos of them, so I didn't know which one. Whoever it was, he seemed to be okay, aside from uncombed hair, torn clothes, and dark circles under his eyes. From the way he was staring, I guessed the circles were from watching too much of the big-screen TV.

I focused my attention on what was playing on the Creepy Room Network. Or maybe it was the Discovery Channel? Animal Planet?

A small deer walked through tall, yellow grass. I recognized it as some kind of antelope. A hot African sun shone brightly above trees in the background.

A lion exploded out of the grass. The antelope had no chance. The lion leaped on the deer, slamming the animal to the ground with its huge paws. The carnivore's powerful jaws closed around the thin neck of its prey—

Michael-or-Greg started shrieking like an animal. He jumped up and down in his seat, straining against his straps, which I realized were made from duct tape. He stared at the screen, moaning, growling. The veins in his throat were exposed and throbbing. The chair rocked slightly forward each time he pushed against his restraints.

It was as if he wanted to join the lion in its feast.

"Isn't it amazing," said Sharp, "that he still gets so excited about this kill even after seeing it six hundred times?" He had to speak louder now that my companion was so full of energy.

Six hundred times? Was he serious? Why would the boy be forced to watch a lion attack a gazelle hundreds and hundreds of times?

The boy flexed his muscles and pushed violently against the tape. He drooled, and his spit flew through the air as he shook his head back and forth. A thick stream of saliva smacked the side of my face. The chair began to inch across the floor as the crazed child pushed forward.

"Michael!" shouted the dentist. "Enough!"

But Michael wouldn't stop. He kept growling and spitting and pushing and shaking. He wanted to be a part of the action, especially now that, on-screen, the lion tore pieces of the fallen antelope off in bloody chunks.

"I said, ENOUGH!"

Sharp turned the television off, shrouding the room again in darkness, *but not before I caught a glimpse of the fangs in Michael's screaming, drooling mouth.*

45

THIS TIME I found the ability to scream. I screamed so loud and for so long that my throat began to hurt. All the while, Michael growled, grunted, and jumped in the darkness nearby.

"SHUT UP! BOTH OF YOU!"

The doctor's anger stopped me, and it even seemed to quiet Michael. The dentist chuckled. "That's better. That's how you obey your master."

Master? I didn't have a master! The closest thing I had to a master was Mom, and the only true power she had over me was the power to not pay allowance.

Michael moved in his seat, and it caused me to lean as far to my left as possible. It was difficult to move too much, because I was taped to a chair, but I at least wanted my throat as far away from the guy's fangs as possible.

"What's *wrong* with him?" I asked.

"Nothing is wrong with him." Sharp's voice floated around the room. It was getting harder to figure out where he was.

"What did you do to him?" I said.

"I made some improvements," said the dentist.

"I don't know what that means!"

"Of course, you don't, but you'll find out soon enough."

I started to cry. "No...no... I want to go home!"

"To your mommy, is that it? Too bad. You're mine now. You'll do as I command. Soon enough your mother will hardly remember you at all."

"That's not true! She's looking for me! The cops are going to find you, and—"

"You don't even know what you're talking about, boy." The doctor had been calm, but the mention of the police brought an edge to his voice. "You don't know where you are, your mother doesn't know where you are, and the police don't know where you are. *Got it?*"

Blurry shapes were made blurrier with my tears. I closed my eyes tightly. "Why are you doing this?"

"Because you and your stupid friend couldn't mind your own business. You took the files, you took the MyPod. I'm not sure what you know, but you know something, and in this case, knowledge is dangerous."

"I...I won't tell anyone *anything!*"

"Don't make me laugh." The dentist chuckled anyhow. "Of course, you're going to tell *me* what you know."

"If I do, you'll let me go?"

"Not only are you a spy, but you're a comedian. No, I won't let you go. Like I said, you and Braxton are now mine."

Why did he keep saying that, like we weren't people, but *things?* My stomach began to hurt. "I don't feel good," I said.

"You are so *weak*. We have a lot of work to do to get you on track with the other boys. Even Braxton is handling his situation better than you are!"

"I'm not Braxton."

Sharp said, "No, you certainly are not. At least you eat meat. And that bite—*wow*. That is one heck of a bite you have in that whiny little mouth of yours."

Oh, no. After I left his office, he must've measured my bite pressure on that mouth guard. Was I now a "candidate" for whatever twisted plans he had? Was that why I was tied up in a dark room?

"You figured that out, didn't you?" said Sharp. "The bite pressure? You screamed it out before you pushed me onto the needle."

I didn't answer. Didn't want to talk to him anymore. His true colors were out now, and all I could see was darkness.

Sharp said, "Was pushing me an accident? I suspect it was, but with you, I just don't know. You're a smart one. Should applaud you for all you've done. You've proven your worth, and you've certainly kept me on my toes."

A hand rested on my shoulder. Couldn't help but tremble. The itch screamed.

"There, there," said the dentist. "I understand why you're frightened. This must be quite overwhelming. My goal is not to hurt you. It's to help you become something more than you ever imagined you could be.

"Before that happens, I need to know all that you know so that no one's able to get this close to uncovering my project again. As you can probably guess, Braxton hasn't been very cooperative in the information department so far."

I gulped. "No matter what I tell you, you won't let us go?"

"Don't want to lie to you."

I opened my eyes. The tears were gone. Tears were for the weak, just as he'd said. If there was any way at all to get out of the straps and out of that room, I needed to stop feeling sorry for myself.

I had to be strong. *A hero never surrenders.*

I said, "Then, you know what, Dr. Sharp?"

"What?" I could feel the man's hot breath on the back of my neck.

"If you come near me again, my whiny little mouth is going to bite off your ugly face."

46

Sharp released his hand from my shoulder. Must not have wanted his face bitten off. I don't think I could have bitten someone's face off if I had to, but I wasn't going to tell him that.

"Didn't expect that from you," he said as his footsteps moved behind me. "Pleased to hear it, though. Shows that you have some ferocity after all."

"So what if I'm ferocious?"

He chuckled again. "Don't think so. First, you tell me what you know, and then I'll tell you what you want to know."

I shook my head in the darkness even though Sharp probably couldn't see it. "Nope. First, you tell me what I want to know."

There was no answer. All I could hear were Michael's wheezes. It was risky to make Sharp angry, but he'd said he wouldn't hurt me. If he wouldn't hurt me, that showed weakness on his part, right? I had to attack that weakness as much as possible, and push, push, *push*.

"Do you love your mom?" he said. "How about your grandpa? I bet you do."

The image of Grandpa lying on the floor flashed through my mind again. A different image of Mom lying next to him appeared.

Neither of them moved. I knew it was all in my imagination, but it was still terrible.

"Leave them alone!" I cried.

"That won't be happening, but I assure you I can prevent them from getting hurt. I also have the power to make them hurt *very much* if I feel it's necessary."

Mom and Grandpa. On the floor. Unmoving. *Dead.*

"No!" I screamed.

"Then cooperate!" He was in my ear now, yelling. "If you don't tell me what you know, they are going to get very, very hurt, Jase!"

I almost started crying again, but I held back the tears. Sharp knew he was winning, but I couldn't give him the satisfaction of knowing he was winning by *so much.*

Grandpa told me fear makes you stronger. I had a lot of fear, so I had to be full of strength somewhere... I needed to find that strength to find a way out of that room.

In films and books, people in situations like mine reacted to threats against family members. They usually made the same deal with their captors.

"I want to hear from my mom and grandpa first," I said. "Want to know they're okay. When I know they're okay, I'll tell you what you want to know."

"Seen too many movies," was the reply. "I'll let it happen, though, if for no reason other than to let you know I'm only a phone call away from making bad things happen to your family."

I couldn't believe how evil he was. He was meaner than I thought any person in real life could actually be. He was also more confident than I thought any person in real life could be. He didn't think he could do anything wrong. That made him very dangerous, but it also showed another weakness of his.

Everyone is human. Everyone messes up sometime.

If Sharp messed up, he wouldn't see it coming. He wouldn't be prepared for it. All I had to do was make him mess up somehow. That's when I would have to make my move.

Sharp said, "I'm making a call to my sister. I know you made my family connection to Alexis long ago. We're twins, actually. She was a doctor, too, at one point. But, of course, you know about that, as well. You know about her incredible talent for hypnosis. You found things on the Internet, right? Good work. Even our stupid receptionist doesn't know that much about us."

Behind me, I heard a cell phone ringing. Seemed to be set on speakerphone.

Alexis answered, "How are the brats?"

"Jase is proving to be quite the challenge," her brother said.

"So are his mother and grandfather."

"Oh, yeah?" said the dentist.

Thank goodness. Mom and Grandpa were alive!

"As you know," said Alexis, "some people just don't respond very well to hypnosis. I'm progressing, but slowly. Doesn't help when I have to be interrupted all the time."

"This isn't 'all the time.'" Sharp sounded annoyed. "Jase won't share what he knows until he knows for sure his family is okay."

"He's been watching too many movies."

"Alexis, just put one of them on."

"This isn't such a good idea, Xander."

"Are we not in control?"

Alexis hesitated for a couple of seconds. "We are, but—"

"*Are we not in control?*" Sharp seemed to have major anger issues, which would've surprised me earlier, considering he smiled all the time in his office. Smiles were the friendliest masks one could wear.

"Fine!" said Alexis. Seconds later, she said, "Tell your son you're okay."

Mom argued with Alexis for a couple of moments, apparently confused, but then she said, "Jase? *Jase!*"

"Mom!" I didn't care anymore. I let the tears flow. "Are you and Grandpa okay?"

"Oh, honey, it's *so good* to hear your voice!"

And it was good to hear hers, too. A billion times better than good, actually. She didn't sound hurt at all. If she wasn't hurt or hypnotized yet, that meant she could probably still get away from Alexis and rescue—

Wait, *what about Grandpa?* The last time I saw him, he was on the floor, unconscious. Was he okay?

"How's Grandpa?" I asked.

"I don't know, honey, I don't know," said Mom. "Haven't seen him. She got me right when I walked through the front door. I hear him yelling, but she won't let me see him. She has us both tied up and blindfolded, I think. Don't even know where we are..."

Mom paused for a bit, and then she said, "You're so brave, *so brave*. Don't worry about us. We'll find a way out of this, I promise you. Are you okay? That's all I've wanted to know. Are you and Braxton fine? If anyone's hurt you, so help me, I'll—"

"You'll do nothing!" interrupted the dentist. "Your time is up. Bye-bye."

"You monster, when I get my hands on you, I'll rip your heart out! Your hear me? *I'll rip your heart out!*"

I couldn't help but smile. If Mom came across Sharp, she *would* rip his heart out. And then smack him in the head with it.

Sharp's confidence showed its ugly face again. "You'll never find us," he taunted. "Never! How does that make you feel, knowing that your son is forever lost to you?"

"Where are you?" said Mom. "*Huh?* I *will* find you! I will find you and I will *kill* you!"

"A big, yellow house on a hill!" a voice called from my right.

Sharp cried out, "No!" He ended the phone call. "Why did you say that? *Why did you say that?*"

No more darkness. The dentist must've flipped a light switch. I didn't feel his eyes aimed at me. Instead, they must've glared at Michael, who wasn't acting like a crazy animal anymore.

He was now speaking like a ten-year-old boy.

47

SHARP STORMED between our two chairs and pointed a long finger at Michael. "You aren't supposed to be saying anything! *Anything!* How long is all this supposed to take? *How long?*"

He stood there in front of us, as if waiting for some kind of answer. But neither Michael nor I said anything, because the doctor's eyes were the eyes of a crazy person.

Crazy people are almost as dangerous as stupid people.

"That's good," he said, wagging his finger. "Keep your words to yourself. You'll forget them soon enough, anyway." He left the room, slamming the door shut behind him.

I looked at Michael, but he didn't look at me. His head was bent forward as he stared at his legs. Perhaps it was something he practiced often. If he looked at his legs long enough, he could forget where he was.

"Hello? Michael?" I wanted to take advantage of the time alone with him. Especially if he wasn't screaming and spitting like a beast. "My name is Jase."

I waited a while for some type of reply, but I got nothing. He just stared, and stared, and stared. Was probably already in his Happy Place, and I didn't know how to bring him back.

"Michael, we're in a big, yellow house? Are you sure?"

There was no answer. A little wheezing, but no words.

I said, "I know where this house is. So does my mom, and I'm sure she heard what you said."

In reality, I would have crossed my fingers if my hands weren't tied. Mom might not have heard Michael at all, but if she had, she would know where to come to find us. I hoped. There was no way she could forget about the house. It's what all the secrets were about... Wasn't it?

"Are we in the basement of the yellow house?" I said. We couldn't have been in the attic, because the attic at least had one window from what I saw earlier. If we were in the basement, the stories Chip had heard about a mad scientist being in there were actually kind of true.

When Michael still didn't speak, I decided to switch subjects. I said, "I talked to your dad." If he liked his dad, maybe he'd want to hear more.

"Dad?" he asked. I would've jumped on top of my seat and danced if I could.

"Yes, I spoke with Mr. Huntley. Huntley is your last name, right?"

Michael turned his head to me. His eyes were vacant. "I...I think it is."

"You *think* it is?" How could he not *know*?

"I have trouble... remembering things. Soon I won't be Michael anymore."

I gulped. "Who will you be?"

"What."

"I said, 'Who will you be?'"

"No, you mean, '*What* will I be?' There's a battle going on inside my head. My mind... is losing. Things they're doing are making me... not human. I'm hungry and angry all the time. Pretty soon, there won't be any of me left." He looked back at his legs. "You'll be next."

"But we're kids!" I said.

"Not anymore. They're making us into…" He didn't finish what he was saying. Tears rolled down his cheeks.

I said, "You know why we're here? You know why they're destroying our lives? 'Cause that's what they're doing! They're destroying our lives! Your dad thinks you're in Colorado some-where! They've tricked your family into thinking you're someplace safe when you're here tied to a chair!

"Right now they're trying to do the same thing with my mom and grandpa! They're making us disappear so that nobody asks questions! Why do they want our families to let us go? *What do they need us for?*"

I stopped, because I wanted to give Michael an opportunity to say something. Also, I was losing my voice, and my heart was beating so fast my chest ached. Sweat trickled down my forehead.

"They make me watch… bloody things," said Michael. "I can't get them out of my head. *Red*. All I see is red. All I smell is blood. All I taste is meat." Another tear rolled down his cheek. "I think I used to like to eat fruit. Apples. Grapes. Oranges. But…but I can't remember now. Do they smell good? Do they taste good? Or are they… just blood and meat?"

I didn't know how to answer. I thought apples, grapes, and oranges were okay, but what was he even asking me? He wasn't making sense. He was actually freaking me out.

He suddenly sat up straight in his chair. He sniffed the air. "Blood," he said. His eyes glowed. "*Meat*."

I sniffed the air, too, but all I could smell was my own sweat. "Michael, don't go crazy on me again."

He licked his lips. He took a longer whiff of the air. He jumped up and down in his seat. "Meat!" he cried. "*Meat!*"

"Michael, stay here!" I begged. "Stay with me! Stay on Planet Earth, Michael!"

He was losing his grip on reality, and I didn't want to lose my grip on him. I said his name as much as I could. I didn't want him to forget who he was. He was Michael, a boy, like me.

He jumped more in his seat, pushing on the tape. He whined

when he realized he couldn't break free. He tried to turn his head to see the door, but of course he couldn't. He screamed.

"Your name is Michael!" I shouted over the noise. "Your last name is Huntley! You like apples, grapes, and oranges! Yum! Do you smell that? Apples, Michael! Warm, apple pie! Your dad's baked some apple pie for us! Can't you smell it? It's so delicious, Michael, you can almost taste it!"

I really needed to shut up. My stomach was beginning to believe some apple pie was actually around, and my stomach's growl could rival Michael's growl any day.

The door opened behind us. "Snack time," said Dr. Sharp.

Michael was as wild as ever as the aroma of smoked meat filled the room. I didn't want to think what I thought at that moment, but I just couldn't help myself.

Meat. Give me meat.

It was the most amazing thing I'd ever smelled. Way better than some lame apple pie. Mom's cheese enchiladas didn't stand a chance. Fresh-out-of-the-oven chocolate chip cookies were rotting garbage.

Meat. Give me meat. Now.

I found myself trying to reach the meat just by moving my neck the right way. Why couldn't I be a giraffe? If I were a giraffe, I could swing my neck over there and tear that meat away from the dentist with my teeth.

No, Jase, NO. Be strong.

I drooled. Couldn't help myself.

"Doesn't it smell good?" asked the doctor.

"*Yes,*" I forced out. "I'm so *hungry...*"

He chuckled. "Bet you are."

"But... No, I *can't...*"

"If I feed you, you must promise to behave."

I shook my head. "But I don't want—"

"If you don't eat now, I will *never feed you again.* Understand?"

I cracked. "No! Fine! Maybe a little bit..."

"Ah, children. Always put up a fight, but in the end, you are so easy to control."

The smell grew stronger with each step Sharp took toward us. He finally appeared between the chairs, balancing a mountain of steaming meat on a plate with his strong hands.

I didn't know if it was beef, pork, chicken, turkey, alligator, buffalo, moose, monkey, or hippopotamus on that plate. I didn't care, either. Whatever it was, I had to have some.

Michael must've thought Sharp was taking too long. He snapped at the dentist with his fanged jaws. "Just for that," said the doctor, "you get to go second."

Michael howled in pain. Sharp turned his back to the boy. He then lifted a chunk of meat between his fingers and held it above my head.

"Open wide," he said, "and don't forget to chew."

I tilted my head back and opened my mouth like a baby bird. The meat fell from his fingertips and tumbled my way. I snatched it out of the air with a quick bite.

Delicious.

48

FORGET Mom's chocolate chip cookies. That meat was ambrosia.

I'd never tasted anything like it before, and I wouldn't ever taste anything like it again. I'd always been pretty good with words, but no words could describe just how awesome it was.

That's why it was so difficult to spit the fifth chunk of meat back into the doctor's face. My tongue begged for the taste's return as soon as it was gone.

With the back of his hand, the dentist wiped spit and bits of meat from the spot on his nose where I'd nailed him. Hadn't really aimed, either. Not bad at all.

"Think that's funny?" Sharp's voice told me that *he* didn't think it was funny. He glowered, gritted his teeth.

"I'm full," I said.

"You're full? You haven't eaten for hours."

"I'm full."

"After only four pieces? I put extra spices on this." He looked at the plate of meat. "You should be wanting to tear this out of my hands."

Michael carefully chewed on an extra-large strip of meat that hung from his mouth. My stomach found the wrong moment to growl.

Sharp smiled. "You're lying to me, Jase. I can *hear* your lies." He lowered the plate in front of my face. "*Sure* you're not hungry for more of this scrumptious stuff?"

I closed my eyes so I wouldn't have to look at what he held before me. Closing my eyes, however, did little to hide the plate's contents from my nose. My mouth watered for the ambrosia.

"No," I said. "Something is wrong with it."

"Wrong?" said the doctor. "What do you mean? You don't like how it tastes? The way you were scarfing it down a minute ago seems to say otherwise."

"No, you *did something* to it."

"Yes, I made it extra enticing. It's my secret recipe, and I made it *just for you*. I wanted you to like it."

I opened my eyes and head-butted the plate. The plate flipped over in Sharp's grasp and all the leftover meat spilled to the ground. It reminded me of the Infamous Burrito Drop. If Mom were there, would she have scolded me for making a mess?

Michael whined softly at the sight of his spilled treat, but he was working too hard on what he was chewing to give much attention to what was now on the floor.

Sharp said, "Don't worry, Michael. The floor is clean." The dentist kneeled down and started scooping meat back onto the plate. "As if you would care."

I said, "What's so important about being a carnivore? What is all this *about?*"

Sharp smiled. "Just don't give up, do you?"

"No. I don't want to do whatever it is you want me to do. I won't eat anything you give me."

He stood, gripped the arms of my chair, and leaned into my face. "*Then starve,*" he said. Not surprisingly, he had pretty good breath. It was minty-fresh.

I said, "I would rather starve than let you brainwash me and turn me into something like Michael."

The doctor backed away from the chair, leaving the plate and meat on the floor. "Brainwash you?" He chuckled. "You really *are* smart for a dumb kid."

"Give me some answers!"

"No."

"Why not? You know I'm never going to get out of here, that sooner or later I'm going to be some weird freak like Michael over there!"

"Don't try to play mind games with me, boy. It's a mistake the bad guys always make in the movies. They reveal their plans at the end, and they always get caught because of it."

"You're *afraid*?" I said. "Afraid of an eleven-year-old kid?"

"Not at all." Sharp smirked. "But you've proven to be unpredictable."

"You're afraid."

"I'm not."

"Afraid."

"Not."

"*Afraid.*"

"*Not.*"

"Yes, you are!"

"Shut up!" Again he leaned across the chair to get into my face, fuming. "*You* should be afraid of *me*."

"But I'm not," I said.

"You're just trying to hide it."

"No, I'm not."

"You are."

"Not."

"Are."

"*Not.*"

"*Are.*"

I smiled. "This is fun!"

He backed away from me again. "Fun? You're having *fun*? That's too bad. Now it's *my turn* to have some fun."

I hesitated. "What're you going to do?"

"I'm getting your friend, and I'm bringing him over here."

"Why?" I gulped.

"Want to know the *truth*, right? The *reason* you're here? *Why* I'm doing all this?"

"Yes."

"Then I'll show you. *Both* of you."

49

A MINUTE LATER, Braxton began to shout in the hallway. Sharp had left to bring him back to the room with me. From what I could hear —which wasn't much—Braxton was not excited to see the dentist again.

The door opened, and Braxton shouted behind me, "No! Not another room! What're you doing?"

"Braxton!" I yelled over my shoulder.

"Jase? Is that really you?"

"Yes!"

"You haven't been watching any TV, have you? *Have you?*"

"Let's not talk about that just yet," said the doctor.

Something heavy dragged across the floor, and then Sharp placed Braxton, taped to another chair, six feet to my left. If we'd been making a sandwich, I would've been the filling and Michael and Braxton were the extremely unique slices of bread.

My partner-in-crime managed to smile when he saw me. His hair was a mess. His clothes were stained with sweat. "You look okay," he said.

I said, "Could be worse."

"Oh, yes, it definitely could be," said the doctor. He stood before us, in front of the television. "*Much* worse."

Braxton said, "I saw what you did to Greg! He's like a monster now!" He looked past me. "And... Michael too?"

Greg and Michael. Taken by Sharp and Alexis and turned into... something.

Jase and Braxton. Taken by Sharp and Alexis and *not yet* turned. Still some*one*, not some*thing*.

"What's that smell?" said Braxton. "Think I'm going to be sick..."

Sharp smiled at the plate of meat on the floor. "Stupid vegetarian," he said to my friend. "That isn't tofu you smell."

Braxton looked over at Michael chewing ferociously. "I'm going to throw up," he said.

"Go ahead," said the dentist. "All over yourself. Then I'll make you lick up your own puke."

Braxton closed his eyes, seemingly concentrating on holding back the stuff rising in his throat. When he opened his eyes again, he looked better and more focused. He forced a grin my way.

"Show us," I said.

Sharp smiled. "Show you *what?*" I wanted to punch that smile right off his face. Of course, I couldn't with my arms taped down.

I said, "You brought Braxton over to show us why we're here."

"I did, didn't I?" Sharp looked at Michael. "Then let's get on with it."

The doctor walked over to Michael's chair and pushed it in front of us. Michael still chewed on the same strip of meat. Without the use of hands, it was difficult to eat quickly. He seemed to be happy with what he was doing, at least.

Sharp pointed to him. "*This* is why you're here."

I wanted to scream at him for calling Michael a "this," but I decided it was better to be quiet and listen. I looked over at Braxton. He literally bit his lip to keep himself from yelling.

The dentist said, "Michael isn't perfect yet, but, as you can see, he's *near* perfection. He and Greg are both in the final phases of their transformation."

I asked, "What're you transforming them into?"

"You mean, 'What have I *transformed* them into?' As I said, they're already in the final phase. They're more what I made them than they are anything—or anyone—else."

"You're making them into some kind of animal," I said.

I wasn't going to let him tell me they were *already made* into something else. Michael had just talked to me. There was still some part of him left. Maybe not much, but there was still some left.

Sharp's eyes now seemed to smile at me, too. "Humans are animals, Jase," he said. "We're just the *most intelligent* animals out there. Deep down, when you look past our so-called intelligence, there are basic animal instincts. The need to eat and the need to live longer than anything else, *no matter what.*

"That need to live longer, to be stronger—it's everyone's dream, isn't it? Especially in our selfish nation. We want to be the best at everything, to allow no one to get the upper hand on us. If another country has something we don't have, we need to get it, and we need to make it ours, to make it bigger, better, and stronger than ever."

Braxton and I looked at each other, confused. Sharp caught our faces.

He said, "I'll just get right to it, then."

"Good," I said.

Sharp grinned. "I don't think you're ready for what I'm about to tell you, but if you want the truth..."

"We do," said Braxton.

The dentist nodded. "Our military is strong—perhaps the strongest in the world—but is still weak. Many nations continue to be threats to America. Why? Not because of their guns or bombs, but because of the lengths they are willing to go to defend themselves. For example, they allow their children to fight.

"In America, you have to be eighteen—an adult—to fight for your country. In some nations, they train children younger than you how to fire a gun, throw a grenade, detonate a bomb... One can look at that as foolish desperation, or he can look at it as amazing strategy."

"How is that good strategy?" said Braxton. "Kids aren't smart enough to be soldiers."

"Don't have to be too bright to be an effective soldier," said the doctor. "Just have to know how to kill. From a young age, children can be taught math and science, so why can't they be taught how to hurt others?

"During battle, an average American soldier doesn't expect an innocent child to attack him. That's our military's weakness. We have fought in places in the world where they are not above putting a weapon in the arms of some kid. For decades, our soldiers have approached and ignored the kids, thought everything was safe, and then… When the children attacked, it was often times too late.

"My father fought in a war a long time ago. A boy about your age shot him. Father never saw it coming. Lucky for him, he survived."

I remembered the article that said Dr. Sharp, Sr. had been injured in a war. I almost said something about it, but didn't want the dentist to know how much we knew. Not yet. It was smarter to let him talk if he wanted to talk.

The doctor continued. "Father was inspired by his attacker. Even when he went home after his injury, Father stayed in contact with the military. Made a deal with a general. Father would try to make the ultimate weapon for the United States: a better, stronger, killer child."

"That's insane!" said Braxton.

"It's brilliant," said Sharp. "Hypnosis has been in our family for centuries. Father thought he knew how to control children to make them kill. His dream was to sell his ideas and methods to the military."

Braxton said, "The military wouldn't support that! It's wrong to make kids do those kinds of things! And using hypnosis is not the way the Army or whatever works!"

Sharp shook his head. "What do you know? Soldiers' minds have been messed with for decades to prepare them to see—and do—horrible things when they go off to fight in war.

"As for the killer kids, the U.S. military loved Father's idea. They wanted to be put on an even playing field with other countries. At whatever cost it took."

I didn't know how much more Sharp was going to tell us, but it seemed like he wasn't going to stop any time soon. His eyes were bright. He was actually excited to tell someone his crazy plan.

He said, "Father failed many times to make his 'innocent weapons,' as he would call them. It was his secret project from the world, what kept him going for many years. He let my sister and I learn from him while we grew up.

"Once, he did come close to finally creating his weapons. It was years before you were born."

Were Kirk Mason and Eric Christopher, the teenagers who killed animals in 1997, actually "innocent weapons" Dr. Sharp, Sr. had brainwashed into being murderers? It was beginning to make such terrible sense to me. Couldn't tell by the look on Braxton's dumbfounded face if he was making the same connections to Grandpa's articles as I was.

The dentist said, "But that effort, too, failed, and the military gave up on Father. He died without ever fulfilling his dream."

So, Dr. Sharp, Sr. was dead. Our trip to the yellow house earlier really had been for nothing.

The dentist said, "My sister and I have taken Father's ideas and methods and made them better. Stronger. We are going to complete what he could not. The military will welcome our family back. No longer will there be shame connected to our name. We will be national heroes when we show everyone that America has 'innocent weapons,' as well. Father's legacy will survive."

Braxton said, "Maybe the old Navy or whatever would've wanted killer kids as weapons, but things are different now. Right, Jase?"

I nodded. "It's sick. You'll get in trouble for this, Dr. Sharp. The military won't let you do this to us. We're kids, not weapons. They'll know it's wrong."

The doctor flashed a wicked grin and shook his head. "Don't act like I'm delusional," he said. "They'll think it's perfect. The American government will do anything to protect our country's assets abroad. *Anything.*"

50

"Wait," I said. "How can we protect anything? We're kids."

Sharp looked at Michael. "Obviously, you can be so much more than that. Instead of holding a weapon for battle, you could *be* the weapon. Pit bulls and Doberman Pinschers are bred to defend and attack at any cost. They're incredibly loyal to their owners.

"But they're also stupid. Clumsy. They make mistakes. You boys are dozens of times smarter than the average guard dog. A ten-year-old boy's intelligence is leaps and bounds above that of a mere beast."

"I'm eleven," I said.

Sharp shrugged. "Even better."

"We don't want to be guard dogs!" cried Braxton.

"But you'll be so much more than that. You'll be sent out to attack American enemies before they even get the chance to attack first."

"Like ninjas?" said Braxton.

"A special kind of assassin," said Sharp. "One who can attack with the savagery of a wild animal but also use human intelligence. No one would expect a little American boy to be capable of the things I'll prepare you for. You look so innocent. You're only children, after all." He licked his lips. "Oh, I can already see the surprise on their faces as you tear out their throats."

I couldn't believe what I was hearing. The man was obviously crazy for kidnapping his patients and hypnotizing their parents, but what he was saying now took his insanity to a whole different level.

"Before I can train you," he said, "I have to transform you. That's what we have here." He waved his hands over Michael. "It's a complicated process, to say the least."

Michael was now done with his snack, and he sniffed the air for more. There was still the plate of meat on the floor, and he growled and lunged for it, still strapped to his seat.

"I believe he's hungry for more," said the doctor. "And that's good. Very good. He needs to have a taste for meat and blood if he's going to be a successful weapon."

"That's why you don't like vegetarians," I said. "They don't have the taste for blood and meat."

Sharp pulled a big piece of meat off the plate and held it in front of Michael. The boy's jaws snapped shut around it. Soon, he was silent again, chewing.

The dentist said, "You boys are smart. Definitely proven that. Right now, your intelligence has made things very difficult, but soon enough I'll be able to take full advantage of what it can offer.

"You somehow discovered the messages on the MyPods. I found one of them in Braxton's pocket." He clapped. "Bravo. How'd you think of it?"

"We're not going to tell you," I said. I didn't want Chip to suddenly be on Sharp's Enemy List.

"That's fine," said the dentist. "Probably nothing more than a lucky guess, anyhow." Good. Chip was safe.

"You and your sister are terrible people!" screamed Braxton.

"Yet we're not the worst out there," said Sharp. "We at least love each other. We're a team. Always have been. She does her part—the brainwashing—and I do mine—the training. She's much better at hypnosis than I am. Without her, none of this would be possible. She's very gifted.

"She's also good with technology. Knew about putting messages on the MyPods. Made all the videos that you're going to watch over and over and *over* again."

"No!" Braxton looked at me. "Don't watch them, Jase! Greg was watching them, and they're... They're disgusting!"

Sharp said, "They're to show you not to be afraid of the things you'll eventually have to do. Takes many, many viewings to get used to it all, I know, but you'll get used to it. You'll even grow to learn from it, to *love* it."

"No!" Braxton pushed against his straps. "Get me out of here!"

"Why fight?" said the doctor. "It'll only make you weaker. Need all the strength you can get."

Braxton pushed for a couple of more seconds, and then he stopped. I'd never seen him so tired and beat up.

"You come across the computer virus?" Sharp asked. "How Alexis did that one, I don't know."

I ignored what he said. "How long have you wanted to do all this? Your whole life?"

"Pretty much," said Sharp. "Father began to let Alexis and me help him a little on his project when we were about your age. Think it was after he scrapped the notion of making us the first 'innocent weapons.' Mother didn't agree with the idea too much, and Father didn't like having to hypnotize her more often than he had to.

"Wasn't until some years ago, after Alexis moved back out here, that we decided to finally finish where Father left off. To strengthen America... to make military contract money... It's a difficult thing, taking over someone's mind. Requires months and months of small steps. Michael and Greg listened to those MyPod messages for almost a year before we felt enough seeds were planted for their transformations to go smoothly."

I said, "But I've only been your patient for a week!"

"That's right," said Sharp. "Your transformation will be a real challenge. Fortunately, we have lots of time. If the way you reacted to the meat is any indication of how easy you'll be to control, then it won't be so difficult after all."

"My mom and grandpa will never let you—"

Sharp laughed. "Your mother and grandfather are very soon going to think you're away at military school in Colorado. They won't be able to help you. We already started hypnosis with your mom that day at the office, just in case things got worse, which they did. As I said, Alexis is extremely talented, and she thinks of almost everything."

I remembered them having a "private meeting" with Mom after Braxton called Michael and Greg's parents. How could we have been so dumb to just *let* it happen?

I said, "But she's heard Michael talk about the big, yellow house on the hill!"

"Big, yellow house on a hill?" said Braxton. "Is that where we are?" He sounded a little too happy about it.

I said, "Michael almost escaped once, right? That's how he knows where we are."

All the dentist said was, "Your mother didn't hear anything. Michael was too far away from my phone for her to hear. Alexis confirms it."

I hoped he was lying, but he seemed too comfortable to believe that his hiding spot was exposed. I screamed inside my head. Couldn't Mom and Grandpa just *guess* that we had been brought to the yellow house? They already knew the Sharps' connection to the place.

Or did they even realize that the Dr. Sharp they knew from long ago was connected to the dentist and his assistant? Maybe they didn't. They could've just thought the last name was a coincidence. I would've done anything to know what Mom and Grandpa knew...

"What about my mom and dad?" said Braxton. "Even though they might not like me very much, they're going to notice I'm missing."

"Ah, yes," said the dentist. "The fools. Their weak vegetarian minds will make them particularly easy to hypnotize later on."

"Don't want them worrying about me and calling the police, do you?" Braxton said. "They probably think I'm at Jase's house, and if they can't reach Jase's mom, they might freak out."

What was Braxton doing? He didn't want to talk to his parents, did he? Weren't they at the health spa anyway? He had something up his sleeve.

"We'll call them, then," said the dentist. "Tell them you're spending the night at Jase's house. Tonight, Alexis will make her way over to the Grunk residence, and your family will no longer be a problem."

The doctor pulled out the cell phone again. "What's the number?" he said.

Braxton looked at me. "Do it," I told him.

Do whatever crazy thing you're about to do.

51

"LET'S GET SOMETHING STRAIGHT," Sharp said. "If either of you tries anything funny, I will pull out your teeth without any anesthetic."

On second thought, don't *do whatever crazy thing you're about to do*!

"Braxton," I said. "Are you sure this is for the best?"

"What's wrong?" asked Sharp.

"Need to call my mom and dad," Braxton assured me. He said to the dentist, "The number is…"

I knew Braxton's phone number. The number he told Sharp to dial wasn't the number to his house. Wasn't exactly sure who was called until the person picked up after the first ring.

On speakerphone, a voice said, "This is Chip. I put the 'hip' back in—"

Sharp scowled. "What the—"

Braxton interrupted Sharp by yelling, "Dorito, it's Braxton! Help! They've got us in the big, yellow house!"

All Chip got to say was, "Braxton?" before the dentist hung up.

"*Who was that?*" Sharp yelled, full of fury.

We didn't say anything. Maybe Chip wasn't so safe after all…

The dentist's eyes burned with flame and they tried to melt Braxton's face. "You cause nothing but problems!"

My friend wasn't looking at the doctor. Instead, he stared at me. "Sorry," he said, "but I thought it was the only chance we had."

I nodded, because I understood. Who knew, maybe Chip had actually understood what Braxton had yelled at him. Even though he'd acted strange earlier, maybe he'd believe it, and maybe he'd be able to find help and rescue us.

But I doubted it.

"You're so *stupid*!" Sharp boomed. "So *useless*!"

"I'm not useless," argued Braxton.

"Yes, you are! You don't eat meat! The messages probably had no effect on you, did they, because you're vegetarian? And your bite is laughable. All you do is stick your nose into places it doesn't belong. You're good for *nothing* when it comes to what I need you for! I'm already going to have to start you from scratch!" He let out a deep breath. "Unless I don't even bother."

"What does that mean?" I asked.

He patted Michael on the head. "Let's see how far along this one has come. Maybe he's more ready than I think."

"What're you going to do?" asked Braxton. He actually sounded scared now. "Pull out my teeth?"

"Yes," said Sharp. "And..."

Braxton began to cry. "And *what*?"

52

WITH A FINGER, the dentist pulled back Michael's upper lip. The boy didn't seem to mind. He kept eating. He was happy as long as he had something to chew on.

"Aren't they beautiful?" asked the doctor. "The fangs?"

"No." I was trying to be as honest as possible.

Sharp removed his finger from under the lip. "No? That's too bad. At least I can appreciate my work." He stared at Michael for a moment. "Look at how they slice through that meat. It's so effortless."

"You carved his teeth to look like that?" I asked.

The dentist laughed. "Oh, no, that would be ridiculous. Human teeth aren't strong enough to survive that. I made special covers for his teeth called veneers. Veneers are quite common. They're usually made to replace broken or decaying teeth so that a person's smile can look absolutely perfect."

He stopped to admire his handiwork. "But these fang veneers I've made for Michael and Greg are perfect in an entirely different way." His eyes met mine. "Don't worry, Jase. Soon enough, your bite will be the deadliest of them all. You have such strength in your jaws, and when you finally have razor-sharp fangs to go along with them, you'll be—"

I shook my head. "I don't want fangs. I like my teeth."

"But your teeth," said the doctor, "can't rip human flesh clear off the bone."

I almost threw up at the thought of chewing on raw human. So I stopped thinking about it. "Couldn't ever do something like that. Especially if it was for you."

Sharp said, "You'll learn to obey me, Jase. I'll be your master *and* your father." He smiled. "Don't you want a father?"

I burned red. "I get along just fine."

"Is that right?" He turned to Braxton. "How about you? Wouldn't you enjoy having a father who actually respected and loved you?"

"My dad wouldn't strap me to a chair and torture me!"

"Give me credit, Braxton. I haven't tortured you yet." He put a hand on Michael's shoulder. "Greg and Michael don't like their daddies." If Michael didn't like his dad, is that why trying to talk to him about his father didn't work too well?

Sharp continued. "I like to think I'm here for my boys. My own father targeted children with rough upbringings for his project. More likely to be loyal to him, more likely to be happy to obey a new master."

Grandpa's article said that Kirk Mason and Eric Christopher had problems at home and that Dr. Sharp, Sr. became a "mentor" to them. Braxton caught my gaze. Still couldn't tell what he had figured out.

"Tell me about those kids," I said. "The ones your dad got close to brainwashing."

If I could get the dentist to talk about his father's project for long enough, maybe he would forget that he wanted to pull Braxton's teeth out. There was also the chance that Chip could show up and save the day. If I stalled the dentist long enough, the Hipnotist could reach us before anything else happened.

"You don't get to hear about Father's greatest failure," said the dentist. "Maybe someday, but not today. Have to pull some teeth, remember?"

Darn, he didn't forget. It *had* only been a couple of minutes. Braxton had stopped crying, but he started up again at the thought of removing his teeth.

"Don't be such a baby," said Sharp. "Should be used to all the tooth work by now."

My mouth reacted without asking my brain for permission. "Don't hurt him," I said. "Pull my teeth instead."

Was it possible to go back and change what I said? *Nope.* As weird as things had gotten, time travel was still impossible.

Sharp crossed his arms. "You want me to pull your teeth? You'd put yourself through all that pain just for your friend?"

My heart spoke instead of my mind. "Yes, I would."

"Now *that* is loyalty. Have to admire your willingness for sacrifice, even if it is incredibly dumb." He tapped his foot against the floor. "Once I have control over you, your loyalty and sacrifice will be *for me and your country.*"

"Please," I said.

The doctor smiled. "What do you say, Braxton? Should he take the punishment for you? What should happen to your friend?"

Braxton stopped sobbing long enough to say, "Don't do it, Jase. I messed up, not you."

"No," I said. "I can handle it."

"Yeah, right!" Sharp chuckled. "Coming from the boy who couldn't have a cavity filled with the help of anesthetic!"

"This is different," I said.

The dentist nodded. "So it is, so it is." He paused to think for a moment.

What had I *done?*

"Okay, you can have your teeth pulled, Jase, if that's what you want."

The butterflies in my stomach flapped their wings all at once. "Yes, it's what I want." The itch burned a hole in my hand.

Sharp chuckled. "*After* I pull Braxton's out first."

"What?" I said. "No!"

"Don't like that deal?"

"It's not what I meant!"

"Then sit there and keep your mouth shut." He pointed to Braxton. "Don't waste any strength on this piece of garbage. He's not worth it."

I said, "He's my *friend*."

"If you want to help your friend, tell him to do as I say next time."

Braxton began crying louder than ever. Sharp covered his ears, didn't say anything else, and walked out of the room.

The tears suddenly stopped. "Good," said Braxton. "He's gone."

"Wait, you weren't *really* crying?" I said.

"Tears were real, but not the emotion. Learned a long time ago that adults don't like to be around crying for longer than they have to be."

I said, "You got him out of the room, but what next? He won't be gone too long."

Braxton slipped his left arm out from under the duct tape. "Surprise!"

"No way! How'd you get loose?"

"I wished it would happen, and it did!" With Braxton, it was the best explanation I was going to get.

"Wish some more! I want out, too!"

He said, "I've tried, but I think it's a decade of unanswered birthday wishes answered in one big wish!"

"How long have you been able to get out of that?"

"Since I was in the other room." He sighed. "I'm not left-handed, though."

"Can't you pull the other straps off?"

"I've tried, but it's duct tape, Jase. No one can peel off duct tape with his left hand!"

"So, what're you going to do?"

"Wanted to ask you what you thought I should do."

"I don't know, *I don't know*." Now we literally had a kind of upper hand on the situation, and there didn't seem to be any way we could use it.

"Don't worry," he said. "When the opportunity comes, I think I'll know what to do. It has to be destiny. *Has to be.*"

The door opened, and Braxton slid his arm back under the tape. Sharp walked over to him and grabbed the back of his chair with one hand.

In his other hand, the dentist balanced a ball of clear, plastic wire and a pair of long, sharp scissors.

53

"As a dentist, I know lots of methods for pulling teeth. Didn't have to go to dental school, though, to learn my absolute favorite method." He raised the hand that held wire and scissors. "Cut a piece of fishing line. Tie one end of the fishing line to a tooth, and tie the other end to a doorknob. Then—"

"Oh, no," I said.

"—SLAM!" Sharp stomped his foot loudly against the floor. Michael whined softly at the noise, but he kept chewing. Pretty soon, he'd need more to snack on.

"That's what you're going to do to me?" said Braxton.

The dentist nodded. "Doesn't it sound like fun? When the door slams, your tooth will be yanked right out of your head."

"Please, don't do it!" I begged. "It only works if a tooth is already loose! My grandpa did it for me in first grade, and it hurt even then!"

The dentist shrugged. "Then I'll just slam the door harder. At the very least, his tooth should be loosened quite a bit, and we'll yank it out on the second try."

Braxton didn't say anything about that. He looked at the floor and seemed to be in a whole other world. He was either trying to think happy thoughts or he was planning a way to get us out of there. I hoped it was the second choice.

The doctor stepped in front of us, unraveling a long piece of wire from the ball. The scissors now stuck out of his right pants pocket. "This fishing line is able to hold up to three hundred pounds. Can you believe that? This thin, little wire."

Nobody answered him. He looked at the wire he held between his fingertips. He liked the length, so he took out the scissors and cut it from the ball. The snipped fishing line twirled to the floor.

The doctor asked, "Ever been fishing, Jase?"

"No, don't like seafood."

"Not your kind of meat, eh?"

"Think I'll be a vegetarian from now on."

Sharp ignored that. "Don't have to eat fish to go fishing. They're two different things. I'll take you fishing someday. Father took me on occasion."

"I don't want to hurt any fish," I said.

"Oh, come on. It's a thrill. Your blood gets pumping real fast. When that fish bites, you have this creature fighting against you in a kind of tug-of-war, and it's up to you if you're going to win or if it's going to win. A game, like almost anything else. A real exciting game."

"You think all this is fun, what you're doing to us? Is it like fishing?"

The dentist smiled. "Kind of making me feel like I'm fighting against a great white shark here."

I said, "Thanks," because it sounded like he gave me a weird compliment.

"Only reason I don't gag you, is that sharp shark's mouth reminds me of my own at your age. You're truly something special, Jase. Not like these others, so easy to manipulate. I appreciate the challenge you're presenting."

He leaned over and picked the fishing line off the floor. "Your friend here, though, is chum. Blood in the water." He looked at Michael. "And here's the barracuda. He'd do anything to taste some blood."

I shook my head. "Not if the great white has anything to do about it."

"That's just it, *Jaws*," said Sharp. "You won't have anything to do about it."

Sharp put the ball of fishing line in his left pants pocket. The scissors went back in his right pocket. He pulled Braxton's chair out of sight, scraping it across the floor behind me. My friend went wordlessly, lost in his thoughts.

Was he planning anything?

"I want to see," I said. Did I *really*?

"That's what I like to hear," said Sharp. "Breaking you down already."

He wasn't breaking me down. I just had to be able to see if things got too out of hand. Also wanted to witness whatever Braxton was going to do, if he was actually going to try anything.

Sharp spun my chair around, and now I faced the door. The dentist grinned in my face. Michael chewed on the last of his treat behind me. Braxton was a few feet from the door, still silent, now staring at a different part of the floor.

Sharp walked over to the door and opened it wide. All I saw outside was an empty hallway with white walls. Didn't look like we were in a basement, after all.

"On with the show," said the doctor.

He tied one end of the fishing line to the rusty doorknob. He had cut about three feet of wire. He walked the other end of the fishing line to Braxton, who didn't sit there with his mouth hanging open, waiting for his tooth to be tied. He just stared.

"Hey, chum." Sharp waved a hand in front of Braxton's face. "Earth to chum. Open wide. Need to hook something I can throw back as bait."

"He won't listen to you," I said.

"That's okay. I'll just force his mouth open." The dentist put one palm against Braxton's forehead, and the other against Braxton's chin. He put pressure against both parts of Braxton's face, and my friend's lips parted.

That's when Braxton lunged forward and bit down on the doctor's right thumb, which had been pushing against his chin. Sharp howled as Braxton bit down harder on the stubby little worm. *Harder.*

So much for his laughable bite, eh, Dr. Sharp?

Braxton growled, twisting in his seat, tearing on the thumb. The dentist screamed and cursed. He pushed on Braxton's face with his other hand, forcing the mouth open. His thumb was released, but even from where I was sitting, I could see it was painted red with blood.

Sharp stumbled away from Braxton, dropping the fishing line, shouting some of the worst language I'd ever heard. *Grandpa let me see quite a few R-rated movies, too!* The doctor's cries made it seem like his thumb was going to fall off. I almost laughed.

I could hear Michael sniff the air. He'd caught the bloody scent. He began to struggle against the tape, wanting a taste of Sharp's gushing thumb. It was pretty scary to realize just how far gone Michael seemed to be.

"My thumb! Oh, my blankety-blank-blank-blanking THUMB!"

The dentist stared in disbelief at his hand. It was pretty gross, but I was sure it could've been worse. I'd seen nastier thumbs before. Not in real life, of course. In the movies.

"I can't believe it! How did this happen?"

What Sharp didn't seem to realize was that Braxton bit down on his thumb not only to cause him great pain but to also distract him while the scissors were taken out of his pocket. If you looked at Braxton, you would probably expect him to be clumsy, but he'd lifted the scissors easily and silently off the doctor—*all with his freed left hand and without looking, too!*

As the doctor complained very noisily about his poor, blankety-blank-blank-blanking thumb, behind him, Braxton carefully cut the tape away from his right arm and legs. He stood away from his chair.

He'd been planning something, after all.

54

SHARP TURNED TO BRAXTON, ready to shout more bad words in his direction, but the dentist fell silent when he saw my friend *standing in front of* the chair instead of *sitting in* it. There were a couple of seconds when the only sound in the room was Michael struggling against his straps.

The doctor began to smile. "Clever little idiot," he said. "What're you going to do now? Stab me with those scissors?"

Braxton held the scissors in his right hand. Their points were aimed at Sharp, but the doctor was about five feet away. "Don't know what's next," said Braxton, "but somehow Jase and I are going to get out of here!"

"Maybe you can leave, but your friend stays here with me." Sharp slowly backed over to my chair. "Jase isn't going anywhere."

Braxton didn't move. I didn't move. Sharp didn't move. Only Michael moved, and he moved a lot from the sound of it, shrieking and wrenching in his seat. The chair started to screech against the floor, making a noise like nails on a chalkboard.

Still, no one else moved. It was an Old West showdown. Who would draw first?

My hand itched *so much*.

Even if the tape was all cut away from my arms and legs, the amount of sweat on my back would've probably kept me stuck to the back of my seat. Felt like I was sweating everywhere on my body, even in places where I didn't know I could sweat, like my ears. In those moments, when my fate truly hung in the balance, all I could think about was how badly I needed a shower, and how much I *absolutely hated* taking showers.

The sound of four duct tape strips splitting apart at once was much like the sound Velcro made. Loud and annoying. But, there, at that time, the sound was closer to music, sweet and harmonious. I snapped out of my trance to see Michael breaking free of his restraints.

Beside me, Sharp turned to the sound. His eyes were wide flying saucers in his head. He actually *caught* Michael as the boy leaped onto him, but he also made the mistake of allowing his bloody thumb to get too close to Michael's fangs.

I thought the words Sharp had yelled before were too much for children's ears, but—WHOA—he found much worse things to scream as Michael tried to chew his thumb off.

The doctor stumbled and twirled around the room as he fought to push his insane experiment away from him. Michael held on strong, though, not letting go of the thumb, gripping Sharp's shoulders with his hands. It was the most awkward dance I'd ever seen, and Grandpa once tried to show me how to do the Macarena.

But I wasn't watching for long. Braxton took the opportunity to race over with the scissors and slice through my duct tape like butter. His eyes met mine, sharp and gleeful.

I stood up, massaging my wrists, which were red from the tape that had been rubbing against them. I'd never felt so alive in my life, never so free. My fingernails were finally able to ease the itch. I was a balloon ready to just float away to happiness. Tears of joy began to form.

Sharp didn't seem to notice or really even care that we were both now free. He was too busy trying to keep his thumb attached to his hand.

"Jase, *come on!*" Braxton grabbed my elbow.

Oh. We weren't out of there yet.

"*NO!*" Sharp screamed louder than ever before. Thought he was screaming at Michael, but his eyes were fixed on us.

"Run!" I yelled.

Sharp grabbed Michael by the throat with his free hand, and threw the boy off him. Michael crashed against the floor, landing hard on his side. He stopped growling and began to cry, an injured child.

The dentist charged. We raced for the door. *He was going to cut us off, block our escape!*

We were three steps away from the hall, Sharp closing in fast. His legs, and strides, were longer than ours.

Two steps away from the hall. *He was closer.*

One step away. *He was next to us.*

I grabbed Braxton's shirt and pushed my friend out the door. He slid past Sharp's grasp, but I ran straight into the doctor. He grunted, grabbed for me, and I dodged his bloody hand.

Instead, I grabbed his other hand and bit down as hard as I could on his uninjured thumb. *Now it was injured.* His weakness really must've been bites to the hand, because he cried out again. Only, this time he was able to throw me down to the floor before I could do any major damage.

There, right in front of my face, was the loose end of the fishing line. I grabbed it and turned around to see Sharp bending over to reach for me. I crawled quickly between his legs. There was Braxton, out in the hall, already free, but he seemed to be waiting for me. What a pal.

I wasn't ready to leave just yet. Sharp would be able to catch us if we ran away. He was faster than us, and he was familiar with the territory. What if we got lost or even made one wrong turn? He'd have plenty of time to get us.

So, I tied the fishing line to his right ankle. I tied it tight, just like how Mom taught me to tie my shoes in second grade. Wouldn't take just one knot to get the job done or even two. Had to be quadruple-knotted. Mom taught me how terrible it would be if I ever lost a shoe, so I was used to the quadruple-knot. I'd been tying my shoes for years, and nobody in the world quadruple-knotted faster than me.

Had three knots tied before Sharp even realized what I was doing behind him. "Hey!" He tried to lift his foot, but I held it down. "Let go of me!"

Done. Four knots. I reached for the open door as the doctor turned for me. Braxton gestured for me to hurry. I grabbed the doorknob, ducking under Sharp's arm. I ran, pulling the door shut behind me.

From the other side of the door came a thunderous crash. Sharp's foot must've been pulled out from under him and he fell. Very hard. I prayed the fishing line held. Didn't think the dentist weighed more than three hundred pounds.

There we were. No longer in the room. Now in the hall.

Now what?

"I'm coming for you!" Sharp's voice sounded louder than ever before, even though he was on the other side of a closed door. He was really, really, really, really, REALLY angry now.

"Go!" I pushed Braxton ahead of me, because I was probably faster than he was. Didn't want him to fall behind. Didn't bother to tell him the dangers of running with scissors.

The hall didn't extend very far. Only a couple of other closed doorways on each side. Reminded me of the dentist's office, where it all began.

The hall turned right, so Braxton turned right. I didn't hear a door open behind us, and when I looked back, the hall was still empty. We were in a bigger room now, one filled with old, dusty boxes and furniture.

"There!" I pointed to big, sliding doors on one wall. Pale moonlight spilled through the glass doors. Yep, not in the basement.

We sprinted over. Braxton seemed to be okay. Wasn't wheezing or anything. Neither was I. Things were happening too fast for us to even think if we were feeling okay or not.

But being in the same building as Dr. Sharp = NOT OKAY.

I figured the sliding glass doors wouldn't open. They'd be jammed. Things hadn't really been going our way except for in the last few minutes.

Braxton slid the doors open with no problem at all.

We stepped outside, and I closed the door behind me. If Sharp came after us, he would have to open the door, and that could buy us a second or two we might need.

We were next to a large, empty pool. The only water in it was a small puddle of old, dirty rainwater in the deep end. We must've just left a pool house, because on the other side of the pool was a monstrous building—a mansion—covered in peeling yellow paint.

"Go around!" I shouted.

55

We raced through weeds and over cracks as we made our way around the pool. We reached a rusted gate that was built into a high, cracked brick wall. The gate looked like the only way out.

I twisted the gate's knob, and it didn't stick. It turned, and I pushed through, into a side yard of the big, yellow house. All around us were dead, brown bushes. Didn't seem to be any way out of the yard.

"The only way out is through the house!" Braxton sounded scared. I didn't want to go into the house, either. We'd definitely get lost in there.

Behind the bushes on our right was another tall brick wall. In front of it was the huge tree we'd seen from outside the gates of the house. It was where Braxton claimed to have seen someone watching us from the shadows.

If we climbed the tree, could we jump to the other side?

Braxton saw where I was looking. He said, "Primates and I might share a lot of the same genes, but I'm not a monkey!"

"I'm not, either, but it's the only way!"

Even though he wasn't too excited about it, Braxton made his way over to the tree. I cupped my hands so he could step on them and raise himself into the branches. He put his sneaker into my palms, and I pushed him up as he jumped. He was lighter than I thought he'd be.

Within seconds, he was definitely a monkey in that tree, climbing around spider webs, making his way over to the wall. The tree creaked some and even swayed, but it didn't slow my friend down any. Not even holding scissors seemed to bother him.

"What's on the other side?" I asked.

He looked down to me, a shadowy figure in the night. "Just the empty driveway and lawn," he said.

"Okay, good. We're almost there, Braxton!" Behind me was the gate to the pool. It swung in the breeze. "I'll be back in a second."

"Wait! Jase, where are you going? Don't leave me!"

"Don't worry, just have to close the gate in case he comes after us!"

I went over to the gate and began to close it when I saw Sharp in the pool house, behind the sliding glass doors. He saw me, too.

I slammed the gate shut and ran. "Braxton, he's coming! *He's coming!*"

A second later, doors slid open in the distance. "Come out, come out, wherever you are!" shouted the doctor in a sing-songy voice.

Once back under the tree, I jumped up and grabbed a branch. Pressed my feet against the trunk and began to walk up it slowly. My feet slipped on decaying bark, but I caught myself before I fell back to the ground.

"Braxton," I whispered. He was now close enough to the wall to jump on over to the other side. "Is it safe?"

"Don't know. The dead grass doesn't look soft enough to land in."

Footsteps smacked loudly against the ground poolside. The doctor was running our way. "Jump," I said.

"But—"

"*Jump.*"

Braxton dropped the scissors over the wall, jumped, and landed with a grunt on the other side. I didn't hear anything else, thought the worst for a second, and then he yelled, "I'm okay!"

Awesome. *Now it was my turn.*

I was all the way in the tree at that point. Sharp exploded through the gate, looked left, and then looked right. My white shirt couldn't camouflage me in a leafless tree at night. The dentist's eyes met mine. He came for me. I climbed faster.

Below, Sharp said, "Haven't climbed since I was a kid, but this was always my favorite tree. Actually had a little practice earlier tonight. Came up here just for the heck of it. And, wouldn't you know, there was some car sitting just outside those gates in front, and I had to get down before someone saw me. Spoiled the moment a bit."

I didn't know if he was telling me that so that I knew he saw us in Chip's car or because he wanted me to know he was a good tree climber. Either way, I had to get moving.

"*Let's go, Jase, let's go!*" shouted Braxton from the other side.

The tree shook as Sharp ascended. Yep, he was part-monkey, all right. Just my luck. He was standing in the tree within seconds.

I tried not to lose valuable seconds by scratching, but millions of ants seemed to be crawling across my hand.

"*Jase?*" Braxton called. Couldn't yet see him. Still had a few branches to get through.

Sharp pulled himself toward me with ease. He gained a couple of feet on me each second. He may have been big, but he made his way through the tree like some kid who climbed trees every day instead of playing video games. His bleeding hand didn't slow him down one bit. He didn't even try to go around any of the spider webs. He pushed them away. I saw him crush one spider with a squeeze of his hand.

He wanted to get to me *badly.*

After he crushed the spider, I decided I couldn't look at him anymore. He was distracting me, slowing me down, and really freaking me out.

"Jase, you're mine," he taunted. "Why even try to get away?"

Because I knew I could. I'd already made it that far when things had looked so bad, like there wasn't a chance in the world I could get away. And there I was, in that tree, only feet from dropping to the next level of escape.

Over the wall, I could now see Braxton. He looked up, waving me on with the scissors. "Hurry! He's behind you, *behind you!*"

As if I didn't know.

All I had to do was get over one branch and crawl down to another one. Then I could drop twelve feet to that soft pillow of yellow grass and weeds.

A bloody hand tugged on the bottom of my shirt. "*Gotcha.*"

I didn't even look back. I just kicked, and it sounded like my shoe crunched against Sharp's face. *What did that sound like?* Like:

"Ugh! My face!"

The doctor released my shirt. I climbed over one branch and down to another one. I let myself fall. Gravity worked pretty well. I hit the grass sooner than I expected. The stuff was itchy and prickly. I was already itchy enough, so I didn't roll around in it too much. I secretly thanked whoever had been too lazy to mow the lawn and had let it grow tall and thick, and then I was on my feet again.

Braxton was next to me. "We have to keep going!" he panted. "He's still coming!"

Sure enough, even a kick to the face hadn't fazed the dentist for too long. He was almost to the branch I jumped from. If he got to us before we got to the street, all our efforts would be for nothing.

56

WE MADE it through the grass and onto the long, empty driveway. It was about seventy-five yards to the street. But, even if we made the trek to the road, we'd be trapped behind the locked gate and tall, deadly fence.

As we approached the street, I saw Jason Root impaled on spikes, reaching out to Braxton and me for help. I saw Mom and Dad looking in at us, asking us to run to them. What I didn't see was a realistic way to escape.

The doctor dropped to the ground just as we reached the gate, which had the same sharp tops as the fence. We pushed and pulled on the gate. It rattled but didn't open. The chain and lock that held the gate shut seemed to be brand-new, not rusted at all. Sharp and Alexis had replaced it recently, to keep intruders out.

Or to keep prisoners in.

The dentist said from behind us, "Going to need me to open it for you, and guess what? I'm not going to do that."

We stopped rattling the gate and turned to see him walking our way, not in any hurry. Scarier than if he ran. His walk was so calm, so *confident*. It said that he knew we couldn't get away. We had no chance. Game over. Nice try.

"What do we do?" I said to Braxton. "There's nothing to use to climb over."

"Try to squeeze through!" my friend offered.

Braxton tried to push his body through the six-inch gaps between each post on the gate. The gaps were just as wide on the fence. I did the same as my friend, but I could only get my arms through up to the shoulder. Braxton was desperate, trying to squish his head through. It looked painful, like if he pushed any harder, his skull would be crushed.

"My brain!" he cried. "It's too big! My head won't fit!"

"That strategy doesn't seem to be working too well for you, boys," said the dentist.

I didn't want to look back, to see how much ground he had gained, but it sounded like he was much closer now. I kept my eyes on the dark street before us, kept them on freedom.

"Just yell!" I said. "Yell for help! The other houses aren't that far away. Somebody will hear us!"

Braxton said, "None of the lights are on! Everyone's probably sleeping!"

It was true. In the distance, each house was dark and lifeless. I had no idea what time it was, but if we screamed loud enough, someone had to hear us. No one would ignore our calls. Adults don't like kids shouting in the middle of the night.

"HELP!" I shrieked. "HELP US! WE'RE BEING HELD WITH A BAD MAN! A BAD MAN!"

Braxton followed my example. His voice was so loud and annoying, I would have asked him to quiet down if the circumstances were any different.

"Save your breath." Sharp raised his voice to be heard over our shouting. "We're too far away. It's too late in the evening. Or, might I say, it's too early in the morning."

Couldn't help myself. Had to look back. Sharp was only forty yards away now. He came toward us, deadly calm, in no hurry whatsoever.

"HEEEEEEEEEEEEEEEEEEEEEEEEEEEEEEEEEEEEEEEEEELP!"

Braxton screamed.

No lights came on in any of the houses along the street. I looked at Braxton, almost ready to give up, tears collecting beneath my eyeballs.

Then, at the end of the street, a car turned the corner. The headlights were small, but they were coming our direction. Perhaps hope wasn't lost after all.

I rejoined Braxton in the screaming. We had to get that driver's attention. I turned to look at Sharp. He was only thirty yards away now.

"Braxton!" I warned.

My friend turned and held the scissors in front of him. "Stay back," he told the doctor.

Would he actually do something with the scissors if he had to? I had no idea, but Braxton knew how hard we had worked to get to that gate. He wouldn't let anything or anyone take it away from us.

The doctor stopped in his tracks, his face wary in the dim glow from the faraway streetlight. It seemed that Sharp wasn't so sure about Braxton anymore, either. You probably lose trust in somebody when he tries to separate your thumb from your hand.

"Can't just let you leave," he said.

"Hold those scissors tight," I told Braxton. I turned sideways so I could see both the street and Sharp at the same time. "AND DON'T STOP SCREAMING!"

Braxton kept his scissors pointed at Sharp and continued to cry for help along with me. The car hadn't turned into a driveway yet. It still climbed toward us on the hill, but it was nowhere near close enough yet.

"Whoever that is," said Sharp, "don't be stupid enough to think they're coming for you. No one's been here for years. As far as anyone knows, this place is vacant. That car will stop at one of those houses, and that will be the end of this little game."

But the car didn't stop. It kept coming. It drove right past the last houses on the street. Its headlights were eyes opening wider for us by the second.

"*No way!*" shouted the doctor.

We could hear the rumble of the car's engine as it approached. The driver zoomed up the hill.

"Yes!" I said. It was weird. I was so excited, I started to laugh.

Sharp was less happy. He came a step closer, but Braxton swung the scissors his way, his eyes wild. "Stay right there! I'll stab you!"

Who was in the car? Chip? Was he actually coming to rescue us? Was it *my mom*? Had she somehow escaped Alexis?

I jumped up and down, shaking the gate, waving my hands, screaming at the top of my lungs, "WE'RE HERE! WE'RE HEEEEEEEEEEEEEEEEEEEEEEEEEEEEEEEEEEEEEEEERE!"

"Shut up!" cried the doctor.

But I didn't shut up. And Braxton joined in. He jumped up and down, screaming for help, still facing the dentist, the scissors sharp blades pointing right at the doctor's guts. The moon was definitely bright enough for the driver to see us.

"NO!" Sharp must have decided to forget the scissors. He came toward us again. "YOU CAN'T GET AWAY!"

The car was right there, fifty yards from us. We could hear it very clearly, we just couldn't see past the bright headlights.

Hurry, hurry, HURRY!

"HELP!" shouted Braxton.

Sharp was only feet away. He looked at Braxton, then at me. I was the one who was unarmed. I knew he was going to lunge for me even before he did.

The doctor leaped forward, his bloody hands reaching for my throat. I dodged his attack, and he slammed against the gate, clanging it loudly. That was great and all, but now the doctor was between Braxton and me.

We had been separated, and Sharp knew which one of us he wanted. *The one without the scissors.* He turned to me, smiled, growled, and charged again. I stumbled backward, scrambling to get away.

Tires screeched. Headlights sliced over us. A banged-up white car screamed to a stop in front of the gate. Sharp came to a screaming stop about three feet from me.

"It's Pringle!" exclaimed Braxton, looking over his shoulder.

It was Chip, all right. I could see him through the driver's side window. He was there to help us, but it didn't look like he knew what to do.

"Please!" Braxton cried. "We're locked in here!" He shook the gate for the Hipnotist to see. "Dr. Sharp's going to hurt us!"

Sharp stared at Chip for a few seconds. He must have recognized the man as one of his new patients. I saw the confusion and fear in the doctor's eyes. He stepped back, away from me, toward the house. Messing with an adult was different than messing with a kid, wasn't it? What a tough guy. *Not.*

"This isn't over," said the doctor. "Your family still isn't safe, Jase."

Sharp made sure to give me that stab to the heart before he sprinted up the driveway. I watched him run for a couple of seconds, and then my attention turned to our hero on the other side of the gate.

57

"GOT YOUR CALL, BRAXTON," said Chip as he climbed out of his car without turning it off. "What the heck is going on? How'd you guys get here? Was that Dr. Sharp?"

"Just get us out of here!" begged Braxton. "He'll be back soon! I know it!"

"You guys okay?"

"Not really," I said. "Braxton's right. He'll be back."

"You said the gate's locked?"

I nodded. "We don't know how to open it."

"Looks old," said Braxton. "Maybe you can drive through it."

"You want me to *drive* through it? That's gnarly." Chip shook his head. "Know my front bumper looks like a crushed can, but that was an accident. Don't make enough money to just ram my car into things without caring about how much it will cost to fix the damages."

"It's the fastest way," said Braxton. "We need out *now*."

"Right," said Chip. He pulled a phone out of a pants pocket. "Didn't know what was going on before I got here, but now maybe I should call the cops. Wow. Feels weird to say that..."

"Don't you dare!" shouted Sharp from up the driveway. "If you do, Jase's family *dies*."

We all turned to look at the dentist. He was almost to the front porch. He said, "I will make sure your mother and grandfather are killed immediately, Jase, if he makes that call."

I scratched my hand. My heart was a hummingbird trapped behind my ribcage. "No!" I said. "You can't!" The tears were back.

"They will die without ever saying goodbye to you," Sharp threatened.

"Man, that is gnarly," said Chip. "This guy really has your family somewhere?"

"Yes," I said. "Just like he took us!"

"Dr. Sharp's lying," Braxton said to me. "He won't hurt your mom and grandpa." He yelled to Sharp. "You're lying!"

"I've been pushed too far," said the doctor.

"If he's going to hurt my family..." I started to cry. "We can't let him hurt my family..."

"I have to call the cops," said Chip. "What else can we do?"

Braxton and I locked stares. "We don't have any other choice," my friend said.

"Wait," I said. "Just *wait*, all right?"

I began to jog up the driveway toward the dentist. "Hold up, Dr. Sharp!"

"What's he doing?" I heard Chip say.

"Don't know," said Braxton. "Jase, stop!"

"Just stay there!" I said to him.

I stopped three-quarters of the way up the driveway. Sharp said, "What's your plan, little boy?"

"I don't have one," I admitted.

"No?" he said. "I doubt that."

"Can't we make a deal?" I spoke low enough for only him to hear. I didn't want Braxton and Chip to be involved in this conversation.

"What type of a deal?" Sharp spoke in a quieter tone, too.

"What can I do to convince you not to hurt my mom and grandpa?"

Sharp paused, thinking. Finally, he said, "If you, Braxton, and that spy you sent to my office all agree to have a chat with me inside the house here, your family will remain untouched."

I looked back at Braxton and Chip. They paced in front of the car's headlights, darting glances up the driveway at me and Sharp. What would they think of Sharp's offer?

It seemed like a set-up to me. As soon as we were inside the house, Sharp would attack. He would probably hurt Chip first, because he was the biggest, and then Braxton and I would be right back to where we started.

I turned my attention back to the doctor. "Don't know if they'll do it," I said to him.

"Yes," said Sharp. He pointed behind me. "Apparently not. Sorry, Jase. Your family's fate has been sealed."

I looked back to Braxton and Chip. The Hipnotist had his phone to his ear, and he appeared to be talking to someone on the other end of the line.

"No!" I cried. I sprinted back down the driveway. I stopped at the gate, pounding against it. "Chip, what're you *doing*?"

Braxton said, "I told him we should we wait."

Chip talked to a 9-1-1 operator. I heard him say "kidnapping" and "murder" a couple of times. He mentioned an address—where we were, I guessed.

I looked back up the driveway. Sharp was gone. The front doors of the yellow house were wide open.

"He's inside," I said. "We have to get him! We have to stop him!"

I ran toward the house. Braxton chased me. Chip shouted after us in confusion.

"Even I think this is a bad idea," said Braxton.

"You don't have to come," I said.

"Yes, I do."

"The cops say to wait!" Chip yelled. "Wait, guys, wait! That isn't safe!" He shook the gate behind us in frustration.

But we didn't wait. We raced up the front porch, and I led us inside the dark, hungry mouth of the yellow house.

58

BEHIND ME, Braxton gripped the collar of my T-shirt. The open front doors were behind us, and moonlight shone only a few feet into the house. I had stopped right where the shadows started.

"Yeah, well, I smell *fear*," I told him.

Angry, I looked back at my friend. However, it was so dark in the house I didn't think he could see my face too well. My family was in danger. I hadn't come so close from so far to wait for help and waste more time. I had to fix this. Mom and Grandpa wouldn't, couldn't, shouldn't die because of me.

"You're scared, too," said Braxton.

I scratched my hand. "That can't stop me," I said. "Not now."

"It's not stopping me, either, Jase."

"Good." I paused. "Can you see anything?" My eyes were taking a while to get used to the darkness.

"It's too dark," said Braxton. "Dr. Sharp could jump right out at us. It's like we're blind."

How could I stop the dentist from calling Alexis and telling her to hurt my family if I couldn't even follow him into this scary old house?

I had to bring him to me...

"DR. SHARP!" I yelled as loud as I could. "LET'S TALK!"

"So much for the element of surprise," said Braxton.

"He left the doors open," I said. "He expected us to come in after him."

"Which isn't very smart. We just did our best to get away, and now we're trying to get him to come to us!"

"I know that!" Braxton was starting to annoy me. "I need to do something! I have to try to stop him!"

"Fine," he said. Then, he shouted, "DR. SHARP, DON'T KILL JASE'S MOM AND GRANDPA! THAT'S REALLY, REALLY MEAN!"

We stood in silence, but there was nothing to hear. No voices, no footsteps. Not even any police sirens in the distance. Help wouldn't arrive in time. That was for sure.

"Let's find a light switch," said Braxton.

"Lights won't work," I said. "It's an old house."

"The pool house is an old pool house, but the lights work there."

"You're right. Let's try it."

Braxton released my shirt. "I'll try over here," he said as he left my side to search the darkness for a light switch.

As I moved, I held my hands out in front of me to make sure I didn't bump into anything. I reached a wall, sliding my itchy hand across it, searching. Wallpaper peeled off at my fingertips.

From across the room, Braxton said, "I can't find it."

"Just keep looking," I said.

After a few more seconds of zero success, I realized my eyes were getting used to the lack of light. I could make out shapes in the shadows. I left the wall, and, hands out in front of me, I began to quietly walk deeper into the house.

I didn't tell Braxton. He didn't need to follow me. He'd be safer if he stayed by the front doors. Besides, it was my fight. My family was in trouble, not his.

A hand grabbed my shoulder. My body froze.

Dr. Sharp had found me. He'd been waiting there for us all along...

"Jase," Braxton said in my ear. "I can kind of see better now. Maybe we should just try to keep going without the lights on."

Just could not get rid of the guy. To be honest, I felt a little safer with him by my side. He was the one with the scissors, after all.

"Let's go," I said.

I took another step into the darkness, and then the room lit up.

Braxton and I turned around to find Chip with his hand on a light switch right next to the front doors. The Hipnotist said to us, "So gnarly. Thought there'd be no way the electricity still worked."

"Frito!" Braxton exclaimed.

"Why were you guys walking in the dark? Didn't you try the lights first?"

"How did you get over the fence?" I said.

Chip said, "I climbed, man. I've had to escape the cops at a few parties before. Fence-climbing comes in handy."

"But you didn't get hurt," I said.

"Yeah, well, I have some serious skills." Jason Root could have learned a few things from Chip.

Braxton said, "Why aren't you waiting for the police outside?"

"They know the address," said Chip. "What kind of a jerk would I be if I just let you two kids come in here by yourself? I mean, I know I can be selfish, but that'd be so gnarly." He looked past us. "So, where'd he go? Upstairs?"

The lights had revealed a rotting wooden staircase that disappeared up into darkness and a doorway that led to another dark room. It turned out that I had been leading Braxton and myself to a dust-covered table with a cracked vase on it, not anywhere near Dr. Sharp.

"Don't know where he went," I said. "But we have to hurry!"

Chip held a golf club at his side. More specifically, a putter with a rubber end. He raised it. "Always thought I kept this in my car for my love of the mini-golf game, but right now I'm ready to hit a hole-in-one against this fool's head."

The hypnotist walked over to us. He looked up the staircase and said, "Before we go up there, we make sure the first floor is clear."

I nodded and took a step toward the doorway to the other room. Chip grabbed my shoulder and said, "I'm armed. I'm an adult. I go first."

Braxton said, "I have the scissors, I go second."

I glared back at him. "Don't think so." To Chip: "Hurry up! We'll follow."

Chip raised the putter to his shoulder. He was a righty. He didn't look very scared, even though I wasn't so sure he could do much damage by swinging the mini-golf club. He was tall, but pretty skinny, and he didn't look like anyone who'd played baseball past Little League. But he was our best chance, and he'd already proved he was there to help, so I didn't say anything.

We crept through the doorway to the other room. Chip paused for a moment to flip the light switch. Light switches were always near doorways. Didn't know why I hadn't thought of that before, instead of searching in the darkness like some idiot.

We were in a living room. It was at least three times larger than the one at my house, but had hardly any more furniture. There were a couple of chairs, cabinets, a couch, and a coffee table covered in sheets.

Dr. Sharp was not there. A doorway led to a dark hall.

The Hipnotist nodded at us and we began to move quietly across the room when the front doors slammed shut behind us. I didn't think it was the police. Chip and Braxton's eyes went wide. They didn't think it was the police, either.

Chip held a finger to his mouth, telling us to be quiet. We slowly moved back to where we had come from. Putter and scissors raised, ready for defense or attack.

Standing by the closed front doors, phone in bloody hand, was the dentist. "Hi," he said. He actually waved to us.

"You make the phone call?" I demanded, stepping forward. Tears made the words come out more slowly than I hoped they would.

Chip held his weapon out in front of me, stopping me from going for Sharp. "Calm down. I'll handle this."

Sharp smiled. "Yes, boys, do let the men talk."

"Did you make the phone call?" Chip asked.

"Same question?" Sharp scoffed. "Might as well have let Jase speak for you."

Chip pointed to Sharp with the putter. "I *will* hurt you."

"Don't even think that speaking to me like that will get you the answers you're looking for. Be nice."

"Nice?" I said. "*Nice?* You aren't nice to us!"

"So I'm not." The doctor looked at his watch. "Was waiting to make the call, actually. So don't start your bawling, Jase."

"We're here to talk," I said. "Remember the deal you wanted to make? All three of us are here to talk to you about things."

"Bossy, aren't we?" said Sharp. "But, yes, let's talk."

"Tell us where my mom and grandpa are," I said.

"Yes," said the dentist. "Bossy, indeed."

"Give us the phone," said Braxton.

Sharp smiled at the device in his palm. "No. Actually, I was thinking about making another call. Not to Alexis. Just give me a moment, okay? Then we can talk."

"No!" I took a step forward, but Chip grabbed me by the shirt.

The dentist dialed a number without setting the speakerphone. He put the phone to his ear. It was a private call.

Or so I thought.

Another phone began to ring. Thought it was coming from behind me, but when I looked, all I saw was Braxton looking behind himself for a ringing phone. Then, I realized what was happening.

I looked up at Chip, but his eyes weren't on me. They were on his jacket pocket. He was confused.

"Cheeto?" Braxton now realized our ally was ringing.

"Why're you calling him?" I asked Sharp. "He's right in front of you!"

The dentist held up a finger to silence me. He just kept smiling. *Oh, man, I wanted to knock those teeth out of his head more than anything in the world.*

"Don't answer!" cried Braxton. "He's put a bomb in your phone!"

I'd been thinking the same thing, but I quickly pushed it out of my mind. First off, how would Sharp even get Chip's phone to put a bomb in it? Secondly, Sharp wasn't moving, and there was no way he was going to blow up the room that he stood in.

Chip dug his hand into the pocket, pulled out his phone, pushed a button, and put it to his left ear. "Yes?"

"Is this Chip the *Hip*notist?" asked Sharp.

"Yes, it is. May I ask who's calling?"

Braxton and I shared the same look.

What the HECK was going on?

"This is Dr. Xander Sharp, D.D.S."

Deadly Dr. Sharp.

"Yes, Dr. Sharp." Chip's eyes glazed over.

"Thanks for helping us with the kids, Chip. We make a great team."

"Yes, Dr. Sharp."

The two men now shared the same evil grin. I backed away from the hypnotist and pulled Braxton with me, because he was still trying to figure things out.

Chip wasn't our ally, our friend.

He'd betrayed us.

59

"WHERE ARE YOU BOYS GOING?" Sharp asked. "There's much to discuss."

There *was* a lot to discuss, but I was sick of being around people who wanted to hurt us. I was literally getting sick to my stomach, and I didn't want to deal with any of it anymore.

I pulled Braxton back toward the living room, then stopped abruptly. Michael was on all-fours in the doorway, back arched, and hissing. He would definitely make a good weapon. He showed his fangs and looked fully recovered from being slammed into the floor back at the pool house. An olive-skinned boy with short black hair —Greg—crawled into the doorway next to his fanged brother. If it was possible, Greg's teeth looked sharper than Michael's.

Braxton almost fell over in shock. He hadn't expected them to be there, and neither had I, but I actually wasn't too surprised. Was pretty much to the point where nothing else could shock me.

"Don't worry," said the doctor. "They won't attack anyone unless I order them to do so. I suppose they do have some kinks I still need to work out." He looked at the bloody thumb Michael had bitten earlier. "But they're more mine than they are themselves. My innocent weapons."

Braxton's knuckles around the scissors were bone-white. We were armed, and we weren't going down without a fight. Although, Sharp knew that already.

Chip stared at Michael and Greg. They seemed to make him speechless, and even frightened. He, too, clutched onto his weapon for dear life. He trembled some, and Sharp noticed it.

"If you appear to be weak," said the dentist, "they may attack. I can't be responsible for their actions. I promised them meat if they did as I asked, but sometimes even that isn't enough. They've attacked me on occasion." He again looked at his thumb. Was he surprised it was still there?

Chip tried to stand as tall as possible, but he still shook. When he spoke, his voice shook too. "Y...Yes, Dr. Sharp."

The dentist said, "Be strong, Chip. Don't stare at them too long. Try to forget they're here. Who knows if they'll feel threatened by your eye contact?"

"Y...Yes, Dr. Sharp." Chip turned his back to them, even though he still seemed uncomfortable with it.

"Why is that all Dorito's saying?" Braxton said. "Why is he only saying, 'Yes, Dr. Sharp'?"

"Because," Alexis said as she appeared in the doorway behind the innocent weapons, "that is all we instructed him to say."

"Where's my mom?" I said to her. "Where's my grandpa?"

"Don't tell him anything," Sharp ordered his sister.

"I won't. Calm down." Alexis wore all black. Probably to match her soul. She sneered at us.

I looked over at the dentist and said, "Thought she was some-where else with my family? You called her right in front of me!"

"We are not discussing this right now," was the doctor's reply.

"Where are my mom and grandpa?" I demanded. "Did you already hurt them?"

"Maybe," said Alexis. She laughed.

"Where are my mom and grandpa?" I said again.

Sharp and Alexis only stared at each other, smiling, chuckling. They enjoyed seeing me freak out.

"If Alexis is here," said Braxton, "then they're probably here, too. Right?"

The smiles and chuckles stopped. Alexis looked briefly to the staircase. The look said it all: *Mom and Grandpa were somewhere upstairs.*

That's all I needed to know. I dashed for the staircase.

"Chip, get him!" ordered Sharp.

"Yes, Dr. Sharp," said the Hipnotist.

I reached the first step. Only twelve more steps to go.

The second step. *Here I come, Mom.*

The third step. *I'm almost there, Grandpa.*

Chip pounded up the stairs behind me. His legs were longer and faster than mine. He reached me at the fourth step, pulled back on my right shirtsleeve. I turned and punched him in the shoulder, causing him to drop the putter. He still pulled me back to him, and I still punched. The hypnotist was caught off-balance and he stumbled, slipping on his weapon where it rested on the third step. He fell hard onto his side, but he had me in his grasp, and I fell down the stairs with the traitor.

I lay at the bottom of the staircase, looking up at the ceiling. Michael's fanged face suddenly appeared above my own. I sat up quickly, backing away from the innocent weapon and into the wall. I could see that Greg had blocked Braxton from getting anywhere near me.

Chip sat at the bottom of the stairs, wincing. His right elbow was scraped up pretty bad. Good. He deserved it.

Sharp said, "Chip, stand up and get your club."

Chip didn't seem to hear the doctor. He was too busy looking at his elbow.

"Chip, stand up and get your club," Sharp repeated.

The hypnotist still ignored Sharp. He stared at his bloody arm almost as if he was confused how he got hurt.

Sharp was angry now. He yelled, "CHIP, STAND UP AND GET YOUR CLUB!"

The Hipnotist snapped out of it. "Y...Yes, Dr. Sharp." He stood up and grabbed the club.

Alexis said, "Xander, you're losing your hold on him. He's hesitating far too much."

"Shut up," said the dentist. "It'll be fine." He looked at the hypnotist. "Chip, go to the living room and stand by the couch."

Again, Chip seemed to ignore Sharp. He now stared at Michael, who stared hungrily at his bloody arm. The Hipnotist shivered. Michael licked his lips.

"Michael, do not attack," said Sharp. "Now, Chip, go to the living room and stand by the couch."

Chip stared at Michael, and the man's entire body shook. Michael growled.

"Xander," Alexis said impatiently. "They're not listening to you."

"Shut up, Alexis." Sharp rubbed his forehead. "Chip, go to the living room and stand by the couch *or I will kill you.*"

"Y...Yes, Dr. Sharp," Chip said.

He slowly stepped away from Michael and walked toward the living room. As the hypnotist walked by, Greg snapped at him with deadly jaws. Alexis stepped aside to let Chip into the living room.

"You hypnotized a hypnotist?" Braxton said. "That's why Pringle's helping you? You hypnotized him?"

"Who would've thought such a thing was possible?" said Alexis.

"He's been pretending to help us all along?" I said.

"Not all along," she said. "Just long enough."

We'd been tricked. Chip hadn't come to our rescue tonight. Sharp probably told him to come over, to make us think we were safe. The doctor only pretended to be surprised when Chip drove up outside. The dentist or Alexis probably even unlocked the gate to let the hypnotist in. Chip couldn't climb the fence any better than Jason Root could.

"The police aren't coming?" said Braxton.

Sharp smiled. "When I talked to Chip after you tied my feet up with the fishing line, I told him to come over and fake a rescue for you however he could. So, no, that phone call was not real. But I did use it to my advantage to get you inside the house here."

"You think you're so smart," I said.

"Smarter than you know," said the dentist. "Want to know how smart?"

I said, "No," and then I screamed up the staircase, "MOM! GRANDPA! I'M HERE! CAN YOU HELP US? HELP US!"

Michael snarled at my loud voice. Alexis said, "They can't hear you where they are. Believe me. We've thought of everything."

"Now, boys," Sharp said to Braxton and me, "enough of all this nonsense. Time to cooperate." He looked up the staircase. "That is, Jase, if you want to see your mother and grandfather again."

He knew where to find my Achilles heel. Achilles was a powerful Greek warrior finally defeated when he was shot through the heel of his foot—his weak spot—with an arrow. My love for my family was both my strength and my weakness.

"Okay," I said, getting to my feet. "Let's make that deal."

"This will be quite the chat, boys," said the doctor. "To the living room."

60

MICHAEL AND GREG hissed at Braxton and me as they crawled after us on the way to the living room couch. The dentist followed behind his innocent weapons, but I noticed he kept a safe distance from them. It was very creepy that they acted so much like animals. They were too far under the Sharps' control.

Alexis stepped away from the doorway to let us past her and into the room. Then she reassumed her position, probably guarding the doorway in case I tried to make another break for the staircase.

"This talk isn't necessary," she told her brother. "We should just take the brats back to the pool house and continue where we left off. There's no deal to be made. You know that. All you're going to accomplish is giving them more unnecessary information, and they know too much already."

The doctor didn't even look back at his sister when he said, "Stop second-guessing me. I want them to taste this possibility of freedom just so it crushes them more when they finally realize all hope is really lost."

I stopped walking. Braxton bumped into me. Greg snarled.

I turned to Sharp. "That's not why we're talking. We're going to make a deal."

"Sure, we are," said the dentist like he wasn't sure at all.

"We're going to make a deal," said Braxton, "or I use the pointy part of these scissors."

"We should take those away from him," said Alexis. "He could poke his eye out."

Sharp smirked. "So what? Who cares?"

"If you try to take them away," said Braxton, "I will poke out Michael's eyes. Then Greg's."

My friend was lying, of course, but it shut the Sharps up for a second, at least. The dentist said, "Just sit down next to where Chip is."

The Hipnotist stood in a trance by the couch. He stared at Michael and Greg, his mouth opening and closing like a fish drowning on air.

Braxton said, "The sheet over that couch looks dusty."

"It is," said Alexis. "Hasn't been taken off there for about ten years. Go ahead and sneeze."

"Okay, but my snot will get everywhere."

Braxton and I walked around the cobwebbed coffee table. A cloud of dust rose as we sat on the couch. Braxton didn't sneeze like he had promised. Instead, it was Chip who let out a loud, "ACHOO!" Michael and Greg jumped back a little, startled by the sudden noise.

"Wipe your nose on your sleeve," said the dentist.

"Y...Yes, Dr. Sharp." Chip rubbed snotty nostrils along the arm of his sweatshirt.

"That's a good boy," said Sharp.

"What an idiot," muttered Braxton.

"What was that?" said Alexis.

"Cheeto," said Braxton. "He's an idiot! A jerk!" Bleary-eyed, my friend looked over at Chip, who didn't even bother to look our way. He was too fixated on the innocent weapons. "I trusted you! I called you for help instead of my parents, and you turned out to be even worse than them!"

This time, I think my friend's tears were the result of real emotion, real hurt and pain. His parents had picked on him his entire life. His dentist was a psycho. The hypnotist he befriended was a traitor. Adults never turned out to be very good to him.

"See?" Sharp said to Alexis, grinning. He was enjoying the tears, drinking them in. "We owe these boys the truth! He backstabbed two ten-year-old children. It's only fair that we tell them why he did it. It would be the *hip* thing to do, wouldn't it, Jase?"

All I said was, "I'm eleven, not ten. Don't want to say it again."

Sharp snorted. "You seem to enjoy saying it nonetheless." He paused. "Go on, Chip. They deserve to know. Tell these boys what happened."

Chip didn't reply. Sharp groaned. Alexis said, "I told you your hold on him was wearing off."

Sharp said, "Chip, tell these boys how you came to be here, working with us. They deserve to know."

Chip still didn't say anything. He stared at Michael and Greg more. Sharp groaned louder.

He said, "CHIP, TELL THESE BOYS—"

"*Xander,*" said Alexis, annoyed. "Shut up, will you? I'll tell them."

Sharp sighed. "But Chip should be the one to—"

Alexis ignored her brother. She said, "Your friend, Chip, called us a few days ago, right after you first told him about us. He said that after he heard your story, he realized someone really under-stood and respected the power of hypnosis. He wanted to learn from that person. That person being me, of course." She seemed proud.

"But we turned the tables on him. He thought he could become my student, but he became our guinea pig. His mind's weak. We put him in a fairly permanent hypnotic state, where he has to do what-ever Xander tells him to do." Alexis paused. "Which I think is a mistake, since he's not really listening to my brother very much anymore. Should have been my commands he obeyed."

"Enough with that," said Sharp. He stood on the other side of the coffee table. His smile was now bigger than ever as he looked at us on the couch. "Everything you've told Chip, he's told us about right afterward. That's what I told him to do. We knew about your

Internet searches, that you were going after the MyPods, that you were coming here tonight. That's how we've always been a step ahead of you. However, we were surprised you figured out the bite pressure so quickly."

"Biting on wax isn't common dental practice," added Alexis. "Just what we do to help determine who will be—"

"Good candidates for your sick plan," I finished.

"Impressive," said the dentist. "You never had enough info to put all the pieces together. No way you could've guessed what was really happening.

"You see, we let you think you were in control. Had to let you feel confident. In actuality, we took every precaution to make sure you ended up where you are right now. *In our grasp with nowhere to go for help."*

"All thanks to your foolish Not-So-Hipnotist friend," said Alexis. "Maybe he never actually meant to hurt you, but he set you up from Day One."

"You guys are evil!" said Braxton. "You made him fall in love with Beth!"

"No," said Alexis. "We made him a patient at the office only so that we would have more time for his hypnosis. Beth... Well, let's just say, he's still his own person in a lot of ways. He can still make bad decisions on his own."

I scratched my itchy hand and said, "You really know everything?"

Sharp said, "You mean, how you found out about this house? About your mother and father, Jase? How they're connected to our father? Is that what you mean?" The dentist's teeth glowed. "Chip mentioned you found an article or something. Care to give us all the details?"

I looked at my feet. "No."

"We'll get more out of you later," said Alexis. "Or out of your mom and grandpa."

I looked up at the ceiling. Were Mom and Grandpa really up

there? They had to be. Alexis wouldn't leave them alone if they weren't nearby, would she?

Sharp said, "We'd like to know more about the connection between your family and ours, Jase. Chip was kind of unclear on all that. But we aren't too worried. Have all the time in the world to figure it out."

Before Sharp or Alexis could say anything else, Michael sprang for Chip. The hypnotist should've known to never expose his bloody arm to a vicious, unstable creature. Even the other two didn't see it coming. Greg did, though. He jumped for Chip a split second after Michael did.

Fangs flashed. Flesh tore. Chip screamed.

61

THE HIPNOTIST PUT UP A FIGHT. Even with two eighty-pound boys scratching and biting him, he managed to punch, kick, and swing the putter. The problem was, his blows hit only air. Michael and Greg were too quick and wild for him.

"MICHAEL! GREG!" yelled Sharp. "I DEMAND THAT YOU STOP OR NO MEAT FOR A WEEK!" But his creations only had one thing on their minds: KILL.

Didn't take long for Michael to dig his fangs into Chip's right arm, forcing him to drop the putter. Took even less time for Greg to tear on Chip's left calf, bringing him to his knees. All the while, Chip screamed for help, for his life.

The rest of us could only watch. Braxton and I scooted to the far end of the couch, while Sharp backed away. Would've been crazy and stupid to risk being attacked along with the hypnotist. Michael and Greg were ferocious. They'd spilt blood and they wanted more of it.

"Please," Chip begged. Couldn't tell if he was still under hypnosis or not.

He reached a bloody hand out to Sharp and Alexis. They kept their distance, studying the horrific scene. Clearly, it didn't really matter to them if he died. They'd already used him for their purpose.

Michael and Greg now backed away from Chip, allowing his cuts to run with blood, weakening him further. His gray sweatshirt was splashed crimson in many spots. He was sobbing, pleading for help, for mercy.

"They're looking at his throat," said Braxton.

"Huh?" I said. "Who?"

"Michael and Greg."

Sure enough, the two seemed to be staring at his neck, which was turned out to them like an offering as Chip looked to the Sharps for assistance. If the boys sunk their fangs into his throat, that would be it. There would be no turning back. Chip would be dead, and Michael and Greg would be killers.

That didn't need to happen. Even though Chip had betrayed us, he shouldn't have to die for it. Michael and Greg didn't have to go to that point-of-no-return. *But what could we do about it?*

Braxton jumped off the couch without warning. He stepped onto the coffee table, raced across it, and launched himself through the air toward Chip, toward his attackers. He landed on his feet in a part of the floor stained with blood. He was between the boys and their prey. He had the scissors ready.

"You don't have to do this!" he said to Michael and Greg. "Once you take Chip's life, there will be no going back to how it used to be! There's still hope for you, but not if you finish what you've started!"

Michael and Greg's eyes narrowed. Their growls were unfriendly. They hadn't expected an appetizer to drop in.

"Are you crazy?" said Alexis. "Get out of there! You'll be killed!"

"Let him be," said Sharp.

"No," I said to myself, and I followed Braxton's lead.

I stepped on the coffee table, moved forward, and immediately tripped on my own feet. I fell off the table and on top of Michael as he prepared to leap for Braxton.

Michael twisted under me, screeching and snapping his jaws. He was stronger than I was, and he tossed me away. Whatever I landed on wasn't comfortable.

"Thank you," Chip muttered beside me. Didn't know if it was because he thought we were trying to save him, or if he was just happy that Michael and Greg had new choices on the menu.

I reached beneath me and felt the fallen putter. No wonder my spine hurt.

When I plucked the weapon off the floor, Sharp said, "Jase, it's not worth getting hurt for Chip! He doesn't care if you're hurt or killed!"

"I'm not here for Chip," I said. "I'm here for my friend."

I rose slowly, holding my hands out to Michael to tell him to stay put. Wasn't sure he cared, but he didn't attack. He just sat there, licking his bloody lips.

Braxton had his eyes on Greg. "What do we do?" he asked me.

"Yes, what *do* you do?" added Sharp.

"*This.*" I imagined Michael as a piñata, and I swung the putter into his ribs. It was the same side he landed on when Sharp threw him earlier, so I knew it had to be an extra-sensitive area. I was right. Michael shrieked as the putter struck, and he crumpled to the floor, powerless.

"No!" cried Alexis. "Don't do *that*!"

She thought I was going to hit him again, but there wasn't any need. He wasn't going to be a problem now that his side felt like a sledgehammer had connected with it.

Greg turned his attention from Braxton to me. His fangs snapped open, shut, open, shut. *I was ready to sledgehammer again if I needed to.*

Didn't get the chance. Braxton kicked Greg in the side of the face, and the boy stumbled. He tried to shake the pain out of his head.

Before Braxton could waste time with another kick, I grabbed him and said, "Come on!"

Sharp realized we were going for the other doorway, the one that led to the hall we had tried to explore earlier, but this time he was too far away to stop us. Alexis still screamed, "Xander, stop them!"

Yeah, right. We flew into the hall, into darkness. I didn't know where to go. Once again, I couldn't see anything, but I rubbed my itchy hand against the wall, searching for a room.

That's when I realized the hall was where Alexis had come from earlier. She had suddenly appeared in the living room after we met her brother by the front doors.

She came from here. From some room nearby.

Maybe from where Mom and Grandpa were kept.

But where? Where was a door?

Heavy footsteps and the sound of snarling followed us. Dr. Sharp and Greg were closing in.

Where was a door?

Braxton pushed one open on the opposite side of the hall. I couldn't see it, but I heard the door crash against the wall. My friend grabbed my arm, pulling me along with him into a dark space.

Once inside, I slammed the door shut behind me, right in a tall, shadowy figure's face. Sharp had been that close to catching us again.

My bedroom door didn't have a lock on it, but this one did. Even in the darkness, it was easy to find and turn. Sharp jiggled the knob from the other side. He cursed, pounded the door, and cursed some more.

"He's going to break it down!" said Braxton. "Is there anything to block it with?"

He flipped a light switch next to my head. Why did I keep forgetting the switches by the doors?

We were in some moldy bedroom. I looked around the room and tried to ignore the fact that I didn't see Mom or Grandpa anywhere. The empty wooden bed frame would've worked as an obstacle for Sharp if it weren't too heavy to move.

"What about that?" Braxton pointed to a dresser across the room.

I nodded. "We could try."

Sharp sounded like he was taking his own sledgehammer to the door now, although that was ridiculous, because he didn't have a weapon. Did he?

We ran over to the dresser and tried to pull it away from the wall. We pushed on it. Then we pulled on it again.

"It's not budging." My friend's voice was full of worry and defeat.

"Maybe there's something in there," I said, pointing.

I ran over to the closet, threw open its creaky accordion-like doors, looking for something, *anything* to help us, and instead found my missing family members.

62

Mom and Grandpa sat on the floor, leaning against each other. Their eyes were both covered by bandanas wound tightly around their faces. Their hands were duct taped behind their backs, and their ankles were also taped together.

Both had MyPods in their laps that fed them music through earphones.

Because of the bandanas, they couldn't see me, and because of the earphones, they couldn't hear me. They just sat there, unknown to my presence, for a couple of seconds as I fought to hold back tears.

"Oh, wow, there they are," Braxton said beside me. "Are they okay?"

"I...I think so," I said.

Grandpa smiled and bobbed his head to whatever he listened to. Mom looked bored. They were both breathing, which was the best thing. The problem was that each of them was listening to a MyPod. I didn't know what kind of message they were being given or even how long they'd been given it.

I yanked the earphones away from both of them. From Grandpa's set came some Justin Bieber. Out of Mom's earphones country music played.

"Hey!" Grandpa shouted. "I was enjoying that!"

I pulled the MyPods out of their laps and threw them across the room. "It's Jase," I said.

"*Jase?*" said Mom. "*Are you okay?*"

"For now." I untied their blindfolds. Tears were in both of their eyes. "We need to block the door," I said. "Dr. Sharp's trying to get in."

"Um, Jase?" said Braxton.

"Braxton!" Mom looked past me. "Are *you* okay?"

"We're both fine," I said. I looked back at my friend. "What?"

"Doesn't sound like he's trying to break in anymore."

He was right. Except for the music playing from the MyPods across the room, I didn't hear anything. Had the dentist really left? Was it some kind of trick to get us to go back out in the hall? Or did he just leave to get something heavy to break down the door with?

"It's a trick," said Grandpa. "They want us to think they're gone. But there's no way they've left. Would they really leave us here alone to get the police and report everything they've done?"

"What *did* they do to you guys?" asked Mom. "Where did they take you? Are you *sure* you're okay? We should've believed you when you said something weird was going on!"

That was question overload. I asked my own. "Are *you guys* okay?"

"Chloroform to the face can't keep me down too long," said Grandpa.

"Didn't Alexis try to hypnotize you?" asked Braxton.

"She *tried*," said Mom, "but we wouldn't have any of it." She wiggled around. "Time to get out of this tape. Wouldn't you agree, Dad?"

Grandpa nodded. "Yes, definitely."

Braxton leaned over with the scissors, and Mom said, "Thank you, but that won't be necessary."

She snapped the tape apart with superhuman force. Pieces of tape fell to the floor. Grandpa did the same as Mom. It was as if Scotch, not duct, tape had bound their hands and feet. I didn't know what to say. *So much for being all shocked out.*

Braxton said, "Whoa."

I was flabbergasted. "You could've broken out of the tape that easily this whole time and you didn't?"

"We didn't know where you were," Mom said. "Had to cooperate so they would tell us where they kept you. So they wouldn't hurt you."

She stood and then helped Grandpa to his feet. They stepped out of the closet and hugged me.

Grandpa said, "Now that you're safe, they're going to find out they've messed with *the wrong family.*"

Mom clutched my shoulders. "Jase, there's something we never told you."

"Yeah?" What was she talking about?

"A family secret. When you're twelve, your body's going to go through some changes."

"Mom, don't start talking about *that* now! We talked about that all last year in school."

Grandpa laughed. "No, not *those* kind of changes. You'll experience those, but you're also going to start going through... *other* changes." He pointed at my fingers as they scratched my hand. "Think it may have already started."

"Huh?"

"Our family is special, Jase," he explained. "Very special. We're not like other families."

I rolled my eyes. "I already know that!"

"We have lots of explaining to do," said Mom.

"Have to save it for later, Dana," said Grandpa. "Ever since that dentist knocked me out, I've been waiting to get him back. Can't wait anymore. It's time."

"Time for what?" asked Braxton.

"Time to show those fools who the *real* monsters are." Grandpa added to my friend, "Close your eyes. You can't see this. It could kill you."

"What?" Braxton looked at me for help.

Mom nodded and said, "We'll explain later. Just don't want you to get hurt. Close your eyes."

"Don't peek or you'll die." Grandpa's warning to Braxton didn't sound like a joke.

Braxton must have thought the same thing, because he squeezed his eyes shut. Then he opened them, grabbed one of the bandanas off the floor, and tied it around his head, pulling it over his eyes. "I don't want to die," he explained.

Mom said to me, "Don't be scared, honey."

As she said this, her skin grew green and scaly. Her teeth became daggers, and her pupils, reptilian slits. The bones in her fingers cracked at they grew longer and sharper.

Grandpa transformed in much the same way, but his dentures didn't change at all. He said to Mom, "My fangs are back at the house."

I don't think I breathed during their whole transformation. I scratched harder than ever before. Braxton stood against a wall as still as a statue.

Mom placed *a claw* on my shoulder. "Whatever you hear, don't leave this room." She turned and almost hit me *with her tail.* "Come on, Dad. *Let's get these jerks.*"

Grandpa winked at me with a dinosaur-like eye. "And you thought she was angry about you dropping the burrito!"

They opened the door and entered the hall. They closed the door behind them. I locked it. I was too stunned to speak, and Braxton said, "Can I open my eyes yet?"

I scratched and scratched my hand. "I…I guess so."

He pulled the bandana off and blinked at me, his eyes big and round.

And then the screams started. We didn't move.

It was only Sharp and Alexis finally getting what they deserved.

63

A FEW MINUTES LATER, after I bashed the MyPods to bits with the putter and Braxton tore their insides apart with scissors, there came a knock at the door. "It's me," said Mom from the other side.

Braxton went over to unlock it. Before he did, he said, "Are you a killer monster still?" I'd told him what I'd seen Mom and Grandpa turn into. He believed it much more easily than I thought he would.

"No monster here," said Mom.

Braxton still closed his eyes when he opened the door. Mom entered the room. Her hair was kind of messed up, and she had the sheet from the couch wrapped and tied around her waist, covering the bottom half of her body. Besides that, she looked as normal as ever.

She said, "Everything's taken care of."

"What does that mean?" I said. "You hurt them?"

She changed the subject. "You can open your eyes, Braxton."

He did. "Thanks," said my friend.

Mom said, "What did they *do* to those two poor boys out there?"

"Oh, they just brainwashed them and put fangs on them so they'd become some kind of ninja guard dog assassins for the military."

"Okay…" Braxton's explanation didn't seem to satisfy her. "They wanted to do the same to you guys?"

I nodded. "But we got away."

She hugged me. "You're so brave." She pulled Braxton into the hug. "*Both* of you. *So brave.*"

Braxton smiled. "We're a good team, huh, Jase?"

"Yeah, we are." I pulled away from the group embrace. "So, did you and Grandpa *hurt* them? Michael and Greg?"

"We didn't really have to."

I said, "And that means…?"

"We locked the two boys in a bathroom. Wanted to make sure they didn't see us for too long. They can't get out, so they're safe for now." She paused. "Who's the man bleeding in the living room?"

"Oh, that's just Dorito," said Braxton. "He was our friend, but he turned against us. He *was* hypnotized, which takes some of the blame off him, but I don't forgive him too much."

Mom said, "I see…" She put her hands together in front of her and sat on the bed frame. "What usually happens when a person sees Grandpa or me like that—"

"*Usually* happens?" I asked. "You turn into a monster in front of people a lot?"

"We haven't done it for a while. Not since we moved." She sighed. "And only the bad people, Jase. Only the ones who deserve it. It's what our kind does. We're meant to scare nasty people."

Our kind? What was our kind?

I said, "How long have you been doing this?"

"Since I was twelve," she said. "Grandpa's been doing it since he was twelve. His father did it before him. Generation after generation, our kind has taken care of the bad people."

"Our kind—whatever that is—*kills* bad people?"

Mom lowered her head. "No, Jase, we scare them. We warn them. We tell them to shape up or we'll come back for them in the future. What *usually* happens to these people when they see us is that they go crazy. They can't believe what they've seen and they lose their minds. They end up living in constant fear and they don't hurt anyone ever again."

"Those articles about criminals that Grandpa has in that box? Those are about the bad guys you've scared? Some of them ended up in mental hospitals, because what they said they saw sounded crazy? Monsters aren't supposed to be real, and so if they said they saw what you turned into, people would think they were insane?"

Mom nodded. "That man out there? Dorito? He's shaking and talking to himself right now. Alexis? She fainted, and I don't know when she's waking up again. But when they wake up and talk to the police, no one will believe them."

"What about Dr. Sharp?" I asked.

She looked deep into my eyes. "You must understand that we don't wish to ever cause physical harm to others. Violence is a part of human nature, not ours."

"*What about Dr. Sharp?*" I repeated.

"Certain people can't handle what they see to the point that they get...frightened to death." Tears formed in her eyes. "That's the worst part. I don't like it when it happens, but it does. It's why we didn't want you to see us, Braxton. We didn't know how you'd react."

"Thanks," said Braxton, "but I'd probably just think you looked really awesome."

"What about *me*?" I asked. "You didn't know how I'd react!"

"You're immune to the effect we have on others." She stopped. She closed her eyes and began to cry.

"Mom...What is it?"

She waited a few seconds and then said, "Your father, Jase, long ago... He accidentally walked in on my transformation. He was never supposed to know. And he couldn't... He couldn't..." Mom sobbed.

Grandpa appeared in the doorway, back to normal. "Your dad was a good man, Jase," he said. "A very good man. A *great* one." He walked over to Mom and brought her into his arms. "It's okay, Dana, it's okay."

"No, Dad, it's not okay! It's *not*..." She sobbed into his shoulder and noticed the hole in the back of his pants. It's where his tail had poked through. We were shown a half moon. "Dad, I told you to put on a sheet like I did!"

Grandpa said, "Thought it was a little too cold in here for some reason..."

"Wait," I said. "What are you saying happened to Dad?"

Grandpa explained, "It's an incredible secret we have to keep. What we are. Your grandma thought she knew everything about me, but I could never tell her the whole truth. It could have killed her.

"When your dad saw your mom, that was it, Jase. His brain couldn't understand his eyes. His heart couldn't take it. He was such a very good man, but he wasn't strong enough. Some people aren't."

"His face, caught in that scream forever..." Mom choked out. "It was awful, and it's always with me...what I did it to him..."

"It was an accident," said Grandpa. "We know it was."

I didn't know what to do but hug Mom again. Braxton joined in, as well. It was the saddest thing I'd ever heard. When Mom and Grandpa told me that Dad died in an accident, I thought they meant a car wreck. Now I knew the truth, and I didn't know how to deal with it other than to cry some more.

"I like to think I was the one who scared the life out of the dentist," said Grandpa. "Dana, you didn't have anything to do with it."

"But..." said Mom. "I wanted to rip his heart out like I said I would!"

"It's best you didn't," said Grandpa. "That would've gotten messy."

I said, "What do we do now?"

"We call the police," Grandpa said. "We try to explain to them everything that's happened, only leaving out our little secret."

"What about Braxton?" I said.

My friend suddenly looked scared. "What're you going to do to me?"

"Nothing," said Grandpa. "Welcome to the family."

Braxton and I smiled. We high-fived. He said, "Even if I told people you're monsters, no one believes anything I say."

"I did," I said.

"And look where it got us!" He grinned at me, his eyes shining.

"I won't hold it against you."

"That's good," he said, "because you might not know it, but it isn't really easy for me to make friends. People think I'm weird."

"That's okay," said Grandpa. "As it turns out, we're all a little weird, too."

6 4

I SAID, "The articles about you and Dad, Mom? You knew Dr. Sharp's father all those years ago! You knew about this house!"

"'This house'?" said Mom. "Are we really in that horrible yellow mansion? I've been coming up here for weeks to look around, and no one seemed to live here..."

"It's how they wanted it to look," I said. "Like it was abandoned. Why did we come back to this city, Mom? There has to be a reason!"

"This'll take a while," Grandpa said. He sat down against a wall and said, "Maybe I should've gotten one of those sheets. This wood floor isn't warm or cozy."

"There is a reason we came back here, Jase," Mom said. She sat back down on the bed frame. "I wanted revenge. Finally, I wanted some revenge."

I said, "Revenge against who?"

"Dr. Alexander Sharp," she said. "The plastic surgeon. The man who lived in this house all those years ago. The man who *killed* my friend, Jason. Thought he might still live here. Looked his name up online, but the only Dr. Sharp I found around here was Dr. *Xander* Sharp, a dentist. Didn't know if they were related, but maybe they were. And you needed your teeth looked at anyway..."

"He's dead," I said. "Dr. Sharp told me his dad died."

"Oh," said Mom. "Well, that's okay... Kind of good, I suppose. It's just that we were forced to leave here so many years ago, and it always bothered me. We punish bad people whenever we can, but Jason's killer got away, and I wanted to come back here to fix it. No matter how much time had passed. If I could fix it, I would."

"Tried to talk her out of it," said Grandpa. "Just like I was able to talk her out of it way back then, but she didn't want to hear it this time."

"Fifteenth anniversary of Jason's death was a few weeks ago. A horrible milestone to reach. It re-fueled my rage."

"Why do you think Alexander Sharp killed your friend?" said Braxton. "Jason Root climbed the fence, right?"

"Jason did climb the fence," said Mom, "but I think he might've been forced to do it. He was... hypnotized, I think."

She looked my way. "The day before he died, Jason told your dad and me that he learned something horrible about Alexander Sharp. Jason was writing a paper for some class about these two teenagers who tortured and killed animals—Eric Christopher and Kirk Mason. Alexander Sharp kind of became their father figure when they were caught. Sharp visited them in jail, listened to what they had to say. It was all over the news. It was a big deal, because he was the one who fixed up the animals these two idiots attacked."

I said, "We know that. That's what the article said."

"Right," Mom said. "So, Jason told us that he got to talk to these two guys. They were older now. They were still behind bars, but Jason got an interview with them for his paper anyway. He was really excited about it. He thought he'd get an 'A' for sure, because he'd have info straight from the source.

"And when they met, these two guys told him that Alexander Sharp made them hurt those animals when they were kids. They couldn't explain how Sharp controlled them, just that he did. Sharp even told them to turn themselves in. He told them he would visit them in jail.

"Jason explained to your dad and me that he thought these boys had been hypnotized. Something crazy like that. At least, at the time we thought it was crazy."

"You didn't believe him?" I said.

Mom shook her head. "We should have." The tears were back in her voice. "Maybe if we had, we could've helped Jason. But we told him to forget it, that the guys were psychos. That they lied to him, and that was all there was to it.

"And, then, I guess Jason decided to come to this house. He probably talked to Alexander Sharp about what he'd been told... and the man hypnotized him. Framed him. Called the police and made Jason look like some criminal so that his secret wouldn't be exposed.

"Your dad and I knew Jason wouldn't have tried to run from the police, wouldn't have done anything illegal, anything stupid like that. He was a good guy. We thought about what Jason had told us and decided that Sharp wasn't telling the truth."

"You didn't tell the police what Jason told you?" said Braxton.

"Of course, we did," Mom said. "But they didn't want to hear it. They told us if we bothered Alexander Sharp again, we'd be in big trouble."

"And that's when we moved," Grandpa said. "Wasn't worth staying here. Didn't want your mom to be tempted to hurt anyone, to possibly give up our secret."

I explained my suspicions that Eric Christopher and Kirk Mason might have been the Sharps' first attempts at creating "innocent weapons." Everyone agreed it could be true.

Mom wiped tears from her cheeks. "I didn't know for sure if Alexander Sharp had kids. But it makes sense. He passed his evil ways on to his children, and it took me too long to piece it together. Never should have used you as my 'in' at the dentist's office, Jase, while trying to figure things out on my own. So stupid and reckless. Coming back to this town has brought up so much for me, and I wasn't thinking clearly. Almost lost you because of it, and I'm sorry."

"At least we got the guy's kids," said Grandpa, standing. "Let's go check on them, huh?"

ON THE WAY back out to the living room, Grandpa pulled out some pennies from one of his pants pockets. "Never leave home without them," he said. "You've almost run me dry, Jase. I should probably cut back on those candies."

"You won't," I said.

"You're probably right."

"What do you need the pennies for, Grandpa?" Braxton said.

I wondered if my grandfather was going to say anything about Braxton calling him "Grandpa." He didn't. Instead, he squeezed the pennies tight and gestured for us to follow him.

Mom stayed in the bedroom, crying the rest of her tears out. "I'll be fine," she told us. "Until I try to figure out how to explain what's happened to the police."

The lights had been turned on in the hall. At the end of it was a closed door. Faint scratches came from behind it.

"What's in there?" I asked.

"Bathroom," Grandpa said. "It's where we put those other boys. They're much quieter now."

"Hold up," I said. I went over to the door and put my ear against it. There was some movement and whimpering on the other side.

"Hello?" Braxton said next to me. He knocked lightly.

"We...We want to go home," came a voice. Couldn't tell if was Michael or Greg.

"Just wait a little while longer," said Braxton. "Someone has to fix your brains first. Not sure how that'll work, but it'll be okay. I think."

No one said anything else, so we followed Grandpa to the living room. Chip leaned against a wall, sucking his thumb. Some blood spotted his clothing. He rocked back and forth, staring at nothing. I waved a hand in front of his face, but he didn't respond.

Grandpa raised his eyebrows. "See?" he said. "This guy's lost it. We have that effect on people."

Alexis lay on the ground a few feet away. Her hair was a mess in front of her face. She appeared to still be unconscious... *and then she groaned.*

"What's going on?" she said, lifting herself onto her elbows. Then, she brushed the hair out of her face. Her eyes grew wide when she saw Grandpa. She pointed at him, shook her finger, and said, "You!"

"Boo," he said.

She shrieked and fell back on her face, passed out once again. Grandpa said, "I don't think the police will be very nice to her, either."

I said, "Grandpa, what *are* we?"

"Well, Jase, I can only tell you what my father told me..." He said, "We're descended from the Gorgons."

"Like Medusa?" I said. Medusa was a Greek monster, one of three evil sisters called the Gorgons. A good look at a Gorgon literally turned a person into a statue.

"Yes, like Medusa," said Grandpa. "Although, over thousands of years, our power has diminished. A single look can't turn a person to stone." He paused. "Knowing where we come from—essentially, Greek mythology—angers your mother. Especially after what happened to your father. I, as you know, try to accept our origins. It's why I share so many of the stories with you. Don't be ashamed of your heritage like your mother is. You don't have to like what you sometimes have to become, but always be proud of who you are, got it?"

I nodded. "It's all kind of making sense now."

"Let me see your hand," said Grandpa. He scratched where I scratched, although much harder than I ever had before. Oddly, it didn't hurt much, and when he pulled his hand away from mine, I saw that he had *uncovered green scales beneath my skin.*

"Oh, *wow*," said Braxton. "That would be so cool at show-and-tell!"

Grandpa caught my gaze. "Your body's been warning you of the changes you'll be going through. Just wait until other parts of you get itchy. *That* is going to take some getting used to..."

He looked away from me and over to the couch. *Now it was time to visit the doctor.*

Grandpa had warned us that Sharp might "look strange." I'd seen dead people in movies and on TV before, but it was the first time I was going to see one in real life. I was nervous and itchy, and I tried to wipe the sweat off on my pants, but it kept on coming no matter how much I wiped.

Braxton looked as uneasy as I was, and he said, "Maybe I don't want to see him."

Grandpa shook his head. "No, it'll be okay. He needs our help now." He held out his hand, revealing the three pennies he took from his pocket. "Both of you take one. They're not gold *drachmas*, but they'll do."

We hesitated. Why did we have to do this?

"Go ahead," said Grandpa. "Doesn't matter which one you take."

I took the shiniest one. Braxton took the second shiniest. Grandpa looked at what was left in his palm. "Oh, sure, leave me with the ugly one." He grinned. "Just kidding."

We moved across the room to the couch. Sharp sat on the floor against it. In his lap, he held a large pocketknife. His hands were frozen in a tight grip around its handle. He was dead.

"He swung the knife at your mom," Grandpa explained. "So I got right in his face. *Look at that scream stuck there*. That was *all me*." He didn't sound proud, he sounded angry. "Finally, I made a dentist pay."

Sharp's mouth hung wide open, locked in a silent state of terror. I didn't know mouths could open that wide. His eyes bulged out of his head, like they were on the verge of popping out. They looked up, toward the ceiling, but they probably still saw Grandpa's reptilian face in front of them.

"I've dealt with lots of bad guys in my time," said Grandpa. "This man was one of the worst. Apparently, being a dentist was only a tiny part of his problem."

I said, "So those articles under your bed are all about things you and Mom did in the past. You made the criminals go crazy." I paused. "You killed some of them."

Grandpa nodded. "Police were getting too close to finding out what your mom and I were doing to these types of people." He sighed. "Authorities wouldn't understand the truth. They'd think of us as murderers. That's why we can't truly explain what happened here. The two idiots over there are going to try to do that, and they're going to come across as insane." The two idiots were Alexis and Chip. "Understand, boys? We'll think of something to say. We'll all be on the same page before the police arrive."

"Yes," Braxton and I said in unison.

"Good." Grandpa leaned over and put his penny on Sharp's chest. "I'll help him pay his way."

I looked at my penny. "What are we doing?"

"Give him your pennies. He needs to pay Charon the Ferryman."

Braxton looked confused, but I said, "Are you serious?"

"This man doesn't deserve to be lost forever on the Styx, Jase."

"What's the Styx?" said Braxton.

"The River Styx," I explained. "It's in Greek mythology, too, like Cerberus and Medusa. It's the river that leads to the Underworld. Before your soul can cross the river, you need to pay Charon the Ferryman. Otherwise, he won't take you across and your soul is stuck forever."

Grandpa nodded. "This man needs the fare to cross the Styx, so he can burn for eternity in that fiery place he deserves to be."

I nodded. "Let him burn."

"My father taught me this was the right thing to do, no matter how bad the person may be. Your mom prefers to save her money, but it's why I always have pennies. Just in case I need them for someone's payment."

"How many have you given out?" said Braxton.

Grandpa said, "I've been around a long time, and I've given out far too many. There are unfortunately a lot of bad people out there. Always have been, and I think there always will be."

Braxton put his penny next to Grandpa's. "Three cents is enough?" my friend said. "Crossing the river's that cheap?"

I snorted. "Doubt it's a very beautiful trip."

The last penny fell from my palm and into Sharp's lap. I had a bad taste in my mouth for helping the man who wanted to take me away from my family and turn me into some kind of bloodthirsty animal. It tasted like rotten meat.

I took one last long look at Dr. Xander Sharp, D.D.S.

D.D.S.

Dead Dr. Sharp.

I turned away from the body, forever changed and stronger than I'd been before, but still more than a little uneasy about the changes yet to come.

EVAN BAUGHFMAN

Evan Baughfman works in a very scary place: a middle school! (He's a totally-not-evil teacher.) He lives in California with his wife, Ashley, his children, Mason and Story, and their probably-not-evil-at-all black cat, Friday. Evan has been reading and writing for fun since childhood. After disturbing his mom with a tale about killer opossums, Evan knew that he wanted to write a book of his own someday. Evan was so serious about becoming an author that he earned a Bachelor's degree in Creative Writing from University of Redlands.

Evan writes all genres, but horror is where he is most comfortable. His short fiction has appeared in various anthologies, including books from Improbable Press, 4 Horsemen Publications, No Bad Books Press, and Grinning Skull Press.

Evan's first short story collection, *The Emaciated Man and Other Terrifying Tales from Poe Middle School*, is published through Thurston Howl Publications. D&T published Evan's first novella, *Vanishing of the 7th Grade*, in 2022.

Much of Evan's writing success has also been as a playwright. He's had many different plays produced across the globe. Heuer Publishing has published Evan's script, "A Taste of Amontillado" (an adaptation of Edgar Allan Poe's "The Cask of Amontillado"), in addition to a couple of his other scripts. Evan's work can also be found at YouthPLAYS, Next Stage Press, Drama Notebook, and New Play Exchange.

More information about Evan's writing can be found at amazon.com/author/evanbaughfman

ABOUT THE EDITOR / PUBLISHER

Dawn Shea is an author and half of the publishing team over at D&T Publishing. She lives with her family in Mississippi. Always an avid horror lover, she has moved forward with her dreams of writing and publishing those things she loves so much.

D&T Previously published material:
    ABC's of Terror
    After the Kool-Aid is Gone

Follow her author page on Amazon for all publications she is featured in.
    Follow D&T Publishing at the following locations:
    Website
    Facebook: Page / Group
    Or email us here: dandtpublishing20@gmail.com

Bad For Your Teeth by Evan Baughfman

Edited by Jamie LaChance

Cover by Ash Ericmore

Formatting by J.Z. Foster

Bad For Your Teeth

www.ingramcontent.com/pod-product-compliance
Lightning Source LLC
Chambersburg PA
CBHW070659180626
46817CB00006B/2440